REDHAZE: TRILOGY

TRAVIS D. LANE

120904

PublishAmerica
Baltimore

ISBN: 1-4137-6094-5
PUBLISHED BY PUBLISHAMERICA, LLLP
www.publishamerica.com
Baltimore

Printed in the United States of America

This Book Is Dedicated To:
Caleb Angelus Lane
(The best son a dad could ask for)

I'd like to thank my friends and family who believed in me and put up with me during this book's creation. And everyone who put up with me when I'd go on an on about it. A special thanks goes out to Susan Zoon Devlin, The Writer's Hood's Horror editor, who gave me my first break at getting the book out to the masses.

REDHAZE: TRILOGY

BOOK I

BLOOD REIGN

CHAPTER 1

My life changed dramatically the summer before my senior year of high school. It was an unusually chilly Friday night in July when I got home from working at the Pizza Palace in my hometown of Dweller Valley, Pennsylvania. As I walked through the front door, the phone was ringing.

"Hello, Wayne residence," I greeted.

"Trevor? It's Robin," my next-door neighbor and closest friend said from the other end.

"Hey, lady. What's up?"

"I was just wondering if you wanted to come over and watch some movies with me."

"Yeah. Sure. I'm not doing anything," I answered as I took off my work shirt. I wrinkled my nose at the smell of the hundred-plus pizzas that I cooked during my shift at the local hangout. "I'll be over as soon as I shower."

"Could you hurry, please? I mean with all these vampires around, I don't want to be left alone for very long."

"Aw, come on. You don't actually believe all that talk on the radio. Haven't you heard of *War of the Worlds?*"

"No," she answered. "But I'd still be happier if you hurried."

"All right. I'll be there as soon as I can," I said cheerfully.

"You always could make me smile, Trevor. I'll see you in a little bit."

"Okay. Bye."

"Bye-bye," she said as I hung up the phone.

I smiled to myself as I walked upstairs to the bathroom. Robin had been my friend for as long as I could remember. We were as close as two people could be without being related. We were born two days apart and had grown up together in Dweller Valley. Our parents were in the same business, computer sales, and were on the same business trip this weekend.

After my shower, I got dressed and ran over to her house. Even though it was right next door, it was fifty-five degrees out and the dark gray clouds in the sky said it was going to rain soon. When I stepped out my back door, I felt a gentle sprinkle begin to hit my head.

"Aw, come on. Don't even start raining," I said to the sky.

I took a deep breath, sighed, and jumped over the hedges that separated our properties. I rolled when I landed in Robin's backyard. I rose to my feet and headed for Robin's back porch. As I opened the screen door, I heard a wolf-like howl.

Damn! Somebody better put "Rover" out of his misery.

I knocked on the kitchen door. I never went in the front door. It was my own little quirk with her family. Whenever I would come over to visit Robin or drop something off to her mother, I used the back door.

Suddenly a heavy gust of wind blew through the enclosed porch, knocking over boxes and papers. I knocked on the door again.

"Hurry up, Robin! Open the door," I demanded as I shivered. From fright or chill, who's to say?

I saw a shadow move across the wall of the kitchen. Instantly light filled the room and filtered through the curtains. I peeked in one of the windows.

I saw Robin walking toward the door wearing a pair of red and black-checkered boxer shorts and a white tank top. She pulled back the curtains on the window and smiled when she saw that I was standing there. She unlatched the lock. I opened the door and walked in, shutting it behind me. I looked at Robin in disbelief.

"Man, Robin," I said with a grin. "Aren't you cold?"

"No, I'm fine," she answered as she walked over to the fridge.

She opened the door, leaned in and pulled out a bottle of cranberry juice. She took a big swig straight from the container. She swallowed then handed the bottle to me.

"Want some?" she asked with a grin.

"No. That's okay," I answered as I held in a chuckle. "I will have a soda, though. If you have any left."

"I think we do," Robin replied as she lowered her head into the refrigerator once again. I could hear her moving bowls and different food items around as she searched for my drink. "Ah, here we are." She stood up and handed me can of Pepsi. "Last one."

"Thanks." I walked over to the sink and jumped onto the counter.

Robin walked over and jumped up beside me. "So," I patted her on the leg. "What're we gonna watch?" I took a drink of soda.

14

Robin put her hand in mine. "I don't know. I'll leave it up to you." She looked at me. "Either *Buffy: The Vampire Slayer* or *Bram Stoker's Dracula*."

"Buffy." Was my answer. "We'll save the scary one for later." I put the can beside me then hopped off of the counter. I stood in front of Robin and put my hands on either side of her legs. I leaned in close to her face. "But first, there's something we have to do."

Robin wrapped her legs around my waist and said in a seductive voice. "And just what might that be?" She put her arms around my neck and started to twirl my hair with her fingers. She looked into my eyes.

"Popcorn," I replied teasingly. I lifted her off the counter. She hugged herself closer to my body as she let her legs lower to the floor. *Damn, Robin! Getting a little bold now. Aren't we?* "We need popcorn."

"Oh. I'll get it," she said, doing a complete 180-degree emotional turn. She got a bag of microwave popcorn from the cupboard, placed it in the microwave and set the timer.

Noticing that her attitude suddenly changed, I asked a simple question.

"What's wrong?" I went over to my friend and put my hands on her shoulders. We both looked out the window above the sink. "I'm sorry. I shouldn't have been flirting with you after you and Bobby's breakup. I don't know what came over me."

"No, Trevor. It's all my fault. I've been lonely ever since the breakup." She sniffed and wiped her eyes. "And I guess all I want is to be held."

I couldn't help myself. I gave in. I turned Robin around so that we were face to face. I put my arms around her waist.

"Hey. Don't let your breakup with Bobby get you down," I said reassuringly. "Hell. If we weren't such good friends, and it wouldn't mess up our friendship, I'd ask you to go with *me*."

"Oh, Trevor. You're such a sweetheart."

We looked into each other's eyes. *Come on, Trevor. Just kiss her.* Without realizing what I was doing, I gave in to the voice in my head. Robin must have been thinking the same thing, because she leaned her face toward mine. Just as our mouths were about to touch, the beeping of the microwave snapped us back to reality. *What the hell just happened?*

"Cool. Popcorn's done." I quickly went over to the microwave and opened it. Without thinking, I reached in and pulled out our snack. "Ow! Ow-ow! Get me a bowl! Quick!" I begged as I burnt my fingers on the steaming bag. Robin held out a big, yellow Tupperware bowl. I grabbed it and poured in the popcorn. "Thanks," I said as I extended the bowl toward my friend. "Want some?"

"Maybe later," Robin declined as she waved the snack away.

"We have our snack, let's watch the movie," I explained as I headed to the living room. I had to get away from any more temptations.

After about an hour of watching Luke Perry and Krisi Swanson kill vampires, Robin did the one thing that changed my life from that moment on. She was sitting on my right side on the couch as I chowed down on the popcorn. Still chewing a handful of popcorn, I pointed to the television.

"Oh man. I love this part. Luke Perry is funny as hell." I swallowed what popcorn I still had in my mouth and put my hand jokingly on Robin's leg. "And Kristi Swanson. Wow!" Robin reached over and grabbed the bowl from my hand. "Robin. What are you doing?"

"I'm gonna make you forget about Buffy," she said seductively as she turned off the VCR and crawled on top of me.

I didn't do anything as my body responded to Robin's acts. My inner voice wasn't helping matters either. Robin kissed me full on the lips and I didn't do a thing to stop her. Deep down, I liked it. She began to suck the air from my lungs. This took my breath away both figuratively and literally. I started to get lightheaded as she continued. Suddenly, Robin bit me on the tongue.

"Ouch!" I gasped as I pushed her away. "What the hell was that for?"

"What's the matter, Trevor? Don't you like it when I do that?"

"Unfortunately, yes." I put my hand to my mouth. "Everything but the biting." I sat up and looked my friend in her eyes while trying to catch my breath. "That's why I can't." I put Robin's hands in mine. "Like I said in the kitchen. If we get too serious now, it could screw up our friendship later."

"What if I could guarantee," she started, "that later, you'll feel completely different about that?" I thought I saw Robin's eyes glow red as she leaned closer to me.

This is nuts. I gotta go home.

I tried to get up, but Robin adjusted her hips against my waist. Effectively pinning me to the couch. I looked up into her eyes. Two eyes that had once been beautiful emeralds became two glowing rubies of evil.

As I looked into them, my head began to pound. I shook it in a feeble attempt to clear it. My vision began to cloud over in a sort of "red haze." Everything in the path of my vision now had a red hue to it. Whites were pinks. And the blue of her living room curtains transformed into a dark shade of purple. I could feel control of my body slowly draining away.

"Uh. Yeah. Sure." I couldn't believe what I said.

I don't want to do this with Robin. Especially while she's on the rebound. Did she drug that Pepsi? Then, as if I someone else were talking, I heard my own voice say, "I guess I wouldn't have a problem with that."

"Good," she replied with an evil smile. "Then do what you want with me."

My body did what I had the respect not to do. It gave in to my basic desire for physical contact. I grabbed the back of Robin's head, pulled it to me, and kissed her passionately on the lips.

What the hell am I doing? And why can't I stop?

Our tongues danced passionately inside our mouths. My hands roamed up and down her back and legs. Robin stopped kissing me and sat up. I leaned up to continue kissing her, but she pushed me back against the couch. She tore off her tank top and threw it on the floor. She then lowered her body once again onto mine and began to rub against me.

"Let's see," she said. "Where were we? Oh yeah." She began to once again kiss me. Slow little pecks at first, then as I started to rub her chest, she became more animalistic in her actions. At one point she scratched open my T-shirt with her fingernails.

"Oh shit!" I cried out. "Robin! That hurt." I looked down at my shirt then up at Robin. And wished that I hadn't. "What the hell!"

The sight of my oldest friend's face contorting into the face of the undead snapped me to my senses. It was now the face of a vampire. The true embodiment of evil. I tried to get up and run, but I couldn't move. I wasn't sure if it was because Robin was sitting on me, or if it was some kind of vampire hypnosis. But I did know that I had to get out of the house and away from her. My mind began to race through different ways to leave.

Robin grabbed me by the head and leaned my head to the side. She lowered her mouth to the flesh of my neck. I could feel her fangs enter my skin. For an instant her mouth was cold on my flesh. Then I began to lose most of the sensation in my body. I could no longer feel Robin's weight on my legs as they went numb. What little sensation I still had told me that blood was trickling down from the wound in my neck as she fed on me.

Oh shit! This is it. I'm gonna die. I made up my mind. *I can't die this way. I won't die this way.* Then I came up with an idea. *God, I hope this works.*

I began to twitch my body. After a few seconds I stopped. Exhausted, my body went limp. It worked. I felt her sit up and heard her lick her lips as the sensation came back into my body. Robin crawled off of me and stood beside the couch. I opened my eyes a little to see what she was doing. Her face

17

changed to her human one as she put on the red-checkered shirt flannel shirt that was on the back of the couch.

"Was it good for you?" she asked after she wiped the rest of the blood on her arm. She then turned and walked out toward the kitchen.

I felt my strength returning as renewed energy flowed through my body. I sat up on the couch and I put my hand to my neck.

"No," I answered matter-of-factly as I looked toward the kitchen door.

What the hell just happened here? I thought vampires weren't supposed to exist. I walked over to the fireplace and looked in the large mirror that was hanging above it. *Maybe it's a dream?* I looked at the bite marks even more closely.

The two holes were side by side, about an inch apart. It looked as though someone had stabbed me twice with a pencil. They had somehow stopped bleeding. *At least they're healing,* I thought to myself as I touched the one on the top. "Ouch." *Not fast enough though.* "There goes the dream theory."

At that moment, I had a prickly sensation in my temples. And a feeling as though someone were behind me. *Robin's coming back from the kitchen. I gotta hide.* I grabbed the fire poker from the hearth and dove behind the couch. I heard Robin's feet move on the carpet. Then something hit the floor with a thud.

"What the hell! Nooo!"

Wait a sec, I thought to myself. *Vampires don't drink juice. Oh crap. That was blood. It's now or never.* I rose from up from behind the couch, hiding the poker behind me. Vampire or not, I wanted a weapon.

"What's the matter, Robin?" I said with a smirk. "Lose something?" I walked to the side of the couch farthest from my former friend.

"But…but…you were dead. You went limp!"

"Not quite. I was faking. I played dead."

Her eyes glowed red as she once again changed into a vampire. "Then I guess," she growled, "this time I'll rip you apart to make sure you're dead." She leapt toward me at a speed that I never thought was possible. For some reason I noticed that I could see the light from the fireplace flicker off of her fangs.

Thinking quickly, with reflexes to match her speed, I raised the poker and stabbed her in the chest. Her body fell onto the couch and rolled to the floor. "You should know," she coughed, spitting up blood, "this isn't gonna stop me, Trevor."

"Yeah. I know. But it *will* buy me some time to get out of here." I ran to the kitchen and left through the back door.

I ran across town to Dick Harshburger's house. Dick wasn't one of my closest friends, but he was a good enough one to help me out. I just hoped that the vampires hadn't gotten to him. Luckily, he didn't live too far away.

The ducking in and out of peoples' driveways and cutting across a few yards helped me cut a lot of time off my trip. As I went behind the Pizza Palace parking lot, the bells in the united Methodist Church across the street from the restaurant signaled that it was nine o'clock. As if it were on a sprinkler system on a timer, the sky opened up and the rain began to pour.

"Great!" I exclaimed as I looked to the clouds for mercy, "This is all I need." At that time, I got that same strange sensation that I had at Robin's. I ducked into a nearby alley. A car pulled up to the curb in front of my hiding place. The headlights went out and the passenger's side door opened.

Oh crap.

"You'd better get in," The female driver said from inside. "Unless you want to catch your death."

That's a hell of a way to put it. Although it is raining and I don't feel like catching a cold. I crawled inside and looked at the sister of one of my other close friends from school.

"Thanks a lot, Candy." I shut the door and started to put on my seat belt.

"That's all right, Trevor. Anything to help one of Shauni's friends. You won't need the seatbelt. This car has real good breaks and airbags," she replied without taking her eyes off of the road. "What were you doing out in this weather? You could catch a cold or worse."

Tell me about it. I looked out the window and then back at Candy.

"Just going to a friend's house. My car broke down on the way over, so I left it in the Lakeside Store parking lot. Then I started walking and it started raining. And you know the rest."

Candy looked at me for the first time since I got in the car.

"Yeah, I know." She grinned. "I could jump it for you." She looked back to the road, I assumed for a place to turn around. "I have jumper cables in the…"

I quickly put my hand on her arm in desperation. "No! That's okay. I don't think that's the problem anyway. I think it might be out of gas or oil…" I ran out of lies, "or something." I looked out the window in submission.

"You know what I think?" Her voice got deeper in a way that I recognized from Robin's house. "I think you're afraid." Candy stopped the car in the middle of the street.

"Candy! What're you doing?" I turned toward her and saw what I knew I would. "Holy shit!" Candy's face was deformed into that of a vampire. Her

19

eyes glowed and her fangs extended to almost a full inch in length. I fumbled for the door and grasped for the handle.

Unfortunately, between thought and execution, Candy grabbed my shoulders and turned me around. Our faces were inches apart. I could feel her breath on my face. It was musty smelling, like my parent's attic on a hot summer day.

"Man, Candy. You need a breathmint. Whew-wee."

"What I need is your blood."

"*No*. You need a bre—"

Candy bent her head back to take a bite from my neck. Her face contorted even more than it already was. She was now more demon-like in her appearance.

"Now. To finish what Robin started." Her eyes started to glow red as she leaned even closer to my neck.

All my thoughts were beginning to cloud in my mind. The same "red haze" from before was once again messing with my vision. I could still see Candy, clear as day. There was a red cloud around her. She tilted my head to the side and lowered her mouth to my neck. I remember seeing a flash of light, then Candy's vampire face.

And once again, my thoughts were my own.

"Dammit!" Candy screamed toward an oncoming car.

I saw this as my last chance to get away. I butted Candy on the side of her head. She flew against her door with a bang. I opened mine and began to crawl out. As my ribs cleared the door, she grabbed me by the waist of my pants and started to pull me back into the vehicle and her vampire hunger. I bent my right leg and kicked at her. The bottom of my foot connected with her chest.

"Aargh!" She groaned as she fell against the steering wheel. I quickly got out of the car. As I stood up, Candy made a final attempt to dive at me. I quickly slammed the door. It connected with her head with a hollow "thump."

I didn't even look to see if she was conscious or chasing after me. I just had to get out of there. I ran into the darkness to Dick's house.

It was around eleven-thirty when I got there. Being careful not to be seen, I kept in the shadows. When I got there, he was lying on his bed reading an issue of *Weight Lifter's Digest*.

I tapped on the glass. My friend looked up from his magazine and with a look of befuddlement on his face, came over and opened the window.

"Can I come in?" I said as I leaned my head inside.

"Yeah. But be careful," he said as he gestured me to enter. I started to crawl the rest of the way in. "Try not to knock anything—" My foot hit a cheerleading picture that was on the stand near his bed. It fell to the floor. "—over."

"Sorry about that," I apologized as I picked it up and handed to Dick.

"That's okay. It was the one Beth gave me last year. I'm gonna ask her for a new one this school year anyway." We laughed at the situation. An inside joke between the two of us.

"By the way," Dick looked at me with seriousness on his face, "what the hell are you doing here so late? And why couldn't you have just used the front door?"

"Vampires"

"Vampires?" he repeated. "What? Did you want to borrow one of my movies? Why couldn't you have waited till tomorrow?"

"No, Dick. Not movie ones. Real life, blood sucking, pain in the neck vampires."

"Are you serious? I mean. I just heard reports about them on the radio, but I didn't think they were real. I thought they were publicity stunts for that movie that's coming out this spring."

"Oh they're real all right. One just chased me here. And another gave me these." I pulled down my collar and showed Dick where Robin had bitten me.

"You can't be serious. I know you're lying now," he said as he looked at my neck. "They don't look that bad. They look like scars that you've had for years."

"What do you mean, 'they don't look that bad'?"

I went over to the mirror that was sitting on the dresser that I had just crawled past. I pulled down my collar and checked the bite marks. To my surprise he was right. They looked like I did have them for years.

"Who did this to you?" Dick asked.

"Robin Green," I said as I continued to look at the bite marks.

"Oh shit."

I turned around and looked at my friend.

"What?" I asked in a serious, "this ain't good" voice.

"Are you sure that it was Robin Green?" I nodded an affirmative. "She just called." I turned and walked over to Dick. "She said she wanted to come here for some fun. If you know what I mean?"

"Yeah, her kind of fun." I rubbed my neck to make my point. "When is she supposed to be here?" I asked as I grabbed the broom from the corner of his room and my Swiss Army knife from my pocket.

"Twelve. Why?"

"So we can have some fun with her. If you know what *I* mean," I answered as I sharpened the hand of the room.

We waited for what seemed like an eternity. Finally, about ten after twelve, my temples began to throb and the back of my neck began to tingle. *It must be nerves.* Then there was a knock at the kitchen door. I hid in the den, right beside the living room. Dick answered the door. I opened the door and peeked out so that I could see what was happening.

"Robin," he said in a slightly scared voice.

"Dick," she began, "sorry I took so long, but I had some unfinished business to attend to." Then she noticed his actions. "What's wrong, Dick? You look frightened."

"Who? Me? No, I'm okay."

"Good. We wouldn't want anything to spoil tonight, would we?" She said in an evil voice as they made their way to the couch.

"No. We wouldn't," he replied in a stupor.

Robin looked at Dick. "Dick. You look tense. Let me give you a back massage." She walked a spaced-out Dick into the living room and onto the couch. "Now, just relax and let me take care of you."

She began to massage Dick's neck. She kneaded the flesh, kissing it as she rubbed. Dick was relaxing and becoming completely oblivious to his surroundings.

"How do you feel, Dick?" she asked as her eyes glowed red.

"I feel good," he replied in his magical stupor.

"Get ready to feel even better," she said evilly as she bent back his neck to take her prize. One I was all too familiar with.

"Get away from him, Robin!" I yelled as I appeared from the doorway.

"Trevor! It's good to see you again," she growled as she looked up at me.

"Wish I could say the same," I sarcastically replied.

"Now we can finish what we started back at my house," she said as she leapt at me with her mouth open and her fangs glaring. She seemed to float through the air. As though she were jumping on the moon.

"I don't think so." When I saw her face and how it was transformed into the disgusting guise of a vampire, the same fear as before came over me. But nevertheless, I reached behind my back and grabbed the makeshift stake. I plunged the old broomstick handle into Robin's chest. She screamed an unearthly howl and slumped to the floor. I ran over to Dick to see if he was okay.

"Hey man, are you all right?"

"Yeah, I'm fine," he replied. Shaking his head as I helped as I helped him to his feet. He looked down and saw Robin's body lying on the floor. "Holy shit! What happened?"

"Oh, nothing," I began. "You just missed all the fun. If you know what I mean."

CHAPTER 2

For the next few weeks, Dick and I prepared for my return to Dweller Valley High School. I may have been considered missing, but that didn't mean I still shouldn't try to get an education. Plus I figured it'd be the best place to ensure my friends' safety from the vampires.

First we made up papers that said that I was Dick's cousin, Dylan MacLeod, from New York. I got the name from my two favorite television shows. They also said that I was staying with him until my parents got back from a business/year-long vacation in Europe. Next, we made the proper manuscripts from "Dylan's" old high school to get him enrolled in Dweller Valley. You'd be surprised what you can do with a computer, a scanner and a printer if you know where to look.

Finally we worked on what "Dylan" would look like. I never cut my hair during the summer months. Some people thought I was nuts. That's not true; I was just too busy having fun to get it cut. We decided to let it grow longer than usual, dye it blond and put it in a ponytail when I got to school. Then I tried on some of Dick's old clothes. After all, I couldn't go back to my house and get mine. Last, but not least, I put on an old pair of Dick's sister's glasses. It worked for Clark Kent, why not me?

All too quickly the day came when we were to see if our little deception would work. That's right, the first day of school for Dylan MacLeod. When Dick and I arrived at school, I headed straight for the guidance counselor's office. After a long-winded talk, getting my schedule and a Dweller Valley High rulebook, Mr. Waters told me I would be reporting to my fourth period class.

"Welcome to Dweller Valley High, Dylan. I'm sure you'll feel right at home here," he commented as we walked out of his office.

"I'm sure I *will* too," I replied with a hidden smile.

25

"Your next class is Geometry-Trigonometry with Mr. Finnish. It's in room twelve. Would you like some help getting there?"

"No. That's okay. I think I can find it. Thanks anyway." I headed down the hall.

"And Dylan," I stopped and turned around, "if there's anything you need help with—any problems—my door is *always* open to the students."

"I'll keep that in mind, sir."

Yeah right.

I headed down the hallway toward my destination. Before I turned down the final hallway, I stopped to look at the trophy case that was right next to the main doors to the building. It was something I always did. One of my many quirks.

I only really liked to look at two of the pictures. One of them was a picture of me when I played basketball my junior year. We won the state championship that year. It was great. The second was probably even more personal. It was a picture of the cheerleaders. One of my friends and the only girl I really ever had feelings for, Shauni Collins, was on the cheerleading squad during basketball season. She was mainly in band during football season. We always had the whole friendship thing going, so I had to keep my feelings a secret. She was also the cousin of my best friend.

I quit reminiscing and decided to head to class. I walked down the hallway to the classroom. I could hear Mr. Finnish as I neared the doorway. He was giving one of his lectures on the American justice system and why we should just kill everyone as soon as they commit a crime.

"…should bring back public hangings. I mean, come…" He turned toward the door when I knocked. "Can I help you?"

I nervously walked into the room and handed him my schedule card. I could feel the twenty-five pairs of eyes watching my every move. I also heard a few murmurs. *I hope no one figures out who I am, or I'm screwed. Dick's in this class too, so that's a plus.* I saw my "cousin" sitting in the back row. He gave me a "go ahead" gesture.

"Uh, Mr. Waters said that I'm supposed to get all my teachers to sign this. I'm your new student, Dylan MacLeod."

"All righty then," he said as he signed my card. He handed it back to me and pointed to an empty desk in the second row from the window. "You can sit there. The student that was supposed to sit there was supposedly killed by *vampires* or something." Mr. Finnish turned back to the class as I headed to my seat.

"Now that Mr. MacLeod has gotten my attention back on teaching. Baby, would you please do number fifteen on the board?" Ann "Baby" Jackson got up from her desk, behind Shauni's, and headed to the chalkboard with her book.

I looked to where he had pointed. The desk was right beside Shauni's. *Great. Just perfect.* Shauni was the last person that I wanted to sit beside. Although I cared for her a lot, I didn't really want her to see through my disguise.

I tried to hide my face as best I could, without her noticing that I was trying to hide it from her. I sat down at my desk and started to act like I was paying attention to Mr. Finnish. Then I noticed that he didn't give me a textbook. I was just about to raise my hand and tell him when someone hit me on the arm with a pencil. It bounced of my side and rolled to the floor.

"Hey, Dylan."

Oh, man. That's Shauni's voice. Maybe if I ignore her, she won't bother me.

No such luck. She called my name again. I turned in her direction.

"Can I help you?"

"Can you pick that up for me?"

"But you just threw…" I began. But thought better of it. With Shauni, it was useless to argue. I bent down and picked up the pencil.

"Thanks. You're so kind," she said with a flirtatious smile.

That can't be good.

"No problem." I handed her the pencil. "Here you go." I turned back to Mr. Finnish, who was watching Baby finish working out her equation. *So much for getting his attention.*

"You're new here, aren't you?"

"No. I've been sitting here the whole year and you just never noticed."

"Ha-ha. Very funny," she said with a smile. "I overheard Dick say that you're his cousin from New York."

"Uh-huh," I answered quietly. Trying not to get Mr. Finnish's attention.

"That's nice. I went there before with Project Upward Bou…"

"Shauni. And—Dylan?" Some of the class clowns in the back snickered as Mr. Finnish interrupted our in-class conversation. "Would you two like to teach while *I* talk?"

"No, sir," we answered in unison.

"Very well. Dylan. Can you come to the board and do number seventeen before class ends?"

"No, Mr. Finnish. I can't." I might as well tell him, now that I have his attention.

"And why not?"

"Because you didn't give me a book yet."

The class burst into laughter as the teacher went to get me a book from the storage closet. He came back with a book entitled *Geometry/Trigonometry Phase I.*

"Nobody likes a smartass, Dylan," he said as he handed me the book.

"Thank you, sir."

"*Now,* will you do number seventeen?"

The bell rang, signaling the end of class.

"Guess not." A voice that I recognized as Tommy Bayer, class goof off and junior year president remarked.

Mr. Finnish turned around and gave me an evil-looking stare. I shrugged in a way that said, "It isn't my fault." Everyone shuffled out the door, giggling as they walked past the teacher's desk. I grabbed my books and followed. When I entered the hall, Shauni was waiting at her locker. *Damn. She knows it's me.* I tried to avoid her as I made my way through the other students. No such luck.

"Dylan. Hey, Dylan. Wait," she said as she ran to me. "I almost forgot to tell you my name. It's Shauni, Shauni Collins."

"Well, Shauni Shauni Collins." I grinned. "What can I help you with?"

"Ha ha. Very funny. No, I was just wondering if I could see your schedule card for a second."

"Yeah sure. No problem." *Yeah. Like saying "no" would really help.* I handed her the schedule.

"Oh rats," she said after scanning my classes.

"What's the matter? Is something wrong."

"Huh? What?" She handed back the schedule. "Oh no. Nothing's wrong. We only have fourth, sixth and seventh periods together."

"Gee. That's too bad. And I was looking to spend the whole day with you," I said with a smile. *At least she won't be hounding me all day.*

"I guess I'll see you in chemistry class."

"Yeah, see you then. I better get to," I looked at my class schedule,"Current Events," I replied then headed down the hall.

Nicole Watson watched me as I walked to my class. She walked over to Shauni.

"Shauni. I wouldn't get too friendly with him if you know what I mean. He

28

looks like he's got a secret. He might be one of those vampires that I heard about on the news."

"Yeah right, Nicole. If he's a vampire, then I'm *Pippi Longstocking*. He's about as harmless as Trevor was," she replied to her friend as she closed her locker door.

Fifth period went by so slow that I thought that I was going to fall asleep. The bell rang, as I was about to doze off for the third time. Our class had "B-Lunch," which meant that we were scheduled to go to the cafeteria before class.

It was the usual excitement for a school lunch. Aside from trying to figure our what the main dish was, nothing much happened. Dick introduced "Dylan" to some of his friends. They all were pretty nice to me.

I got bored during one of Tommy's bad jokes. Without warning, I noticed that I could hear the lunch ladies bitching about the conditions that they had to work in. I laughed, just in time for the end of the joke.

I guess timing is everything.

Just then, the bell rang that signaled us to go to chemistry.

After the ten minutes that it took everyone to get in the room and settle down, the teacher, Mr. Poser told us to get into lab groups.

"But before we do that," he began. "We're going to have a pop quiz." There were a few "boo's" and a couple hisses from the back of the room. "Anyone that wasn't here yesterday doesn't have to take it," the teacher continued. "Okay. Who wasn't here?" About half of the class, including me, raised their hands.

"All right. Let me rephrase that," Mr. Poser said as he waved his hands in an attempt to get order into his class. "Who wasn't here *physically?*" There were a few snickers and some laughs as the jokers lowered their hands in defeat. After which, only four hands were left raised. "Well, Dylan. I think you have a good excuse."

"Just making sure, sir."

He handed out the papers for the quiz. I just stared out the window for most of the time. Other than that, I doodled on my tablet and put book covers on my books. I *even* leafed through my chemistry textbook. What can I say, I was bored. When my fellow classmates were finished asking him to repeat certain questions, Mr. Poser collected the quiz papers then told us to get into our lab groups. I didn't know what to do so I headed to Dick's group, in the back of the room.

As fate would have it, good or bad I do not know, I was drafted into Shauni's group. As I was walking back to get into Dick's group, my favorite sensation, which I started to associate with a vampire being near, hit me harder than it had ever hit me since I had been bitten. I leaned against one of the tables for support.

"Dylan, are you all right?" Shauni asked as she grabbed my arm.

"Yeah, I'm fine," I lied. "Just a little headache."

"Good," she said as she pulled me into her group. "Now you're well enough to light the Bunsen burner for us."

"Oh joy," I replied under my breath. I knew it was useless to argue with Shauni, so I gave in and joined her lab group. The others in her group consisted of Kari Little and Baby Jackson. Shauni and I didn't do much of the lab. Against my better judgment, we talked most of the period.

"I see you survived Current Events. I hear that class is really hard."

"Yeah, it is hard." I smiled. "To stay awake in."

I looked back to Dick's group to see how they were coming along. It looked like he was doing pretty well. I wish I could say the same for the rest of the group. Dick's group consisted of himself, Tommy Bayer, Doug Ewing (my real cousin) and Beth Everett. Doug and Tommy were the only ones in the group that were working on the lab. Dick was working on his own chemistry, with Beth.

I knew it was an invasion of privacy, but I just *had* to hear what lines he was using on Beth this time. I concentrated my slowly developing vampire hearing to listen to his conversation.

"...doesn't give you the kind of attention I do. And he's your boyfriend."

"Dick. I've already told you that you're like a brother to me. I've told you things I didn't even tell Joey. That's why we will never be more that just friends. I don't want to lose that. You understand?"

Deja vu. That sounds familiar. I laughed to myself. Or so I thought.

"What's so funny, Dylan?" Kari asked in a disgusted voice. "If you think you can do any better," She threw down the striker. "Go ahead."

"I wasn't laughing at you," I replied. "I was just thinking to myself."

"Chill out, Kari," Shauni interjected.

I turned to Shauni. "She sure is in a bitchy mood. Or is that just her usual warm attitude."

"That's her usual. Nowadays."

"It's just," she leaned in closer and began to whisper, "ever since last Friday she's been acting strangely."

"Did she do anything out of the ordinary last week? Did she have any unexpected appointments?"

"Well. Last Thursday she had a spur-of-the-moment meeting with Mr. Cross, the music teacher. And when I asked if I could go in with her. He said 'your time will come soon enough,' " she explained. "Why? What's up?"

"Nothing. I was just wondering," I lied. "And speaking of wondering."

Don't do it Trevor. You can't risk it.

It's very seldom how often I listen to myself.

"Yes, Dylan?"

"Are you going to the bonfire tonight?"

You're gonna regret this, man. I'm telling you.

"And if you don't have a date. I was wondering if you'd like to go with me."

"Yes, I am. No, I don't. And yes, I would. Pick me up at seven?"

"All right then. Seven it is."

I'm screwed.

During our after school training exercises, I told Dick about chemistry class and how I can apparently sense vampires when they're near. And about asking Shauni to be my date to the bonfire.

"You're screwed." Was his only reply.

I pulled into Shauni's driveway a little before seven that evening. I adjusted my glasses and tightened my ponytail. I looked in the rearview mirror.

"I hope you know what you're doing."

I got out of the car and went to the front door; I knocked to announce my arrival.

"Coming."

Even though she wasn't too keen on the idea, because it makes her feel old, I decided to call her "Mrs. Collins." Trevor Wayne may have been given permission to call her by her first name, but Dylan MacLeod was new in town. And I couldn't afford to give them any reason to be suspicious.

"Yes, may I help you?"

Here goes nothing.

"Hello, Mrs. Collins. I'm Dylan MacLeod," I started. "Is Shauni ready to go?"

"She should be. Let me check." She turned around and called into the trailer. "Shauni! Dylan's here!"

"Okay, Mom. I'll be out in a minute."

Yep. Shauni's never ready on time.

I looked around the small part of town where Shauni lived. Her house was located in a small, I guess you could say "village," on the outskirts of Dweller Valley. It was a nice place. You could look across the Yosemite River and see the cars driving across the newly constructed highway bypass. And, if you walked one hundred feet straight from her trailer you'd be standing in the river. The only bad part about the place was that when it rained enough, the river would rise and cover the road in front of the trailer and part of her driveway.

There were other families that lived there too. Some in small houses. Others, like Shauni's, in trailers. The closest house to hers was a trailer about fifty feet down the road that I had come on.

Mrs. Collins realized that I was still standing there.

"Oh my! Where are my manners? Won't you come in?" she said as she motioned me to enter.

"Now, Dylan," she said as we walked down the hallway toward the kitchen, "if you're going to be friends with Shauni. You must know my number one rule. Call me Maggie. 'Mrs. Collins' makes me feel old."

That was easy enough.

"All right then—Maggie," I replied as we entered the dining area. I smiled to myself. Maggie made a motion to sit at the table. As I pulled back one of the chairs, I had the same sensation as before. I got ready for the worst.

How stupid can you get, Trevor?

"Who's that, Mom?" Candy's voice asked.

"It's Dylan for Shauni," Maggie answered as Candy walked out of the living room, where she had been watching television.

Candy held out her hand for me to shake it. So I did.

"You look awfully familiar," Candy began with a smile. "Have we met before?"

"I don't think so," I said shakily.

She can't spill the beans. Not now.

"You look a lot like a hitchhiker I picked up a while back," she said. The tension between us was becoming almost tangible.

Just play it cool, man.

"Couldn't have been me. I've only been in down for the past week. I'm staying with my cousin."

"Candy. You know that you shouldn't pick up hitchhikers. I thought I taught you girls better than that," Maggie said in mild disgust. "God knows what he might have done."

"Don't have a cow, Mom. He wasn't *that* dangerous," she said as she gave me a small fang-showing smirk.

Wish I could say the same for you.

Candy continued to stare at me. Maggie, seeing that there was some tension, decided to change the subject.

"So, Dylan Were you and Shauni going anywhere after the bonfire?"

"I don't know. It's really up to her," I answered as I took my eyes off of Candy and looked at her mother. "We'll probably come straight home."

"Well if you *do* go somewhere, call. Otherwise be home before twelve."

"We will."

"You mean you're not going to take her to some secluded spot and…"

"Candy! That's enough!" Maggie ordered.

"Don't let Candy bother you. She's just being her usual self," Shauni explained as she came down the hall.

"Oh, that's okay. I don't mind. I have one at home just like her."

"You have a sister?" Shauni asked.

"No," I answered. "I meant my whole family." Shauni and Maggie laughed at the joke.

Candy, on the other hand, didn't. Shauni got her coat off of the table and we headed down the hall to the front door. We walked out onto the porch. Maggie came out to see her youngest daughter off. Candy followed to keep an eye on me.

"I'll see you later," Shauni said as she kissed her mother on the cheek. "We'll call if we go anywhere. Bye, Candy." She got into the passenger's side.

"Good-bye, you two. And Dylan, you'd better be careful. People that hang out with Shauni seem to wind up being killed by vampires. So you'd better watch out," she said as her eyes glowed red.

"Vampires?" I repeated.

"Yep."

"It takes one to know one. Don't it?" I said with a smirk as I got into the car. We pulled out of the driveway and headed to the high school and the bonfire.

After parking the car in the student parking lot, Shauni and I began the search for our friends. It didn't take very long for the simple fact that almost everybody in our grade was already there. The bonfire was considered the biggest event of the high school football season. Every year, Dweller Valley High would have one to motivate the student body for the upcoming Friday night varsity football game against their archrival, Fichenton. This year's bonfire was no exception. Everyone was hanging out and having fun dancing.

At nine o'clock, the really weird part of the night happened. Shauni and I were standing by the soda coolers talking to Baby Jackson and Nicole Watson. As Nicole was asking me a question, I got that weird sensation in my temples. Simultaneously, two vampires wearing Fichenton High School jackets began to terrorize my fellow students as they ran for safety. I grabbed Shauni's arm and pulled her behind a nearby pickup truck.

"We're not here to cause trouble, unless we have to. We're just here for Trevor Wayne," the smaller of the two vampires explained.

Perfect. Just perfect.

"And if he isn't here in thirty seconds," began the larger one, "we're gonna have to hurt someone." He flew over to Tommy Bayer and picked him up by the collar. Just as he was about to throw his ex-girlfriend's Fichenton jacket onto the fire. "Starting with him."

"Oh shit!" Tommy gasped as he was unceremoniously lifted into the air.

I turned to my date. She was watching the events transpire with a mixture of fright and anger on her face. I assumed, not only for Tommy, but also for the rest of our friends. Trevor Wayne was going to show up. Just not the way the vampires, and Tommy wanted him to. I grabbed Shauni by the shoulders and turned her so that she was facing me.

"Shauni!" I yelled over the sounds of the commotion. "Go find Dick. Tell him to go to the car and that it's time to have some fun. He'll know what you mean."

"What are you going to do?"

"Run interference," I answered as I kissed her on the forehead. "Now go." I gave her a nudge in the direction that I had last seen Dick.

"Good luck, Dylan."

"Thanks," I replied as I stood up for Dylan MacLeod's first confrontation with the undead. "I'll need it."

Just as Tommy was down to his last breath, I stepped out from my hiding place. Tommy and his captors looked at me in awe.

"Who the hell are you?" the bigger of the two vampires asked.

"I'm Dylan MacLeod," I started as I adjusted my glasses with my index finger. I then pointed to my Tommy. "And I believe you're hurting my friend."

"Who cares?" he remarked as he tightened his grip around Tommy's neck. "The Leader wants Wayne. If you don't mind."

"Yeah. I do mind." *Dick. Hurry up!* "First off, Trevor ran away a couple months ago. He's probably dead. Second, I don't think you two are staying here much longer." *God I hope I'm right.*

"Oh. You think!" the smaller one said. No longer tolerating my tough act. "Get 'im, Danny."

Danny dropped Tommy and jumped at me, his fangs glaring in the firelight. *Oh, Boy.* I braced myself for the impact. Luckily, one of my vampire abilities that *had* manifested itself was my invulnerability. When he hit me, I saw my life flash before my eyes. Then I smashed into the side of a nearby van.

"Oh shit!" I mumbled. "That hurt." I pulled myself to my feet.

"You think that was bad," the smaller one said, "wait till you get a load of me."

He ran up to me at such a speed that I didn't have time to dodge him. It was as though he disappeared then reappeared right in front of me. We flew across the front of the van and landed on the ground with a thud. It's too bad that vampires are as strong as they are made to be in the movies. But luckily they aren't as impervious to a well-placed foot. As the smaller one stood above me, I quickly rolled to my left side and kicked him in the groin. He groaned in pain and fell to the ground.

"Brian!" Danny yelled from across the parking lot.

"Come on, Danny." I stood up and brushed myself off. "You're next." Suddenly I was in the air with his hand around my throat.

"No, MacLeod." He grinned; showing off a pair of inch long fangs. "*You're* next."

"I don't think so," I managed to say.

Danny arched his back and dropped me to the ground.

"Aargh!" he screamed. He fell tot he ground beside me.

I looked up to see Dick holding a can of Dr. Pepper in one hand and my backpack full of stakes in the other. He extended his free hand to help me up. We started to walk back to the car and head home.

"Thanks, Dick," I began. "I owe you one." Just then, Dick threw his soda can in the air and reached into the backpack. With one fluid motion, he grabbed a stake and threw it straight at me. I used my vampire reflexes to dodge it. Then I heard Brian, who had tried sneaking up behind me, let out an unearthly howl as the stake entered his chest. Dick even caught his soda can before it hit the ground. "Nice get."

"Thanks," he replied with a grin. "Now that's two you owe me."

"Yeah. Sure. No problem," I replied as we got back to our vehicles. "Where's Shauni?" I asked, concerned.

"Jason gave her a ride home. He's become real protective of her since you disappeared."

"That's good. I guess it *is* better that she isn't here. Too many questions that I, that *we,* don't have answers for."

"Thanks for including me."

"Hey, no problem. What are friends for? By the way, are you getting me cake and ice cream tomorrow?"

"No. Why?" Dick started to unlock his door.

"Because *tomorrow* is my birthday," I said as I leaned against the car I was using for the duration of my stay with Dick. "And you're about the closest thing I have to family right now."

I thought about my real family and how they must've been worried about me and sad that I wouldn't be home for my birthday. Dick must have seen the anguish on my face.

"Okay, man. We'll do it after school tomorrow," Dick replied. "I'll pick up the cake and ice cream on the way home. What kind do you want?"

"Chocolate with peanut butter icing. And some chocolate-marshmallow ice cream," I informed him. "Thanks, man. This means a lot."

"Sure. Nothin' doin'. Now, can we go home?"

"Yeah. Let's go." I looked at the two dead vampires lying on the ground. "This party's dead anyway." I got into the car and headed to Dick's house.

CHAPTER 3

When I awoke the next morning, I could have sworn that I was in the middle of an earthquake. But earthquakes are very rare in Pennsylvania. I opened my eyes to see Dick jumping on my bed.

"Wake up ,Trevor," he said as he stopped his tremors on the mattress. He jumped down onto the floor. "It's time to go to school! We got a pep rally to go to!" He got serious for a moment. "Which means we pretty much have half a day." He resumed his carefree attitude. "Then we got the game tonight. And that's gonna be awesome. We're gonna kick Fichenton's ass. Just like we did last year."

"Gee. When you put it that way, how could I not want to get up?" I pulled the covers back over my head. "Give me twenty minutes."

"Ten," Dick bargained.

"Fifteen."

"All right, fifteen. I'll be back, then you're getting ready for school, young man," he said in his best impression of a female.

"Yes, ma'am," I replied.

I didn't get back to sleep. I spent the next quarter of an hour thinking about my mom and how she was going to take my birthday without me. It went by too quickly. Before I knew it, I had to get ready for school.

I got up and went into the bathroom. I drew my bath water and tried something different. I got a bath and shaved with my increased speed. The shaving, I shouldn't have done that fast. I had nicks and cuts on my face. The good part is that they were healed before I got dressed.

Maybe being half- vampire ain't that bad after all. I walked out of the bathroom fully dressed, two minutes after I entered.

"That was quick," Dick said, surprised.

"Super speed," I replied with a smile.

We headed to school. On the way, we decided to stop at the Sheetz store next to the Pizza Palace for breakfast. We headed straight to the fountain drink machine. As we were filling our cups, I had an eerie sensation. It was almost like when I would sense a vampire, but not quite the same.

I turned around instinctively and saw an old friend. It was Rick James Rice, named for the singer, but everyone called him "R.J." He wasn't looking too healthy this particular morning. He came in wearing sunglasses. His clothes were disheveled and you could tell that he hadn't even shaved. Dick turned around to see what I was looking at.

"Whoa! Dude!" he said when he saw R.J. "You look like crap, man. Were you up late last night or what?"

"I don't know, man. Last night I was out with the guys and some of the cheerleaders after the trouble at the bonfire." He leaned against the freezer that held the frozen snacks. "We were all drinkin' and stuff. Me and Kate Hardy were getting," he started to whisper as he made a "well, you know" gesture, "friendly. I remember looking into her eyes." He squinted as though he was trying to remember something else. "Then I'm waking up to my alarm going off. I don't even know how I got home.

Oh crap! Kate Hardy. This is worse than I thought.

Kate was an avid cheerleader and my ex-girlfriend. We hooked up while I was on the basketball team. We had dated for the last six months of our junior year. She broke up with me about three weeks before the situation with the vampires came about. She thought that I wanted to hang out with Jason and Shauni more than I wanted to be with her. She told me that she had had enough, and was tired of competing with them for my time.

If Kate's a vampire, there's no telling what she'll do.

"Hey, Dick. Since you're here. And I'm tired. I was just wondering…"

As R. J. broke off in mid-sentence, I sensed a vampire.

"R.J.? Are you all right, man?" Dick asked.

"Yeah, I think. I was gonna ask you if I could get a ride to school, then I got this strange feeling. As though someone was creeping up on me."

I know the feeling.

"Dick. You can take R. J. to school." I arched my left eye. "I think I'll walk. I have some things to do real quick. If you know what I mean," I said insistently.

Dick, getting the hint, nodded.

"Okay, man. I'll see you at school." He looked at R.J. "Well, Rick. It looks like a seat just opened up."

"Thanks, man. I appreciate it." I heard him reply as I paid for my drink and headed out the door. The vampire that R.J. and I sensed was gone by the time I got outside. The walk to school was equally uneventful.

As I walked down the hallway to my locker, people were looking at me strangely. They would point at me and talk about last night. About me fighting the vampires and how they would have helped, if they didn't have other things to do. I decided to tune in to some conversations.

"...is a real hero. Too bad you can't be more like him."

"Beth. I..."

Sorry about that one, Joey. I continued to swim through the ocean of people in the corridor.

"Shit! I could've taken them vampires out. But I remembered that I had to return a late video."

Yeah. Sure you did.

"...not the point. If Dylan wants some help from me, all he has to do is ask. Especially after he gave up his seat so I could get a ride to school this morning."

I just might take you up on that offer someday, Rick.

I arrived at my locker to see that I had some guests. One was Shauni, whom I expected. The other was her cousin, and my best friend, Jason Pasner. I walked up to them and kissed Shauni on the forehead.

"Good morning. You got home all right I take it?"

"Yeah. She did," Jason replied as he scrutinized my every move. "Who are you?"

Let's see if I can have a little fun with him.

"I'm Dylan MacLeod. Who are you? Her daddy?"

"I'm her cousin. Jason Pasner. You want to make something of it."

"All right, Jason. That's enough," Shauni interrupted. "Jason, Dylan is Dick's cousin from New York." She turned to me. "Dylan, Jason is my overprotective cousin." She smiled. "Now I want both of you to shake hands." Neither of us budged.

Yep. Same old Jason.

"Please!" she ordered. We did as she asked. "Good. Now that we're all friends, we can now go to class." Shauni turned and gave me a kiss on the cheek. "I'll see you later." I waved to her as she walked down the hall. "Bye, Jason," she said as she waved without looking.

I turned to my best friend.

"So. Since we're friends now," I started. "Where's your locker?"

He pointed to the locker right beside mine. "Right here. Locker five-thirty-four. Where's yours?"

Oh boy! I pointed to my locker.

"Right here. Locker five-thirty-five"

"Oh boy!" we said together.

The bell signaling the start of the school day sounded.

"We better get to class before the announcements start," Jason stated as he headed down the hall.

I didn't want to be late. There were no people in the hall and Jason's back was turned. So I got my books and headed to class at super speed. As I walked in the door to the art room. A student's voice started reading off the day's list of activities.

Just made it.

The rest of the day was pretty much uneventful. Until it came time for locker break. Shauni was waiting for me at my locker. And it looked as though she had just finished crying. I walked up to her and gave her a hug.

"Hey, Shauni. What is it? What's wrong?"

"Well, today is Trevor Wayne's birthday. He was Jason's best friend and I just feel sad that he…" She sniffed. "He's probably dead," she replied. "I wonder how his family is taking this whole thing."

I decided to tell Shauni the truth.

"Shauni…" I couldn't do it. "Don't worry. Everything will be all right," I said as I gave her a hug. "I bet Trevor's doing pretty well for himself right now."

"Yeah. He probably is," she said as she attempted to smile. "Jason, him and I. We were like the Three Musketeers. We did everything together. I just miss him, Dylan. I really do. Do you understand what I mean? He was a real good friend."

"I understand," I replied as I gave her another squeeze.

Believe me. I understand.

We got our books and headed for our respective classes.

"See you in study hall."

The day went pretty slow. The only fun part about it was that sixth period was study hall, and the only one during the week that we didn't have Mr. Cross as the supervisor. Plus, it was the only one in which I could talk to Shauni and not get in trouble. We told Miss Kai Ann that we had some chemistry homework to do.

It was the end of the day. Shauni was going to drive me home since Dick was getting my birthday cake and ice cream. I just told her he had some stuff to do. I waited for her at my locker. As I was waiting, the hall seemed to get more and more empty.

This is weird. Shauni should have been here by now.

I went to find out what was taking her so long. Good thing I did too. As I was going to her locker, I heard her scream. I ran down the hall as fast as I could. As I turned down the final corridor, I sensed a vampire. Shauni was nowhere to be seen. Then I heard another scream coming from the band room.

I prepared myself for battle as I went toward the sound. I reached into my backpack and got a baby food jar of Holy water from inside. With it gripped in my right hand and my backpack strapped on my left shoulder, I kicked open the door to the band room. To my horror, I saw Mr. Cross leaning over Shauni with his fangs bared, ready to bite her neck.

"Get away from her now, Cross!" I demanded as I threw the Holy water at him. The jar shattered on the side of his face.

"Aargh!! Now you're going to die, MacLeod! Right after your precious little girlfriend," my former teacher said as half his face melted away.

"She is precious to me, monster, that's why I won't let you touch her!" I screamed as I executed a jump kick toward him.

My foot connected with his shoulder. The momentum of the kick knocked Mr. Cross away from Shauni. While recovering from the fall to the floor, I reached for my backpack, which had fallen off in the struggle. Just as my hands were about to grasp the strap, Mr. Cross picked me up and threw me against the wall. Then he pitched my backpack on the other side of the room. My vampire/teacher then jumped toward me. Just as he was about to land on me, I rolled out of the way. I got to my feet as fast as I could.

Seeing a push broom leaning against the wall, I got an idea. I did a jumping somersault and landed beside the broom. I broke it off and used it was a staff. Remembering my training sessions with Dick, I went into action. I twirled the broomstick over my head, and then got into my attack position. For a split second, I thought I saw some fear on Mr. Cross's face. Yeah right.

He ran toward me once again, but this time with more force and determination. When he was a few feet away from me, I moved to the left and swung the broomstick down on his back. He fell to the floor, slightly dazed. Before he could get back up, I kicked at his head. In mid-kick, he grabbed my foot and threw me backward.

I fell onto the floor, dazed and confused. Mr. Cross got up and was ready to stomp on my head when he let out an unholy scream. As his body fell down on top of me, all I saw was Shauni standing behind him. Tears welling in her eyes, my backpack in her hand and a stake in Mr. Cross's back.

"Are you all right?" she asked as she wiped her eyes.

"Nothing a few hours in a hottub can't fix," I said with a smile as I got up from under my dead ex-teacher. "We better get out of here before the cops come."

We got into the car and headed to Dick's. Shauni was completely quiet the whole way home. I was tired of the silence and decided to start a conversation. Big mistake.

"What's wrong, sweetie? Is something bothering you? Are you okay?"

"What's wrong? Is something bothering me? I'll tell you what's wrong, Dylan MacLeod! I just had to kill one of my teachers, who turned out to be a vampire. And you ask me 'what's wrong?' "

I should have stayed with the silence.

"Well, from what I remember, you never even liked Mr. Cross that much in the first place."

"Dylan, that's beside the…" Shauni looked at me with a look of shock on her face as best she could, while still keeping the car on the road. "How'd you know that? I never told you that."

I hope she buys this.

"Uh. I mean, from what Dick told me. You never really liked Mr. Cross."

"Oh. I thought for a second…" She shook her head in dismissal. "Oh. Forget it." We pulled up beside Dick's house. "Well. I'll see you at the game tonight."

"Wouldn't miss it," I said.

I leaned in and gave her a kiss. I figured I'd try it and see what would happen. She was a little surprised by the gesture and looked at me dumbfounded. I quickly turned toward the house before she could say anything. But that didn't last long. I had to tell her about Candy. I turned back to my, I could say it with pride and accomplishment, girlfriend.

"And, Shauni, one more thing." *Your sister's a vampire.* I couldn't do it. "Don't tell anyone about what happened after school."

"My lips are sealed," she said with a smile as she put her fingers to her lips. "Who'd believe me anyway?" She rolled up her window and drove away.

I waved and waited for her to turn down a nearby side street, then continued to the house. I went to the mailbox and got the newspaper. As I entered the house, I sensed a vampire. I raised my arm, ready to throw the paper at anything that tried to attack me. Dick's dog, Cleo, was barking like crazy when I walked in. Normally this wouldn't worry me, but this time she was barking at Dick.

He has to be the vampire I sensed. But how?

"Come here, Cleo. It's just me." I scratched her behind her ears then looked up at Dick. "What's wrong with her, Dick?" I went to the refrigerator to get an after-school snack.

Dick got up from the couch and walked over to the kitchen. "I don't know, Dylan. She's been acting like that since I got home."

Dylan?

"Probably a vampire around."

Dick got a scared look on his face. "Holy shit, man. Don't get all serious on me. How could a vampire get in here without us knowing?"

I turned back to the fridge. "Unless..."

"Unless what?" he asked, scared.

"Unless I wasn't around to sense them. And one of them made himself look like you." I turned around and chopped off Dick's right arm with my samurai sword that I stashed beside the fridge. "Who the hell are you? And what did you do with Dick?"

"Gee, I thought it would take you longer to figure," Dick transformed into Mark Hollander, one of the people on Trevor Wayne's "Most Hated" list, "out that I wasn't Dick, Dylan."

I just smiled and raised the blade to Mark's neck.

"All right, Hollander. What's going on? And remember," I patted his shoulder with the sword, "you're in no position to argue."

"Okay. Okay," he started, "the Leader said that you're to be at the track behind the school during halftime. Tonight. If you want to see your cousin alive, as opposed to undead."

"Thanks for the info, Mark. Just for that, I should let you go."

"Oh. Thanks, Dylan. I owe you one."

"Then again," I raised the sword for the killing blow, "you forgot the cake and ice cream."

I swung my arm in an arc. The blade of the sword connected with the soft flesh of Mark's neck. Cutting through it like a hot knife through butter. Mark's head fell to the floor, a look of shock eternally frozen on his face.

I went back to the fridge and got a bottle of water. I chugged a few gulps and put the bottle on the table. Next, I did the only thing I could think of at the time. I went to the bathroom. After which I called Jason Pasner. After three rings, he picked up the phone.

"Hello?"

"Hello. Is Jason there?"

"Yeah, this is him. Who's this?"

"This is Dylan MacLeod. I need you to come over to Dick's house right away. He's been kidnaped by the vampires and I have to get him back."

"And this is why you called me."

"Yeah. I need someone to bail me out if things get too hairy. And you were the second person I could think of."

"Who was the first?"

"Luke Perry."

"But what if I don't want to? I mean vampires are supernatural beings. 'Super' being the main word in that phrase."

"Because Dick is your friend, and he'd help you if the roles were reversed. Now there's no time to argue. Just bring the cavalry saber that's in your closet and your water guns," I told him.

"But how'd you…?" he said as I hung up the phone.

About thirty minutes later, Jason arrived. He was carrying a gym bag in one hand and the sword that we use to have sword battles with in the other. These were both good signs. I met him at the front door.

"Are the squirt guns in the bag?" I asked as I motioned him to enter.

"No, I just carry this bag around for my health," he replied as he emptied its contents onto the table. I picked up one of the plastic toys and twirled it on my finger like a cowboy with his peacemaker. The water gun slipped off of my finger and fell to the floor. I bent down to pick it up. "One thing does puzzle me though, Trevor."

"Yeah. What's that?"

Oh shit! That was smart. Learn to pay attention, man. I stood up and put the gun back on the table.

"So? How long did it take you to figure it out?" We both sat down at the table. It felt good. Not having to hide my secret from Jason anymore. Dick was a good friend. But Jason and I were best friends.

The summer before our junior year of high school, Jason and I bought swords and had sword fights like on the *Highlander* television show. I got cut on the back and had to go to the hospital. We both told our parents that I fell out of a tree. I hid my sword behind my dad's toolshed. Jason decided to hide his in his closet, behind a stack of comic book boxes.

"Actually, not that long," he replied.

"Oh, really." I went to the fridge and got us each a Pepsi. I handed one to Jason, then sat with him.

"Shauni told me about your slip after school today. Second, I recognized your voice on the phone." Jason sat back in his chair and took a sip of soda and

44

smiled. "And last but not least—the sword. Only you, Shauni and I knew about even having them."

"I was in a hurry. I should have been paying more attention to what I was saying." I took a drink of my Pepsi.

"With me or Shauni?"

"Both. Does she know about me?" I asked.

"No, I don't think so. We'd both know if she did." He smiled at me. "You'd better watch it, man, or everyone is gonna know your secret identity."

"Secret identity. That's a good one." I took another long swig from my can. "But you're right. I gotta straighten up."

I hope. Because if Candy finds out, I'm screwed. I shook my head and dismissed the thought.

"You ready to get to work? We've got an hour and a half until the game starts."

"Let's do it," Jason replied as he got up from his seat.

I picked Shauni up at her house. She couldn't believe that the vampires wanted me to meet them in the dark in the middle of the football game.

"There has to be some other reason that they want you there during halftime."

"I know. Maybe they don't want to miss any of the game," I replied with a grin.

"That's not funny, Dylan." I could tell by the expression on her face that Shauni was getting worried.

"I'm sorry. Look, the only way I'm gonna find out what they're up to and save Dick in the process, is to meet with them."

"Do you think the plan is going to work?"

"It should. I mean Jason knows where to be and what to do if Dick or I get into too much trouble." I pulled up to the back entrance to the band room. Shauni played the flute during football games. "There is no reason to be worried. Nothing bad is going to happen."

Yeah, keep telling yourself that.

"Be careful anyway."

"I always am." We kissed each other good-bye. I left to go meet Jason at the Pizza Palace. We had to get some of the last minute steps of our plan ironed out.

Jason was there when I arrived. We went over the plan to save Dick as we ate pizza and drank soda. We left for the game around a quarter after seven.

The game was pretty decent. Even though my mind was on what I was going to do, I still tried to enjoy myself. When there were five minutes left in the second quarter, Jason and I went over by the band to stand until halftime. We went over to where Shauni was standing on the bleachers. She looked worried.

"Everything's going to be all right; don't worry," I said, not only to reassure her, but also to reassure myself.

"I hope so."

"Are you ready, man?" I asked, turning to Jason.

"As ready as I'll ever be."

"Good. Just wait about five minutes then come over. And don't forget the code word." I turned to Shauni. "I'll see you as soon as I can." I gave Shauni a kiss then left.

"Be careful," she said as she watched me walk away.

I always am.

CHAPTER 4

After I left Shauni and Jason, I headed for the main gate to the football field. I exited the gate and headed for the track. This gave me a little time to think about my current situation.

I gotta be nuts. I shouldn't have gotten Shauni and Jason into this. Hell! I shouldn't have gotten Dick into this. If I'm not careful, someone's gonna get hurt. But then again, if it weren't for Dick, I probably wouldn't have made it this far.

I cut across the grass and walked toward the storage shed that held the track equipment. As I neared the shed, I sensed a strong vampire presence that made me really queasy. I knew the vampire or vampires were there, I just couldn't see them.

"I'm here, Leader! It's Dylan MacLeod!" I yelled into the darkness.

Just then, the door to the storage shed opened. There was a light behind six people standing there. I could just make out their silhouettes.

How do I know which one is Dick?

To answer my unspoken question, the lights around the track lit up. I saw my friend, his hands were tied and his mouth was taped shut.

"How do I know that Dick isn't a vampire?" I asked, stalling for Jason.

"Use your newly acquired vampire enhanced hearing to listen for his heartbeat," the Leader said.

I did as he suggested and concentrated my hearing. To my surprise, it worked. I could hear Dick's heart beating. And from what I heard, he was nervous.

"Okay. It's him. You remember the deal. Me for him."

"I may be a vampire, but that doesn't mean I'm not a man of my word. Here is your cousin." He motioned to the vampire that was standing behind Dick. The vampire untied the ropes and ripped the tape from his mouth.

"Ouch!" Dick yelled. As he gave the vampire a fierce look. Dick walked to where I was standing. "Hey, Dylan. Now that's just one I owe you," he said as he walked toward me.

"You might get it sooner than you think," I whispered back. I walked toward the Leader. *I hope you're ready, Jace.* "Why do you want me? I'm certainly of no use to you."

"Oh but you are, Trevor." This surprised me greatly. I looked at Dick in surprise. The Leader noticed the astonishment on my face. "That's right, Trevor. I know who you are. I've waited for this moment for a *long* time."

"But how?" I looked once again at my friend, who was now standing beside me.

"Dick didn't tell us anything. Robin called me after you stabbed her with the fire poker. I sent out agents to find you. Do you still think it's a coincidence that Candy found you when she did?"

I was dumbfounded. I thought all the things that have happened in the past few weeks were chance. I should have known better. But what can I say, I was a naive eighteen-year-old. And I was about to get a real big reality check. I just stood there and listened to The Leader. This was the perfect way to get the time I needed for Jason to show up.

"She told me that you were headed to Dick's house, so I asked Robin to set up a rendezvous with him. I didn't even think that you had the head start that you did. Who would have known that you would have gotten there before her." He sneered. "But we don't have to worry about that now."

"Is there a point to this?" Dick asked.

"Fine. Fine. I guess it won't hurt to tell you," The Leader replied. "I'm going to kill you anyway." He moved closer to me. "Did you ever wonder why you never died or became a full vampire when Robin bit you?" I gave him a blank look. I had no clue. "Because of a magic spell placed on one of your ancestors. As it goes, if the firstborn son doesn't participate in a blood exchange after being bitten. He will receive many powers of the vampire, but he will have none of the weaknesses or the hunger."

"But that still doesn't explain why you're after me." I was getting fed up with the banter. An inner voice told me that I had to get to the brass tacks of the conversation.

"Oh. I think that should be quite obvious," The Leader replied. "You have already been bitten. As I said, you have some, but not all of the powers of a vampire. And I can't have someone with the powers of a vampire not under my control." He looked at me and extended his hand. "And besides," his eyes glowed red, "I don't like loose ends."

With these last words, I felt my willpower slowly begin to drain away as that same "red haze" once again clouded my vision. With my last bit of inner strength, I screamed out one word.

"Buffy!"

My plan went into action. There was a "thwpp!" sound in the air. One of the vampire soldiers bent backward in pain and imploded. This distraction gave Dick the chance he needed to run over to where Jason was and help him out. He got Jason's sword and two water pistols out of the backpack. Jason continued to shoot vampires with stakes from his crossbow. Meanwhile, I was about to get the bite of my life. The Leader and a female vampire led me into the storage shed and shut the door.

"Your friends can't help you now, Trevor," The Leader said as he pushed me to the floor. He held me there in a grip that could crush rock. He looked at the female vampire, who I now recognized as my ex-girlfriend Kate. "He's yours now."

Kate straddled my body then sat on my legs. "Bring him across. Then report back to me." Kate smiled at the Leader. "I'm going to grab a snack." With this, the Leader disappeared in a puff of smoke. "Don't fail me like the others!" His voice echoed inside the shed.

"I won't fail, Leader," Kate said to the ceiling. She turned her attention to me. I tried to sit up, but I was too weak. Kate pushed me to the floor with her left hand. "Oh no you don't. You're not getting away from me like R.J. did."

She looked into my eyes. For the second time that night, the "red haze" clouded my vision. All I could see was our bodies in a sea of darkness. Kate lifted her shirt over her head and threw it to the side. She wore a black string bikini top instead of a bra. It was one of her own personal quirks.

Some things never change, Kate.

Kate bent down and kissed me on the lips. My hands involuntarily roamed up and down her back as we kissed. My ex stopped kissing me and sat straight up.

"Just like old times. Huh, Trevor?"

"Yeah," I replied groggily. "Just like old times." It was like I was watching the events happen from inside someone else's body. My hands reached for her shorts and unbuttoned them. My fingers fumbled for the zipper. Kate slapped my hand away.

"Not yet lover," she scolded. "Just lean back and relax."

I did as she commanded. She leaned forward and ripped open my flannel shirt. The buttons flew in different directions. Kate began to kiss my bared chest. Making a trail up to the left side of my neck. She bit into my skin and began to suck my blood. I let out a scream of pain that quickly turned into one of supernatural satisfaction.

Suddenly, I noticed a vampire flying through the door, soaked in Holy water and yelping like a hurt dog. Kate sat up from her evening feast of my blood.

"What the hell!" she screamed in disgust.

My neck started to hurt enormously. *I'm back in control. Thank you, God.* I put my hand to my neck and pulled it away. As I watched the blood drip to the floor, what the Leader said about the spell echoed in my mind.

"…He will receive many powers of the vampire, but he will have none of the weaknesses or the hunger."

Kate looked at the vampire that had smashed through the door.

"What the hell is going on, Jimmy?"

"The good guys are winning," I answered as I punched my ex-girlfriend in the face. She flew against the opposite wall of the shed with a loud crash.

"How could you do this?" she growled as her face and voice changed to that of a vampire.

"Like the Leader said, there has to be a blood exchange for me." I grinned. "I'll never be a bloodsucker. And that's a promise."

"Then I guess I'll have to kill you," she said with a smirk as she flew toward me with super speed. My speed was no match for hers. I didn't have time to dodge her. She hit me like a freight train. Our momentum sent us flying through one of the brick walls of the shed and onto the ground.

Outside, there was a hell of a war raging. A few of the vampires from the game had joined in on the battle.

Just great.

Jason was shooting them with his Super Soaker two-fifty, which was filled with Holy water. It was funny to see the way that the vampires avoided him. As I rose to my feet, I spied Dick lopping the heads off of two vampires that were closing in on him. After he finished with the second one, he noticed that Kate was getting back up herself. Her face was now that of a hungry, pissed off vampire.

"Trevor! Catch!" Dick called out as he tossed my samurai sword into the air. It decapitated a vampire in mid-flight. "Cool!"

Yeah, cool. Except that the midair decapitation changed the trajectory of Dick's throw. The sword was going to fly past me about fifteen feet off the ground. *Too high for me to jump.* I contemplated my next act for about a second. I jumped up as hard as I could. I soared up to the height of the sword and easily grabbed the weapon from the air.

Then again, maybe not, I thought as I floated to the ground. When I landed, I was already in my attacking stance. Right in front of Kate.

"Hello, dear." I sneered as I went into my back swing for my killing blow.

"Good-bye, dear," she replied. Our eyes locked on each other. Then I blacked out.

I came to the next day at around two o'clock in the afternoon with one hell of a headache. Shauni was sitting beside my bed.

"Dick! Jason! Hurry. Dylan's awake!" she yelled toward the kitchen when she saw my eyes open and me smile at her. My two friends walked into the room.

"Hey, Mac. How's it going?" Jason asked me. "You look like shit."

"I'm not complaining. So do you," I joked.

"Are you all right? What's the last thing you remember?" Dick asked in a concerned voice.

"Not much," I began as I sat up in bed. "Just that I was about to cut off Kate's head. I looked at her. Our eyes locked. Then the next thing I know I woke up here."

"We kinda figured that something was wrong when we saw you fall down," Dick started.

"Then Kate and the other vampires disappeared in puffs of smoke," Jason added. "One thing puzzles me though. How did you jump up and catch the sword. It must have been at least fifteen feet in the air."

"As much as I can figure it's because I never exchanged blood with Robin or Kate."

"But that still doesn't explain how you jumped up to catch the sword," Shauni wondered.

"Actually it does," I replied. "The Leader told me and Dick that because of a spell cast on one of my ancestors. And the fact that I never exchanged blood with either vampire, I will have most of their powers," I continued as all three friends listened intently. "But none of the weaknesses. That's why I caught the sword. I flew."

"Good," Jason said. "Now that you have the powers of a vampire, you can beat them more easily."

"We'll have to do that some other time, Jason," Dick replied. Then he turned to me. "First, we have to test the limits of your new powers."

51

"I'm game," I said with a grin as I crawled out of bed. "Just let me get freshened up first." I headed into the bathroom to take a shower.

Three minutes later, I was showered and dressed for testing my powers. We were halfway to the garage when a car came down the street in front of Dick's house. As it neared our location, the back window rolled down and a semi-automatic machine gun emerged. Suddenly bullets started screaming through the air. At that instant, I sensed a vampire.

"Get down!!" Dick had ducked behind the hedges that outlined his yard. I jumped toward Shauni and Jason. I heard the bullets exiting their barrels then I could feel them enter my back. As suddenly as it started, the gunfire stopped. "Shauni? Are you all right?" I turned on Dick's direction. "Hey, Dick. You okay, man?"

"Yeah, I'm fine," he said as he rose to his feet and brushed off his pants. "How about you, Pas? You okay?" There was no answer. "Jason? Are you all right?"

With the silence, I feared the worse. I looked over at my best friend. He was lying on the ground in a patch of blood-stained grass.

Oh God! NO!

Shauni saw her cousin lying on the ground and became hysterical.

"Jason!" she screamed as she went to move to her cousin's side. "Dylan! Dylan, you have to do something! You have to get Jason to a hospital!"

Dick quickly took me to the side as Shauni looked over her cousin.

"He's still breathing," she informed us frantically.

"You do know that it's going to take at least half an hour to get Jason to the hospital. And he's got about fifteen minutes left. Maybe ten," Dick solemnly noted.

"Yeah. But what else do you suggest I do. I have to get him to the hospital as fast as I can. He's one of my oldest friends."

"Okay. Okay. It takes thirty minutes to get to the hospital. Right?"

"I think we already established that." I looked over to my fallen friend. "Get to the point, Dick."

"Just listen. That's not as the crow flies. Right?"

"Uh-huh."

"Well?"

"No. No way. Uh-uh. I don't even know if I can do it in the daytime."

"There's only one way to find out."

Why do I have the feeling that I'm gonna regret this?

I closed my eyes and concentrated on getting off the ground. I took a lesson from the comic books that Jason and I use to read when we were younger. If I thought about what I wanted to do, I would be able to accomplish my goal. I filled my mind with thoughts of floating. Of rising above the ground and soaring into the sky. It was the only thing I could think of. It felt as though nothing had happened. It just goes to show how wrong I was. I opened my eyes and looked down at my feet. To my surprise, I was about ten feet off the ground.

Holy shit!

I quickly came to my senses and floated back to the ground.

"Let's do it."

After carefully picking up Jason and telling Dick and Shauni to meet me at the hospital, I took to the air. I arrived at the Dweller Valley County hospital parking lot a little before three. I ran into the emergency room with my friend in my arms. One of the nurses ran to meet me. When she saw Jason's injuries, she told and orderly to get a gurney.

"What happened to him?"

"He was shot in a drive-by in Oldeston about fifteen minutes ago." I put my friend on the gurney and watched as the orderly rolled him into a nearby room.

"Are you sure that you have your time straight? Oldeston's over twenty miles away. And unless you were going about a hundred miles an hour, I don't see how you could have made it here in that amount of time," she explained.

"It must be the stress of my friend getting shot. I guess it just felt like fifteen minutes." I used my enhanced hearing to listen to the commotion as the ER doctors worked on my friend.

"…unless you flew?" I heard the nurse finish.

"Huh?" I pointed to where my friend was. "Is he going to be all right?"

"Yes. He's going to be just fine." She handed me a clipboard with a stack of forms on it. "While you're waiting, you can fill these out." I turned and walked toward the waiting room. She noticed my T-shirt. "What the hell?" She walked closer to me as I turned to face her. "Holes? And blood on your shirt?"

"Fashion statement," I replied as I went back toward the waiting room to fill out the forms. It was thirty minutes before Shauni and Dick arrived.

"How is he Dylan?" Shauni asked as she hugged me.

"I don't know. Nobody has told me anything yet," I said to her disappointment. "But I know he'll be all right."

I hope.

"The thing is," Dick began, "why would those guys in the car use guns on you if they knew that you're already part vampire and that bullets can't hurt you? It doesn't make any sense."

"They weren't coming for me, Dick." I replied, and then turned to my girlfriend. "They were coming for you, Shauni." Shauni said nothing. Her eyes just got big with a mixture of surprise and fright.

Just then, a doctor approached us.

"Which one of you is Dylan MacLeod?"

"I am," I replied as I shook his hand.

"I'm Doctor Jonathan Harker. I'm in charge of Jason Pasner's recovery."

"How's it look, Doctor?" Shauni asked.

"I'm sorry to say that it doesn't look good, Miss. We recovered two bullets from his left leg. But there is still one lodged in his chest, near his heart. He doesn't have much of a chance unless we operate. And even then," he gave us a sympathetic look. "it's risky. Has anyone notified his parents?"

"I did before we left," Shauni answered.

"That's good. I'll keep you informed of any changes in Jason's condition," he informed us. We each thanked him as he walked away.

We had been sitting in the waiting room for almost three hours. Then a voice came over the public address system with a message that I never wanted to hear at that particular moment in my life.

"Trevor Wayne."

Shauni's eyes got big. Dick and I sat up in our seats, astounded.

"You have a call on line two. Trevor Wayne, you have a call on line two."

Dick looked at me. I looked at Dick. And Shauni looked at both of us.

Finally the silence was broken.

"What kind of sick joke is this?" Shauni whispered in anger. "First the vampires kidnap Dick for your soul. Then they shoot Jace while trying to get to me. Now they're asking for Trevor to answer the damn phone." There were tears in her eyes. She sighed and wiped them away. "And he's probably dead."

"Well! I don't think it's funny!" I stated with my fists clenched at my sides. "I'm gonna go find out what's going on. Dick, you stay here with Shauni. In case they try to get at her again." I turned to my girlfriend. "I'll be right back," I said, and then kissed her on the forehead.

"Don't worry, Dylan. I'll take care of her."

I half ran, half flew down the hall to the nearest desk.

"I'm Trevor Wayne. There's a call for me," I informed the secretary. She handed me one of the phones that was on the desk. I picked up the receiver and pressed the button for line-two.

"Hello, Leader. This is Wayne," I answered sternly. I moved as far from the secretary as possible. I couldn't afford for her to listen to my conversation. "Calling to gloat? Or give up?"

"Neither," the vampire answered with a laugh.

"Then why call? Why not just wait until I leave, then jump me?"

"Too risky. Besides, this call has served its purposes."

"What purposes? To make sure I was here?"

"Yes. And as a distraction. Call you at Dick's at nine," he replied as he hung up.

Shauni.

Just then, I heard the breaking of glass and Shauni's distinctive scream. I dropped the receiver and ran down the corridor at vampire speed. As I neared Jason's room, I sensed a vampire. I burst into the room, nearly tearing the door off of one of its hinges as I did so.

What I saw when I entered was not a pretty sight. Dick was leaned up against the chair beside the window. He had a cut on his head and was holding his left wrist, which was bleeding also.

Jason's bed was tipped over and he was unconscious and bleeding from his bandages. I ran over and turned the bed upright. I then lifted him back onto it. To my horror, I noticed that Shauni was nowhere to be seen. My heart dropped in my chest.

A group of doctors and nurses came running into the room. One of them looked at the door with an expression of amazement. A doctor and two nurses moved me away from Jason. I went over to Dick with Nicole Watson, a candy striper. She began to tend to the cut on his head. Then she cleaned the wound and put a Band-Aid on it. Against our protests, she motioned us out the broken door after giving Dick a clean bill of health.

"Dick. Dylan. I'm afraid you guys will have to leave while we look after Jason." She nodded toward the hallway.

"But..." Dick began.

"Yeah. Sure. No problem." I gave Dick a "we gotta talk" look as I gently shoved him outside. I led my friend into the restroom. The only place I could think of where we could talk in private. After checking the stalls for any eavesdroppers. I started my questioning.

"So talk, Dick. What the happened in there? Where's Shauni?"

"I don't know. One minute we were talking to Jason. He just woke up and Doc Harker said we could see him. The next thing I know, Bart Myers crashes through the window. Then he knocks me down, tips over Jason's bed, grabs Shauni and jumps out the window with her."

"He must be the one I sensed when I came in. I'm going after him." I walked out of the restroom and headed toward the elevators.

"I'm comin' with you, man," Dick barked as he grabbed my arm. "Shauni's my friend, too."

"No, Dick." I replied as we stepped into the elevator and rode it to the garage. "I need you here to watch over Jason."

"His parents can do that. Besides, you need all the help you can get."

All the help I can get. That's a good idea. Rick, I hope you meant what you said in school yesterday.

"Okay. You take the car back to the house. The Leader said he was gonna call at nine." I looked at my watch. "That gives us about two and a half hours to get ready."

"What are you gonna do?"

"I'm going to get some extra help. I should be back at the house at eight-thirty." I paused. "Depending."

I answered as we headed to Dick's car. I needed some weapons. In case I ran into any vampires while I went to get R.J. When we arrived at the car, I went straight to Dick's gym bag, which was in the backseat. I got out two water pistols and six stakes. I had to be ready for anything.

"Wish me luck," I said as I put the last stake in my backpack.

"Good luck, man," Dick said as I lifted into the air.

Finding R.J. wasn't as hard as I thought it would be. He was at the Pizza Palace, the first place I checked, eating a meatball sub when I arrived. I had the same, "not quite sensing a vampire" sensation that I had at Sheetz. He must have had it too, because when I walked in he looked right at me. He motioned for me to sit.

"Sit down, man," he said as he wiped his mouth. "Dylan? Isn't it?

"Yeah, it is. Thanks." I slid into the seat across from him in his booth. "Rick, I need to ask you an important question."

"I'll do it," he replied quickly.

"Do what? What am I going to ask?"

"I don't know. But whatever it is," He took a drink of soda. "I bet it has something to do with vampires. And yesterday in school I told Nicole that if you wanted help against the vampires," he smiled, "all you had to do was ask." Rick got a serious look on his face. "And besides. Ever since the bonfire," he leaned closer to whisper, "I've been having weird sensations whenever I'm around certain people. And I'm having really weird dreams, too."

"So I guess I don't have to go through all the red tape then. Do I?" I sat back and related the events since Friday afternoon.

"Whoa! That's nuts," Rick remarked as he paid for dinner. "Shauni's cool. My friend Trevor Wayne, I assume you know of him from Dick." I nodded. "He used to like her. And I think she still likes him. Even though he's missing and all." We walked out to his car. "I owe it to both of them, and to Jason, to make sure she stays safe."

Whoa! I never knew R. J. thought of me as that much of a friend.

We got in his car and headed to Dick's house. We had a big battle to get ready for, and not much time to do it in.

CHAPTER 5

The ride back to the house was quiet. Quiet until we were three blocks away. Rick and I were deciding on a plan of attack against the vampires.

"So you're telling me that you have all the powers of vampires? And none of the weaknesses?" he said in disbelief.

"Pretty much. Yeah," I answered as we stopped at a stop sign. "Although I'm not sure why you have the powers that you do."

"I am," he informed me. "I told my grandma what happened. I tell her everything." We passed the stop sign and continued down the street. "She told me that my great grandfather, a voodoo priest, had placed a protection spell on a medallion that he had acquired from an English vampire hunter. To prevent them from becoming vampires. If the need arose."

I looked at my friend in awe.

What is it with our ancestors and magic spells?

"I thought it was just a legend. Until she told me about this." He held up the necklace that he been calling his 'good luck charm' since he started ninth grade. "It is the very same medallion that my great grandfather enchanted years ago."

I was amazed that Rick was actually sharing this story with me. He took a right at the next stop sign and continued his story.

"It's what prevented me from becoming a vampire. And gave me some of their powers to boot."

"That's cool. We're gonna need all the extra power we can get against the…"

Rick stopped the car in the middle of the street as I broke off the end of my sentence. I looked at my friend and could tell by the look on his face that he sensed them too.

"Vampires," he finished for me.

"Yep." I reached into the backseat and got into my backpack. I grabbed three stakes and handed the rest to R.J. "Duty calls," I remarked as I exited the car.

Rick did likewise. We looked around the neighborhood for the vampires that we knew were near. I spotted a quartet of bloodsuckers chasing down Jason's ex-girlfriend and her new boyfriend.

"Oh, Mandy!" I whispered. "Okay. Rick. Undead. Eleven o'clock. Fifty yards. Let's roll."

I flew into the air. Rick looked in the direction that I had indicated. I quickly flew at the two vampires on the right. He ran at the two on the left and tackled them. Mandy and her boyfriend ran to the nearest house for protection.

"Hello, boys," Rick quipped as he shoved his closest vampire to the side. He jump-kicked the other. That one flew into a doghouse in the yard closest to us.

I picked up both of my vampires by their collars.

"How's it hanging, guys?" I threw them both toward the other side of the street. They both recovered in mid-flight and flew back toward me. "Shit!" I could see the bigger one throw back his arm to punch. Suddenly I hit the ground, making a big crater in the middle of the street. I looked up to see the bigger vampire rocketing toward me.

Stupid! Stupid! Stupid!

I rolled out of the way at the last second. The big vampire hit my crater with a crash. I grabbed one of my stakes from my jacket and flung it at him. The stake hit him in the middle of his chest. Right through the heart. He arched back and let out a loud roar.

"No! Jimmy!" He flew at me as I stood up. "Now you're gonna die." He grabbed me by the collar and lifted me into the air. In the distance I could hear the blaring of a train whistle. My adversary must have heard it too. "Let's go see the choo-choo," he said with a fang-revealing grin.

He flew in the direction of the sound; dragging me along for the ride. I wrestled with him as we flew. His grip was stronger than mine. It took most of my strength to keep from choking. We landed at a nearby railroad crossing. The train was about a half a mile away.

"You have got to be kidding me." I looked in the direction of the train, which once again blared its horn, then back at the vampire. He still held me in an unrelenting grip. "You'll be killed too."

"Anything to avenge Jimmy." He moved us closer to the oncoming train. "Kinda like how you wanna avenge Pasner getting shot. Huh, Trevor?"

"Yeah, kinda. But you forgot one thing," I remarked when the train was about fifty feet away. "I'm one of the good guys."

In one continuous motion I grabbed him by the collar, leaned back and flipped him over my body. He landed into the path of the train. I quickly got out of the way. My enemy wasn't so lucky. His foot got caught in between the tracks. He tried to run toward me and fell forward. Just then the train wheels cut through his neck, freezing an expression of surprise on his face.

I flew back to R.J. to see if he needed any help. When I got there, I got a surprise. He was sitting on the hood of his car with a mile-wide grin on his face. I landed five feet in front of him.

"What's the smile for?" I asked as I walked up to my friend.

"I just fought two vampires," he jumped from the hood, "and won." He walked to the driver's side as I went to the passenger's door. "Not bad for my first time. Huh?" We got in and fastened our seatbelts. He started the engine and headed home.

"That's great," I remarked as we started toward Dick's. "But remember. It's not all fun." I smiled at my friend. "If you know what I mean."

"Ha! Ha! Yeah, I know." Five minutes later we pulled up to Dick's house.

"I hope Dick's been preparing for tonight," I said as we got out of the car. "We can't afford to be caught off guard by the vampires." We headed to the front door. I opened it and walked in. "Honey! I'm ho…" I noticed that something was wrong.

"Dylan? What's wrong, man?" My friend asked as he shut the door behind him. "Why'd you stop in mid-sent…" Rick then noticed what I noticed, the eerie silence that was in the house. Cleo wasn't even barking.

She barks every time the front door is opened.

I went over to the television and shut it off. The ending credits to the first *Highlander* movie had just faded to the top of the screen as I pressed the "stop" button. I ejected the tape and put it in its box.

"They got him," I said blankly as I walked back into the kitchen. "You'd better go home, R.J." He gave me a surprised look. "I'm going to do this alone. No more of my friends are getting hurt."

"I don't think so, Trevor." I looked up at my friend. "Yeah, I know." He sat at the kitchen table and motioned for me to do the same. "Ever since I got bit. I've been able to sense things. Not just vampires." He began to nervously fiddle with the napkin holder that sat in the center of the table. "I can sense when danger is approaching. And I can even read peoples' emotions. Gram said that it's because my great-grand father was a witch doctor and her mom was a voodoo priestess."

"But that doesn't explain how you figured out who I am."

"In a way it does," he said as he put down the napkin holder. "When I mentioned that Shauni may still like you." He gave me a wide grin. "You got all happy. But at the same time, I felt your despair, anger, and fear. And why would a guy who just met Shauni have these intense feelings, especially happiness, when another guy's name was spoken. Unless he was the other guy."

"You can sense emotions?" I asked in surprise. "That's cool." I got up and went to the fridge. I got out two cans of Dr. Pepper and put one in front of Rick.

"Thanks," he replied as he opened his soda.

"I guess each vampire gets different powers." I smiled as I sat down at the table. "Even us half-vampires." I saluted my friend with my soda can. He returned the gesture.

"Amen."

For the next hour, Rick and I went over the plan to take care of the vampires and get Dick and Shauni back. Halfway through our third revision of the plan, the phone rang. I put down my fourth slice of pepperoni pizza from the Pizza Palace.

Good thing they deliver. I picked up the receiver.

"Hello. Harshburg…"

"Trevor. Oh man. I'm glad you're there."

"Dick!" Rick looked at me with wide eyes. "Are you okay? Where are you?"

"I'm all right. Listen, I don't have much time," he whispered frantically. "They're looking for me. Oh shit!" Dick screamed this last part. "They found me. Trevor, I'm at the sand plant. Aaah!"

"Dick!"

"You heard him, Wayne." The Leader was now on the phone. "We're at the sand plant. Come if you dare." He slammed down the phone to punctuate his point.

I put the receiver on the hook and looked at Rick. He made a "come on with it" gesture with his hands and face. I grabbed my backpack and headed for the door. "Let's go. The Leader's holding them at the Sugarton sand plant."

"The sand plant? Why would the Leader want to meet you at the sand plant?" Rick asked in disbelief as we headed to the final confrontation with the vampires in Dweller Valley.

"I don't know, R.J," I replied as he turned the car down the last road to the battleground. "I don't know."

Rick pulled the car into the workers' parking lot. We got out of the car and looked at our surroundings. There were giant dunes of sand and mountains of sandstone boulders all around us. There were also cranes and large dump trucks used for hauling the sand. The Sugarton sand plant was one of the top five places in the United States for glass quality sand. It was even the runner-up to the sand plant that made the lenses for the Hubble Telescope.

As we walked out of the parking lot, and into the main work area, I didn't sense any vampires. This was a good sign, in a way. Rick and I headed for the big warehouse in the center of the plant. This is where I figured our friends were being held. The sooner Dick and Shauni were free, the sooner we could take care of the Leader.

We were about fifty yards from our destination when my vampire hearing picked up a noise to my right. I motioned for Rick to stay put. I ran behind the bulldozer from which I guessed the sound came from. I got a hell of a surprise when I uncovered its source.

"Dick!" I said in disbelief and surprise. "How? I thought the Leader took you prisoner again."

Dick looked at R.J. and then at me. "You think they would've learned the first time they kidnapped me."

"Yeah. Go figure," Rick whispered gruffly.

"Well it's good to have you on our team," I replied as we headed for the warehouse. "You up for some vampire-butt kicking?"

"Wouldn't miss it," he said with a grin.

Rick watched our exchange with a worried look. Something was troubling him. Something about the whole situation. I guess I should have asked him what it was.

"Lighten up, R.J., everything is gonna be fi..." I sensed a vampire mid-sentence. Rick's facial expression confirmed what I already suspected.

"Be on your toes, guys." I reached into my backpack and gave them each a pair of stakes. I handed the backpack to Dick. "It's party time."

Rick and I kicked in the double doors to the warehouse. They flew about ten feet then crashed to the ground. Surprisingly, the warehouse was empty. Empty except for a solitary figure at the far end.

"Where is she, Leader?" I grabbed one of the stakes from inside my jacket, ready to throw it at him. "Where's Shauni?" I floated into the air. Suddenly, I was flying in an uncontrolled circle. I crashed into a pile of lumber, knocking the two-by-fours to the floor.

"Dick! No!" I heard R.J. call out. "Not you too."

"Oh yes, R.J., me too," I heard Dick growl.

I watched through pain-clouded eyes as he grew taller. His clothes ripped as his size became too much for the material. Dick picked R.J. up with his left hand as it simultaneously transformed into a fur-covered claw. He threw our friend through the wall farthest from me. Rick crashed through the tin wall like a rock going through a glass window. A wolfed-out Dick walked toward me. Drool rolled out of his mouth as he snarled.

"Raahgh!" He bent over and picked me up by the neck.

"A werewolf, Trevor. The only one of minions that your new powers can't detect. Dick here has been a second pair of eyes for me since the night you got bit." The Leader walked toward me and Dick. "Snap his neck, Dick."

I closed my eyes, waiting for the inevitable. The cold and stillness of death. It never came. Dick released me with a wolf-like howl as he arched his back in pain.

A wolf-like howl? I heard one just like it that night on Robin's back porch. Son of a bitch. They planned to recruit me from the beginning.

As I dropped to the floor, I looked behind Dick. Rick was standing in the opening from which he exited the structure. He had a stake in his right hand; ready to throw it at the Leader. In an instant, I stood up and grabbed the Leader from behind.

"Where is she, Leader? This is your last chance." I positioned him so that R.J. would have a better target. "R.J. here has a pretty good aim."

"Sorry, Trevor. It looks like you're going to have to kill me."

"Have it your way. I'll find her without your help." I replied matter-of-factly. I nodded to my friend. "Do it, R.J.!"

Rick threw his stake at the Leader's chest. With speed and strength that rivaled my own, the Leader elbowed me in the chest, catching me off guard. He then pushed me into the lumber pile where Dick had thrown me earlier. He then grabbed the stake from the air and drilled it back at Rick. The wooden pike struck him in the left shoulder. The force of the blow knocked him back through the hole in the wall.

"R.J.! No! Damn you, Leader!"

The Leader once again turned his attention to me. "Now, Trevor." His face changed to the evil visage of a vampire. "Since I just can't seem to make you into a full-fledged vampire, I guess I'm gonna have to kill you." He smacked his lips together to punctuate his point. His blood sucking fangs increased to a full inch in length.

64

"You think?" I remarked defiantly.

I grabbed a two-by-four and smashed it against the vampire. Good strategy, bad idea. He grabbed the end and flung me against the wall near Dick, I fell five feet to the floor.

Whoa, that was close. I can't keep the battle in here. Dick and R.J. might get hurt worse than they already are. Sorry, Shauni, but first things first.

I stood up with a look of fearlessness on my face.

"You wanna kill me, Leader." I smiled at my adversary. "Come and get me." I launched myself into the air and through the roof of the warehouse. As I hoped, the Leader followed.

"You can't get away from me, Trevor. No matter where you run. No matter where you fly. I will find you," he growled.

"That's what I'm counting on. You old coot," I remarked to myself as I flew over the Yosemite River toward the center of town. I looked behind me to see where the Leader was. *I must be flying too fast for....* I sensed a vampire. I turned face-forward. And was instantly grabbed by the Leader. "Damn!" I whined. The Leader aimed me for the river and flew toward it.

"Old coot? Trevor, I'm hurt." The Yosemite River was coming up very quickly. "But not as hurt as your girlfriend is going to be after I kill you."

"You bastard," I managed to say.

I mustered the last bit of strength that I had to turn the Leader toward the river. I lifted my legs and put them to his chest. I boosted myself into the air. The momentum sent him barreling to the water below.

Too bad old Yosemite ain't Holy Water. My job'd be finished—Holy water.

"Perfect."

I just hope the steeple door is unlatched. I don't wanna actually have to break into a church. I flew toward the First United Methodist Church. And with any luck, the salvation of Dweller Valley.

Fifteen minutes later, while sitting on the roof of the Pizza Palace, I spied my enemy.

"Hey! Old man!" I yelled with a smile. "Down here!" I waved.

The Leader flew at me like a bullet.

"Shit!" I jumped out of the way in the nick of time. He crashed through the roof and landed in the dining area. I landed in the parking lot. "I'm glad you got here, Leader. I was getting worried that you chickened out," I said as he burst through a nearby window.

"You're dead, Wayne," he snarled as he ran toward me.

"Aren't we formal all of a sudden?" I joked as I ran toward him. We locked each other in a death grip.

Five more minutes.

The Leader kicked me in the stomach. I rolled with the force of it and landed by a manhole cover. I picked the cover up and threw it at my enemy.

"Hey, Leader. Catch." I caught him off guard. The large iron disc hit him in the stomach, sending him into the dumpster that sat behind my former place of business. I turned and walked to the street in front of the restaurant.

"Maybe I won't need the—Oof!" I uncontrollably flew across the street and into the sign that displayed the church's schedule. I recovered to see that the Leader's appearance had changed. His ears were more pointed. His nose was more prominent. And his hands were now like animal claws.

"Dong!" The bells of the church sounded. As scheduled, the sprinklers came on.

Yes! Now I better act fast. Before they shut off. Or I'm screwed.

"Dong!"

"I said it before, Trevor. And this time, it's true." My enemy snarled as he dove in my direction. "You're gonna die."

"Dong!"

God! Give me the strength and speed to time this right.

In answer my silent prayer, the Leader seemed to slow down. As if he were a normal human swimming against a stream. When he was only two feet away, I grabbed him by the shoulders. I rolled back and planted my feet in his stomach. With every ounce of strength I had, I catapulted him toward the church. He flew, uncontrolled, over the street.

"Dong!"

Suddenly, a single storm cloud appeared in the sky. From it streaked a single bolt of lightning. It struck the Leader an instant before he hit the water barrier of the sprinklers. This caused him to evaporate in a puff of smoke and rainbow-colored light.

"Dong!"

"Not today, Leader. Not today." I flew into the air and headed the ten miles back to my friends.

The flight back to the sand plant was filled with many questions. *Now that it's over, what do I do? Do I go back to my life as Trevor Wayne? Do I stay as Dylan? What do I tell Shauni?* I got my answers when I arrived. Rick was kneeling beside Dick's now human body.

"How's he doing?" I asked as I landed behind them.

Rick got up and walked over to me. "He'll live." He leaned against a pile of crates. "It was weird. Once I got the stake out of my shoulder, I went over and got Dick's out." We walked over to Dick's body. "He shivered and jerked a little. Then he just laid there, motionless." Rick's eyes got skeptical with disbelief. "About ten minutes ago, all his fur shrunk back into his body."

That's around the time I destroyed the Leader.

"I don't think he's under the Leader's control anymore."

"Why do you think that?"

"Because that's when the Leader took his last shower. His reign is over." Rick looked at me, surprised. I knelt at Dick's body.

"You did it! You killed the Leader. That's great!" He was excited. "How'd you do it?"

I quickly explained how I defeated the Leader of the vampires as we covered Dick with a tarp. I then used a nearby phone to call for an ambulance.

"So," Rick began, "that means that all the half-vamps will return to normal."

I looked at my friend, a small smile on my face. I stood up.

"Yep." I walked over to a nearby crate. "The werewolf Dick." I pointed to our friend. "Unfortunately, he's gonna stay a werewolf. It's in his blood. Quite literally." I pointed to my nose. "He just never knew it."

Rick sat down beside me.

"What about me? I mean us?"

"I honestly don't know, man." I ran my hand through my hair. "If what you said about your protection medallion is true. I'm assuming you're gonna stay this way. You may not be as strong as you were, but you'll still be stronger than normal." I untied my ponytail. "And because of the spell on my family 'curse,' I'm gonna stay this way. Unless I find a cure." Rick looked at me with sympathy. I took off my glasses, which I forgot about until that moment. I looked at the spectacles.

It's amazing how these could fool everybody. Even Jason and... With my enhanced hearing, I heard my girlfriend scream.

"Shauni!" Without a word, I dropped the glasses and flew out of the hole in the side of the warehouse and into the direction of my girlfriend's scream.

"Trevor! Oh, God, Trevor...parking lot!"

She's calling for Trevor. Maybe the Leader told her who I really am. Boy, am I gonna have some explaining to do.

I went to the place that Shauni said she'd be. I landed beside the shed. I grabbed the door of the shed and tore it from its hinges, then threw it behind me. Shauni was sitting on the ground in the fetal position. When I tore off the door, she looked up.

"Trevor!" she said through tear-soaked eyes. She stood up and ran over to me, putting her arms around me. "Oh, Trevor. I thought you'd never come."

"Shauni. I—" She stopped me with a finger to my lips.

"I know," she stated as we stood in the doorway. We slid so that we were sitting down. Shauni looked at me in disbelief, tinged with satisfaction that she was now getting a terrible weight lifted from her shoulders. "I've always known. Ever since you, I mean Dylan, walked into Trig Class."

"Shauni. I…" I started. I couldn't think of a way to get around the conversation. Arguing with Shauni was like telling the sun not to shine. It just couldn't be done.

"You didn't really think that you could fool me." She ran her hand through my hair and looked into my eyes. "I've seen you with long hair before. Remember?"

She was right. She did see me with long hair. During the summer before, when Jason cut me with his sword. She was the oldest of our trio and she had just gotten her driver's license. She was the only one qualified, that we could trust not to tell our parents, to get me to the hospital. She had been recording us on video—Jason's idea. So we volunteered her to drive us.

"Yeah, I remember."

And, don't forget. You told Robin that you didn't want to get involved with her because she was like a sister to you. You shouldn't have let this go this long with Shauni.

I sighed.

I can't believe I'm gonna do this. Shauni, please know that I never meant to hurt you.

"And now that I know that you know," I put her hands in mine and looked into her eyes, "I don't think that it'd be a good idea to stay together." I could see tears beginning to well up in her eyes.

"Trevor, I can't believe you're saying this. After all that we've been through these past few days." Her bottom lip began to tremble. "You're just gonna break it off. Like this whole vampire thing never happened." Shauni's voice began to crack and gain pitch as she tried to prevent herself from crying. Something, that in all the time I've known her, I've rarely seen happen. "Do you think I was just acting that way toward Dylan, because he was the new guy in town and I thought he was cute." She forced a smile. "I *knew* it was you."

"Shauni," I repeated.

I stood up and looked to the sky. For answers. An escape. Anything. Just as long as I didn't have to hear Shauni say what I knew deep down in my heart I always wanted to hear. The words hit me like a ton of bricks.

Shauni stood up beside me and looked into my eyes. "I love you, Trevor." The truth of her words was evident in the way she looked at me. "I always have."

What the hell. You know you love her too. Go for it.

It's amazing how quickly "Love" can make a man actually listen to himself for a change.

"And I've always loved you. Since back at Jason's twelfth birthday party," I said with a smile. This lightened the mood. "When you…"

"Hit you with the snowball," she finished with a small laugh.

"I still think it had a rock in it," I remarked as I rubbed the back of my head where the snowball impacted six years before.

"It did." She grinned. "Love hurts," she finished with a shrug.

I had to do something. I had to keep my relationship with Shauni and get Trevor Wayne back to the land of the living.

What would they do on Beverly Hills 90210? *Then it hit me.*

"Yeah, it does sometimes. But usually for the best." I took Shauni's right hand and led her back to Dick and R.J. "Walk with me."

On the way back to our friends, I explained my plan. At first Shauni didn't like it. Then I convinced her to understand that it was all for the good of our relationship. When we got to the main warehouse, Dick was awake and sitting up. He had a smile on his face when we walked in.

"Hey, Trev…I mean…"

"It's all right, Dick. She knows." I smiled at Shauni. "She's always known."

"So what do we do now? The Leader's dead. And there are no more vampires around."

"We go on with our lives, R.J," Shauni answered as she squeezed my hand.

"Even me. Trevor Wayne." I grinned at my two friends. They stood before me with identical looks of anticipation on their faces. I told them my plan for Trevor Wayne to come back from the dead. "…and that's the plan."

"California?" Dick asked, dumbfounded. "That's nuts." He looked at Shauni. "And you're all good to go about this?"

"Yep. We talked about it. And it's pretty much the only option we have to be happy together."

I looked at my watch then at the guys.

"Well, honey. I guess it's time for me to go," I said with regret in my voice.

I walked over to two of the guys that helped me survive the past few days. I first looked at R.J.

"R.J., You were only on the 'team' for a short time. But I wouldn't have had anyone else help me out." I shook his hand. "You're a real hero, man."

"Thanks," he replied in a wavering voice. "Anytime."

I smiled at him.

"I'll keep that in mind." I looked at my friend that was a werewolf. "Well, Dick. I guess I should thank you. I couldn't have gone this far without you." I gave my friend a hug. He groaned in pain. "Thanks. I guess this makes us even." I pulled away from my friend.

"No, Trevor," Dick said solemnly. "I'll never be able to repay you for getting my life back from the Leader. I'm gonna owe you till I die."

"You got it." I smiled at my friend. My hearing picked up the sounds of an ambulance in the distance. "I hope you guys came up with a story to tell the paramedics. They're almost here." Dick and R.J. looked at me with identical looks of shock. I looked at Shauni, then back at the guys. "If you'll excuse us."

Shauni and I walked out of the warehouse and into the parking lot. I looked at my girlfriend. Her bottom lip began to quiver.

"Shauni. We agreed on this." I looked into her eyes. "It's the only way."

"I know, Trevor." Shauni took a deep breath, and then let it out. "I just wish that we had more time together. That's all."

"Me too, Shauni. Me too." I took her face in my hands and kissed her. We reluctantly parted lips. I knew that she, like me, wanted to stay lost in the moment. Forever. "Hey. I'll be back in a few months. Then we'll have all the time in the world," I said, in hopes that it would cheer her up.

"It'll be hard, but I'll wait for you. As long as it takes." She gave me a little smile, took another deep breath and sighed. "Are you going to see Jason before you leave?"

"Yeah. Even though I'm gonna have to go through his window." She looked at me blankly. "It's way past visiting hours," I said with a grin.

"Then I guess you'd better be going." She waved me toward the air, trying to act like it didn't bother her. But I knew it was killing her. I moved closer to her. I leaned forward to kiss her again. She turned her face and put up her left hand in defiance. "No, Trevor. Don't. It'll just make it harder to let you go."

"Then I guess." The pain in my heart started to seep through as I got a lump in my throat. I sighed. "I'll see you in a few months."

70

I floated into the air. My vampire hearing picked up Shauni's last words to me.

"I love you, Trevor."

"I love you too, Shauni."

If I had looked back at my girlfriend, I would have seen a solitary tear run down her cheek.

I floated outside of Jason's new room at the hospital for ten minutes before I actually opened the window. I figured saying good-bye to my best friend would be just as hard as saying it to Shauni.

Good thing that someone decided not to lock his window.

I floated in and landed beside my friend. My eyes instantly adjusted to the dim lighting conditions as I looked at Jason lying on his bed. He looked in pretty good shape, considering the hell that he went through in the previous eighteen hours. I walked over to him.

"I'm sorry, man," I whispered. "I never meant for anyone to get hurt. Especially you." Jason's body began to stir. He opened his eyes a little bit and looked at me. His eyes adjusted to the light.

"Trevor?" he murmured. "Is that you? Or am I dreaming?"

"You're not dreaming, man," I said with a smile when I found that he was able to talk. "It's me. I beat the Leader. Everyone's safe, even Shauni."

"She told me not to tell you, but she's always known that you were Trevor," he wheezed. "And that she always…" Hack…hack…

"Loved me. Ever since your birthday when she hit me with that…"

"…snowball. Heh-heh!" Cough…cough…hack. Jason tried to sit up in his bed, but his ribs and the needles in his hand and prevented that. "That was funny. If I knew she was gonna throw it at you, I wouldn't have put the stone in it."

I looked at my friend.

So he's the one.

"I honestly thought she was gonna hit Mark Hollander with it."

Go figure.

"I thought there was probably a rock in the damn thing. That sucker hurt, ya know." I jokingly rubbed my head again. "She told me that there was one in it. I guess I should've asked her who put it there.

I patted my friend on the shoulder. The monitors by his bed said that his heartbeat was steadily increasing.

Any minute this place is gonna be crawling with doctors. I gotta wrap this up. I changed the tone of the conversation.

"Seriously, Jason. The main reason that I can by was to tell you good-bye."

"Why?"Cough…cough… "Am I dying?" He laughed slightly.

Leave it to Jason to still be joking when he's down-and-out.

"No, you're not dying. I'm leaving. I'm going to California. To make it look like that I, Trevor Wayne, just up and left to visit my aunt and uncle."

The alarm on Jason's heart monitor went off. My vampire hearing picked up a nurse panicking about Jason's vital signs. I pulled out my pocket watch and looked at it.

Damn! It's time for me to fly. Literally. I jumped up onto the windowsill.

"Jason, the nurses are coming in here. I gotta go." I looked down at the parking lot, then back at my friend. "Take care of Shauni for me. And get well soon."

"On one condition."

I could hear the nurses. Their running sounded like thunder in my ears.

"What's that?"

"Get me a T-shirt of Kramer from *Seinfeld* for my birthday. Signed."

"Will do," I replied as Jason's nurse ran into his room.

And I flew to an uncertain future.

BOOK II

DARK DAZE

CHAPTER 1

"Oh man! I'm never gonna get used to these places," I said to myself as I continued my fifteen- minute swim through the main terminal of the Dweller Valley Airport. I was returning home after having spent six months in Los Angeles. A lot of weird situations arose six months ago that made me have to leave my friends and family. I was finally getting to the end of the river of people when I bumped into someone, knocking their armload to the floor. I quickly grabbed two folders before they hit the ground. The person I bumped into was a scholarly looking brunette. She was about my age, with her hair in a bun and the most beautiful blue eyes I had ever seen, which were hidden behind a pair of old wire-rimmed glasses.

"Oh, sorry, miss," I said as I adjusted my gymbag on my shoulder.

"That's okay, Dylan. I'm always so clumsy."

Dylan? Why would she call me that?

"Excuse me, ma'am. My name is Trevor. Trevor Wayne." I handed her back her folders.

She took them and put them on top of her pile of papers. "Oh, I'm sorry. You just look like someone I use to know." She organized the papers and folders as best she could, then headed to a group of chairs. "Trevor, Trevor Wayne? That sure is weird having your first and middle names being the same," she said as she took a seat.

"No. My name is Trevor Wayne. Not Trevor Trev…" I saw her smiling and decided to change the subject. "Do you mind if I sit with you while you wait? Are you waiting for someone? Miss…I don't believe you've told me your name." She suddenly got a serious look on her face. As though she was remembering something important. She looked at the large digital clock that was suspended from the ceiling. "I'm sorry. I have to go," she said quickly. "I've wasted enough time already." She then disappeared into the crowd. "Miss! Wait!" I called after her.

It was no use. She was gone, engulfed by the swarm of people. *Okay! That was weird. I wonder if I'm gonna see her again? I'll just sit here and wait for Jason.* I sat back down and looked at my watch. He's got five minutes. Which means I'll be waiting for another twenty.

"Trevor! Trevor! Is that *you*?" came the voice of my best friend.

"I guess not," I remarked to the ceiling.

"Holy shit! It *is* you! I almost didn't recognize you without the ponytail," he said as he walked up to me. "You look cooler without one an way." He grinned. "I didn't think you were gonna show."

"Yeah right," I said as I stood up to meet him. "I figured since I didn't come home on Valentine's Day. I knew she'd be pissed if I missed her birthday."

"Speaking of which?" Jason said with a smile.

"Oh yeah." I dug into my gymbag. "Straight from the T.V. Show Store," I said as I handed him the *Seinfeld* T-shirt with Kramer on it. "It's even artificially signed by Michael Richards," I replied as I pointed to the computerized signature on the front.

"Cool, man," he said with a grin as we headed to the car garage. "How'd you get it?"

"I met a girl…"

"You what?"

"No, it's nothing like that." I looked at my friend with a "you know better than that look" as we entered the elevator to the third floor of the parking garage. "As I was saying, I helped a girl and her friends with a little vampire problem they had. Her dad works at The Los Angeles Mall. So she talked to her dad to repay me." I smiled as the elevator stopped on our floor. "The job was waiting for me when I got there."

"Was she cute?" Jason asked. We exited the elevator to the third floor of the garage. Suddenly, I got that old odd feeling in my temples, the feeling that means only one thing. *Great. Just great.* "…you can tell me. I won't tell Shau…" Jason looked and saw the expression of determination on my face and my hand reaching for my backpack. "Oh, man! Not now."

"Happy birthday, Jace," was my only reply as three vampire walked out from behind a van.

"Welcome home, Trevor," said the one that looked like Jim Morrison. He was about my height and had shoulder-length hair. He was wearing a black trench coat and a pair of "John Lennon" sunglasses.

He looks a little familiar. I just wish I could place the face. Can't think about that now. I got work to do. I tapped the stakes together.

"Who's first?" The other two vampires, who looked like Bill and Ted, flew at me. "Jim" just stood in place, watching everything. I dodged "Bill's" initial attack and grabbed "Ted" by the ankle using his momentum to swing him against a nearby mini-van. He fell to the cement with a thud causing the van's car alarm to start "whooping." I ran over and rammed a stake into his chest. "Ted" jerked then fell dead. "Bill" and Jason's battle was taking a little longer, considering he was still sort of recovering from his gunshot wounds. He was supposed to be taking it easy. "Bill" swung at Jason with a right and then a left. Jason easily ducked both punches, then proceeded to punch his enemy in the stomach. "Bill" groaned in annoyance.

"Are you gonna help," Jason screamed to me as he caught "Bill's" left leg in midkick. "Or are you just gonna stand there?" Jason pushed "Bill" backward. His opponent recovered and headed once again in the direction of my friend.

"I *guess* I could help." I used my vampire speed to run at the vampire that was fighting my friend. I shoved one of the stakes into "Bill's" back. He bent over and howled in pain. His lifeless body then slumped to the cement.

"Two down," Jason remarked. We both turned to "Jim."

"One to go." I finished.

"You're next."

"I don't think so," he replied with a smirk. "Another time perhaps." With this, "Jim" disappeared in a large flash of rainbow colored light. I looked at Jason. He had an expression on his face that matched the thoughts in my head. *That was* really *weird.* My enhanced hearing picked up police sirens in the distance. "Time to go," I said to my friend. "Cops are coming."

We ran to Jason's car. I threw my bag in the backseat as he did the same with his new T-shirt. He turned on the engine and headed for the exit. "It's great to be back," I remarked sarcastically as I sat back in the passenger's seat. Two police cars passed us on our way out of the airport parking lot. "Gee whiz. A guy leaves home for six months and the cops get *faster*. What gives?" I exclaimed.

"Well, since you left, people've been dressing up like vampires and looting stores and stuff. Trying to scare everyone. So the police decided that they'd be the new 'vampire hunters' for Dweller Valley."

About time they do their job.

"But little do they realize that *those* were real vampires. Something's just not right about this. Somebody's trying to pick-up where the Leader left off."

"Like I need more stress."

"What do you mean?"

"I got a date for my birthday."

"Who? Anybody I know?" I grinned

"I doubt it. She just moved here two weeks ago."

"Ha-ha. Very funny," I replied sarcastically. "So, how's everybody doing?"

"Well, let's see," my friend replied as he stopped at a red light, "Dick's adjusting to life as a werewolf. He locks himself up in his garage each full moon, so he doesn't hurt anybody."

"That's good," I replied. He turned down the driveway to his house. Then I asked the one question I had been holding off on asking. "What about Shauni?"

"Shauni's still waiting for you. She kept her promise."

He pulled up to his house. I was gonna stay with him for his birthday and then head home. His parents were upstate visiting his grandmother, who was sick. We got out of the car. "I didn't tell her that you were arriving today. I just told her that I had a surprise for her."

We went inside the house to drop off our stuff. I threw my bags down on the living room floor and lay down on the couch.

"I'm just gonna crash here for a while. If you don't mind. You can go to Shauni's without me," I said as I grabbed the television remote and propped my feet on the arm of the couch.

"Oh no you don't!" Jason yelled as he slapped my legs off of where they rested. "First off, there's nothing good on. And second, it's been six months. You *are* going to see Shauni *today*! Even if I have to call and ask her to come here."

"You wouldn't." I looked at Jason. The expression on his face as he picked up the telephone receiver gave me my answer. *He would.* "All right! Let's go!" I said with a sigh.

I stared out the window during the ten-minute ride to Shauni's. We left each other on the hope that we would wait for each other until I came back. I didn't want to leave, but it was the only way Trevor Wayne could return to Dweller Valley. She told me that she was all for it, but I could tell that it didn't make her all that happy. During the ride to our first meeting in half a year, our final words to each other echoed in my head as I watched the houses of my hometown pass by. Shauni and I walked out of the warehouse and into the parking lot. I looked at my girlfriend. Her bottom lip began to quiver.

"Shauni. We agreed on this." I looked into her eyes. "It's the only way."

"I know, Trevor." Shauni took a deep breath, and then let it out. "I just wish that we had more time together. That's all."

"Me too, Shauni. Me too." I took her face in my hands and kissed her. We reluctantly parted lips. I knew that she, like me, wanted to stay lost in the moment. Forever. "Hey. I'll be back in a few months. Then we'll have all the time in the world," I said, in hopes that it would cheer her up.

"It'll be hard, but I'll wait for you. As long as it takes." She gave me a little smile, took another deep breath and sighed. "Are you going to see Jason before you leave?"

"Yeah. Even though I'm gonna have to go through his window." She looked at me blankly. "It's way past visiting hours," I said with a grin.

"Then I guess you'd better be going." She waved me toward the air, trying to act like it didn't bother her. But I knew it was killing her. I moved closer to her. I leaned forward to kiss her again. She turned her face and put up her left hand in defiance. "No, Trevor. Don't. It'll just make it harder to let you go."

"Then I guess." The pain in my heart started to seep through as I got a lump in my throat. I sighed. "I'll see you in a few months."

I floated into the air. My vampire hearing picked up Shauni's last words to me.

"I love you, Trevor."

"I love you too, Shauni."

If I had looked back at my girlfriend, I would have seen a solitary tear run down her cheek.

And me being the glutton for punishment that I am, I just *had* to come back for her and Jason's birthdays. Her's is the day after his. We pulled into her driveway, just as Maggie and Candy were leaving.

"That makes it a little easier," I said as I waved to them with a timid smile on my lips. "At least Candy isn't a vampire anymore."

"How'd you…Oh, yeah. I forgot," Jason replied as we made our way to the front door.

"I *could* fly away. Right now."

"But you won't," he replied as he knocked on the door.

"And what makes you say that?"

To answer my question, the door opened. I turned toward it and stared into the eyes of the only girl that I ever truly loved, Shauni Collins. Her mouth was wide in amazement.

"No reason," Jason said with a smile.

Shauni regained her composure. "Trevor!" she squealed. "Oh my God!!" She pulled me into her arms. I kissed her quickly on the mouth. She let me go. She stumbled over her next words nervously. "You look good. I mean," she blushed, "you look different without the ponytail. I never *really* liked it that much anyway." She stepped inside the trailer. "Come in."

I stepped in the doorway. Shauni's increased heartbeat and breathing, not to mention her rambling, told me that she was nervous. I couldn't blame her. Jason gave her a "Surprise!" smile as we walked through the kitchen and into the living room. I took my designated chair from when Jason, Shauni and I used to sword fight together, before the vampires. Jason went straight to the fridge, like he always did when we'd come over.

"Shauni. Whose Sunny Delight?" My best friend's voice said from inside the kitchen.

"Oh, that's Candy's. No one's allowed to have any."

"Trevor? You want one?"

"Yeah, sure," I said as I winked at Shauni in rebellion.

She looked at both of us in mock disgust. Jason threw me one of the juice bottles. I caught it without even looking. "You guys never change."

"It's just who we are, Shauni," Jason replied as he sat on the couch beside his cousin. "And besides, you know you think it's funny." He took a swig from the bottle. Shauni gave him a smile and stuck out her tongue.

"So, Jason," she patted his leg, "where are you and Sam going tonight?" she asked as she took a drink of his juice.

I choked on the drink of juice I had taken previous to her question.

"I thought you said your date was a she?" Jason gave me "the finger."

"*Her* name is *Samantha*," he stated. Shauni smiled at her cousin's defensiveness.

"I'm just joking, man."

Jason turned to his cousin, who was trying to contain her laughter. "Probably to a movie and then to the Pizza Palace. Why?"

"No reason," she replied with a sigh.

Oh boy. Here it comes.

"It's just that," she looked toward me, "*my* birthday's the day after tomorrow and *I* was hoping to have a birthday dinner with my favorite cousin."

Here we go.

From the tone in her voice and the subject matter of the conversation, I knew what was happening. A double date was in my future.

"Well. Why don't you and Trevor just double date with me and Sam tonight? It'll be like old times," he said with a mischievous grin aimed in my direction.

Boy Jason, you are going down for this one, I thought as I grinned back.

Shauni looked at me, looked at Jason with a smile and then looked back at me. "Well, Trevor? If you *don't* have any plans tonight."

It's almost here.

"Do you wanna double date with Jason and Samantha?"

There it is, folks. I know I'm gonna regret this. "No, I don't. And yes I would, Shauni."

"Pick me up at seven-thirty," she said with a smile.

"Seven-thirty then."

CHAPTER 2

Jason and I had about five minutes until we had to leave. "Who we pickin' up first?" I asked my friend as I started to shave.

"Well. Samantha's gonna drive to the Pizza Palace herself. She said she had some things to do," he yelled from his bedroom.

"So it's just gonna be me, you and Shauni in your car?" I asked as I shaved my neck.

"Yep."

I nicked my chin with the razor. "Ouch!" The cut healed instantly. "Great. Just great." I finished shaving and got dressed at super speed. "You ready to go?" I asked as I walked into his bedroom.

"No! I just got started and you ..." he looked up. "Oh yeah."

"Super speed," we said in unison.

Jason finished getting dressed. I thought about taking my sword then decided against it. *What are the chances that we're gonna get attacked again.* We left to pick up Shauni. As usual, she wasn't quite ready when we got there.

"I bet you she's not ready yet," I remarked to my friend as we walked up the cobble stones to the front door.

"Man, you know that's an unfair bet."

"What're you talking about?" We stopped in front of the porch.

"For one, you probably used your vampire hearing."

"No, I di—"

"And for two," Jason grinned, "Shauni's never on time." We both laughed as we stepped onto the porch. Jason knocked on the door. We heard footsteps and then the door opened. There stood Candy.

"Hey, Jason." She looked at me. "Hi, Trevor."

"Hi, Candy. How's it going? Is Shauni ready?" I asked.

"Yeah, I think. She was fixing her hair last I checked."

83

"You got any Sunny D.?" Jason asked his cousin.

"Yeah. Help yourself."

"He always does," I remarked under my breath.

"It's in the fridge." Jason ducked in the house. I walked to the edge of the porch and sat on the banister. Candy closed the door and followed. "Whoa, Trevor, nice haircut. It suits you. You never really did look right with a ponytail."

"Thanks, Candy."

"Seriously though, Trevor," she started as she rubbed her hands together nervously. "I know we were never really friends. But I just wanted to thank you for saving my life last year." She had a look of sincerity that I had never seen her exhibit before. "And I'm sorry for trying to kill you."

"That's all right. You were just doing what you were ordered to do."

While I was talking to Candy, I could hear Shauni talking to Jason inside the trailer.

"I'm ready. You think Trevor will like this outfit?"

"It's fine, Shauni. Trevor likes you in just about anything."

I smiled to myself.

"Where is Trevor?"

"He's outside talking to Candy."

"Then I guess it's time to go," she said.

I jumped off of the banister.

"It's not your fault," I said to Candy.

"Thanks again, Trevor. You're one of a kind. I guess that's why she hit you with that snowball."

Just then the door opened and out walked Shauni and Jason. He drank down the last of the juice from his bottle. "You ready to go, man?" he asked as he patted me on the back. He handed his cousin the empty juice bottle. "Thanks, Candy."

"Yeah. I'm ready." We walked to Jason's car. Shauni's rules dictated that I had to sit in the backseat. I looked at Candy as I settled into my seat. She gave me a slight smile, waved, and then headed back into the house.

"Trevor, what'd you and Candy talk about?" Shauni asked as she shut the car door.

"Not much," I started as we drove away. "She just thanked me for getting her life back from the vampires. She's really changed since then."

"I know," she said with a smile. "But she can still be a bi...her old self sometimes."

"She's only human, Shauni."

"Yeah. *Now*," Jason said with a giggle as he turned down the street toward the Pizza Palace.

"That's not funny, Jace."

"Sorry."

My girlfriend turned around and looked at me. "So, Trevor, what did you do while you were in California.

"I *did* go visit my relatives. They were, needless to say, surprised when I showed up at their front door." I laughed as I remembered Aunt Martha's facial expression when she opened the door and recognized that it was me standing in front of her. "Mom called them when she found out I was missing. She told them that I was dead. I told them it was a big mistake. And that it was my choice to leave."

We turned onto Elm Street, the last street that led to the Pizza Palace. "I called Mom when I got there and explained to her that I just needed to get away for a while. She took it surprisingly well."

"How much did you mooch off your aunt and uncle?"

"For your information, Mr. 'I think I'll drink all my cousin's Sunny Delight,' I didn't mooch off my relatives." I looked at my friend through the rearview mirror. "You know I got a job at the mall by their house. How do you think I paid for your shirt?"

"What shirt?" Shauni looked through the mirror at me.

"A *Seinfeld* T-shirt. It's signed by Michael Richards and everything," Jason started as he turned the car into the parking lot. "He got it for me. For…my…birthday." My friend gave me an "I'm sorry" look. Shauni turned away from me.

"I got your present, Shauni." I put my hand on her shoulder. "I'm just saving it for after dinner."

"Oh. Then I forgive you."

Dodged that bullet.

"So, Jason," I began as he pulled into an empty parking space, "what kind of car does Samantha drive?"

"Don't know, dude," he replied as he pulled into an empty space. He shut off the engine. "She never told me." We got out of the car and headed into the restaurant.

"You mean you've known this girl for the past two weeks and you don't know what kind of car she drives."

"I never worried about it. She just usually meets me."

"Maybe we should wait outside," I remarked. "She might not have gotten here yet."

"Okay." Jason looked at his watch. "It's 8:03 now. If Sam isn't out here by ten after, we'll go in and wait."

"You two can wait. I have to use the ladies' room," Shauni said as she opened the door to the restaurant. She went inside, which left Jason and I alone to talk. Man to man.

"How long did you two have this double date planned?" I looked at my friend with a stern expression. "Before or after you knew I was coming back?"

"After. But before Samantha showed up. We always knew that you'd be coming back to Dweller Valley." He walked back to his car and sat on the hood. "Shauni thought you'd come back on Valentine's Day. Personally, I knew you wouldn't miss her birthday." Jason pointed at me and smiled. "I know you too well. And Samantha and me hooking up last week was perfect."

"Couldn't find a date for your birthday." I grinned. "Could you?"

"Bite me, man!" he replied. I looked at him in astonishment. "Ooh. Bad choice of words." He looked at his watch. "It's 8:11, time to go in." He jumped down from the hood.

We walked to the door that Shauni had gone through and into my former place of employment. I spotted Shauni as soon as we entered the dining area. She was sitting in a booth across from a blonde female who had a pair of familiar, beautiful blue eyes. This, I assumed, was Samantha.

"There are the girls." I pointed where they were sitting. "Over there." We walked over to our dates. "Are you *sure* Samantha's not from around here," I whispered to Jason. "She looks familiar. I just can't remember from where."

"Of course I'm sure," he replied as we sat down. "It's nice one of you came out to get us."

"Sorry, Jason. I was coming in the other doors as Shauni was coming out of the restroom. And we just started talking."

"That's okay, Sam," Jason replied as he gave Samantha a quick squeeze. "We would have come in eventually." He smiled and remembered that I wasn't introduced to his new girlfriend. "Oh Sam, this is my best friend, Trevor Wayne. Trevor, this is Samantha Stevens. Like on *Bewitched*."

Samantha held out her hand for me to shake. I extended mine in response. As I took her hand in mine our eyes locked.

Suddenly, a dark cloud engulfed my vision. I saw images of vampires and zombies terrorizing people. The Leader's "human" face contorting into his "vampire" one.

"Nobody can save them, Wayne. Because of you," he said with an evil grin, "I win."

All at once, I could see again. The sudden change from the light of my "vision" to the darkness of the Pizza Palace interior dazed me. I reached against the table for support.

"Trevor, are you all right?" Shauni asked.

"Yeah, I'm fine," I lied as I shook my head to clear the daze. "It's nice to meet you, Samantha." All I could see was her eyes. *The most beautiful blue eyes I've ever seen.* I looked at her more closely. "I know this is gonna sound weird, but have we met before?"

"No, I'm new around here."

"You just remind me of someone I've seen before."

"I have that kind of face," she replied with a grin.

"Well, shall we order?" Shauni asked with some irritation in her voice. "*Blood Reign* starts at 9:15, and we don't want to be late."

"*Blood Reign*?" I repeated as we looked at our menus. "Isn't that the first movie of that new vampire trilogy they plan on doing? What's the series called again? Oh I can't think of it."

"*RedHaze*?" Jason answered. "It's supposed to be really good."

"Heh. Heh. You remember hearing about the writer/director...Oh, What's his name?" I thought for a second.

"Travis Lane?" Shauni answered for me.

"Yeah." She and Samantha said together.

"Yeah. So?" Jason asked.

"You remember when he was at that comic book convention? And he almost got crushed by the stage lights during his press conference to promote the movie?"

"Yeah," Jason replied. "He moved out of the way..."

"...just in time," Shauni ended. "Trevor!" she yelled in a whisper.

"Oh. Come on, Shauni. What was I supposed to do," I whispered back. I looked at Jason and Sam. Then back at my girlfriend. "Let him get hurt?"

"No, Trevor! I didn't mean it that way." She crossed her arms across her chest. "Mmmph!"

I don't believe it. I think I actually won an argument with Shauni.

"Look on the bright side." I put my arm around my girlfriend and looked into her eyes. "He just might put the experience in one of his stories." Shauni just looked at me, smiled and kissed me on the cheek. I leaned back and closed my eyes, happily thinking of the events that led me to that point in time. While looking at the ceiling I noticed that we were sitting under the exact place where the Leader crashed through during our final battle. The whole ceiling was now a large glass skylight. After about five minutes, the waitress finally came to our table. It was Baby Jackson.

"Hello. How are you guys tonight?" she asked with a smile. Then she noticed me.

"Trevor! Oh my God! How are you? Long time no see."

"I almost didn't recognize you. It's been like, forever. You look good."

"Thanks." I grinned at Jason after noticing Shauni's obvious displeasure with Baby's flirtations.

"Are you ready to order?" she said to the group.

"Ah, yes." Shauni, as usual, volunteered herself to give the order. "Well have a supreme pizza with regular crust. A pitcher of..." She looked at Samantha. "What kind of soda would you like, Sam?"

"Pepsi is fine."

"Okay. A pitcher of Pepsi," Shauni continued, "and a family order of breadsticks."

"Would anyone like the salad bar?" Baby asked. At the same moment, I got that old prickly sensation again. The females raised their hands. Jason shook his head in denial. "What about you, Trevor?"

"We don't have the time. Jason, we got company."

"Oh man!" he groaned.

As he said these words, six vampires crashed through the skylight and landed on the table behind us. It rained glass and metal on the other patrons of the Pizza Palace. Many of them scattered in the confusion.

"Time to go to work," I said as I floated just above our booth. "Jason, you know what to do."

My friend slid from his seat and headed for the closest wooden chair. I flew at the two closest vampires and clothes-lined them before they had a chance to duck.

"Shauni, start getting everybody out of here!" I kicked one of the vampires in mid-flight. I bounced off him and landed in front of a black vampire that was close to six and a half feet tall. "Shit!" I managed to say before "Shaquille O'Neil" picked me up by the neck and slam-dunked me into the salad bar. I rolled over the opposite side and onto the floor.

"Come on, Wayne." It was "Jim Morrison" from the airport. "Make this easy on yourself. Give up." He pointed straight at me. "I would in *your* position."

"Well *you're* not *me*." I caught "Shaq" as he jumped at me. I flipped him in the air and slammed him onto an upturned chair. The last sound he made was a scream of pain as he died.

"You're next," I said to "Jim." He disappeared right in front of me.

Suddenly, I heard Shauni scream. I turned around toward our table. "Jim" was standing there with his arm around Shauni's throat. A kaleidoscope of swirling rainbow colors appeared behind him.

"Sorry, Trevor," he said as he held onto my girlfriend. She squirmed in his grasp. "She's coming with me."

"Trevor! Help!" Shauni gasped as "Jim" pulled her into the portal. It rippled with a myriad of colors as they disappeared into it.

"Shauni! I will." I ran toward the portal. "I wi…Ooof!" A female vampire flew into me, knocking me to the floor.

"I don't think so, Trevor," she growled. "The Boss wants her." She jumped from me and followed "Jim" and Shauni into the portal.

As I watched them the female vampire looked at me. It was a face I was all too familiar with.

"Kate? There's no way?" I said in disbelief.

I snapped to my senses by a bright light exploding to my left. I looked over to see Samantha being carried by another of the undead soldiers toward the vortex. She was unusually calm for someone in her situation. This sent a chill down my spine.

Why does this crap always happen to me? I asked myself.

"Because it's your fate to fight the forces of Darkness, Trevor," Samantha's voice said inside my head as she disappeared into the light.

"Sam?"

"Sam!" Jason screamed as he ran after her.

"Jason! Don't!" I yelled to my friend. I flew in his direction. Just as I was about to get him, the portal contracted, creating a vacuum effect. I shut my eyes in reflex. Jason, me and a few tables and chairs were sucked out of the restaurant. As quickly as it had appeared, the light vanished. Leaving the Pizza Palace empty of humans.

CHAPTER 3

When I came to I realized my eyes were still shut. I opened them and my enhanced vision adjusted quickly to the darkness. I was in a somewhat familiar building. My head pounded with a hangover-like headache. I heard a noise not too far from where I lay. It sounded big, whatever it was.

Damn, I should have gotten my sword from Jason's. I could really use it right now.

A rainbow-colored light appeared in front of me. It disappeared and in its place was my samurai sword. *Don't say I never gave you anything.* Samantha's voice echoed in my head. I grabbed my sword and put it to my side.

"Jason. Is that you?" I whispered experimentally as I went into a defensive posture.

"Trevor?" Came the voice of my friend. "Where are we?"

"I don't know, man." I lowered my sword and looked around at the structure. "It does look familiar though."

Jason looked around with me. "Oh man. I *know* where we're at. We're at the freakin' Pizza Palace." He paused. "I think."

"Shh. I hear something." I concentrated my vampire hearing. "It sounds like someone's coming."

"...said that he'd be here tonight. And that he'd show up here," a voice that sounded like Jason's said. *"She said he'd be our best bet..."*

"What is it, Trevor?" Jason asked.

"What was that?" a female asked.

CHKK-CHKK.

Chkk-chkk? Oh, hell!

"Jason! Look out!" I yelled. I dropped my sword and jumped between my friend and the sound.

"Look out for wha…" BLAM! I saw a flash of light and fell back pinning Jason to the wall. "Oh man that hurt. Thanks," he said as he pushed me off of him. "Now get off. Don't move!"

"Which do you want me to do?" I said as I began to get up.

"Get off don't move!" he answered in stereo. I turned back toward the gunshot to see my friend standing in front of me. It *was* Jason. But it couldn't have been. He had a patch on his left eye, no goatee and he was holding a 20-gauge shotgun in his hands. Behind him were two people. I knew the female because of her eyes.

"Trevor?" Shauni exclaimed as she stepped from the shadows. "Is that you?" She stood behind her cousin. Her hair was shorter, but the green eyes were the same.

"It can't be! You hit him point-blank," Tommy Bayer said as he pointed at my chest. "Look at his shirt. And the blood!" he remarked excitedly.

"Oh yeah. About that…"

"Shut up!" yelled the Jason with the rifle, he aimed it at me again. "Now get up. Slowly!" He turned to his cousin, "Shauni, get a stake." She reached into a backpack and pulled out a foot long piece of wood with a sharp end. "If it *is* Trevor, he's been turned completely."

Something rustled behind me.

Jason! Oh crap! No wonder he hasn't said anything. He must've been struck speechless when he saw his double. And if I don't do something, "Patch" here is gonna kill himself. So to speak.

"Who's that? Show yourself," Patch ordered. Jason crawled out from the garbage and stood beside me. His counterpart looked at him in amazement. Shauni's mouth dropped wide-open. Tommy just stood there, speechless.

I took this moment as my opportunity to pull the odds into our favor. At vampire speed, I took the shotgun from Jason's hands. He just stood there and continued to stare at my friend. I didn't know if it was because I did it at vampire speed or because he couldn't get over seeing Jason.

"Jason?" Shauni asked my friend.

"Yeah?" The two Jason Pasner's answered in unison as they looked at Shauni. Her voice snapped them from their stupor.

"This is wrong," Tom began. "How can there be two Jasons?"

Then it dawned on me.

"Because," I sighed, "I'm who you've been waiting for. I take it you have another vampire infestation. As you know, I'm assuming you do, I'm an authority on these things." I pointed to the Jason that came through the portal with me. "We can help."

"You're not doing anything." Patch went to cock his rifle. It wasn't there. He looked at me with surprise.

"Looking for this?" I said as I waved his gun in the air.

"What the hell?" Tom let out.

"How?" Shauni asked, stunned.

This is gonna take a while. I sat on one of the last remaining tables in the old restaurant. "Something must have happened six months ago where I didn't defeat the Leader." I ran my hands through my hair and looked at the group of listeners. "Something bad."

"But that *still* doesn't explain why there are two Jasons," Tom exclaimed. "How can that be?"

"Because we're from an alternate reality. A parallel Earth." I motioned toward my friend. "Jason and I were transported here through a portal that appeared out of nowhere."

"We're here to save our girlfriends," Jason said. "We aren't vampires and we aren't here to kill you. We're the 'What-If's.'" He motioned toward his double. "And like Trevor said," he took the gun from my hand and gave it to its owner, "we're here to help. So, what'll it be?" He looked at his twin.

"All right. I'm in," Patch replied with a wary eye.

"Me too," Shauni agreed. "If you're anything like the Trevor I know. We can trust you with our lives."

You have no idea how right you are, Shauni. I bent down and picked up my sword.

"What the hell. If they trust you, I trust you," Tom replied. I jumped off the table.

"We should get headed back to camp. The Hunters probably know we're here," Patch remarked.

We made our way out into the parking lot. The only vehicle was a 1989 Pontiac Sundbird. What little was left of the paint job was red.

"Here's my car," Patch informed us. "Let's go."

"You guys go ahead. I'm gonna follow from the air," I said as Patch and Tom opened the car doors. Shauni got into the vehicle.

Tommy stopped as he was getting in. "You're gonna what!"

"You'll see." I almost forgot that he never knew about my powers. I pointed to my chest. "I'm not exactly a normal human. I can fly too." I sensed vampires. And the feeling was strong. I put my sword in the loop of my belt. *Gonna have to find a long coat.* "You have to go. Now! We're about to have company."

"I guess you can sense vampires too," Tom said sarcastically.

Jason and the others gave a confirming nod as they got in the car. Tommy shook his head and got in. Patch turned on the engine and sped away. I grasped onto the handle of my sword and flew into the air. When I was about a hundred feet in the air I spotted a car pulling into the Pizza Palace parking lot. Two passengers got out of the back.

"Sorry, guys. They just left," I remarked to them from the air.

"Damn!" Lewis screamed. "They should be lying here. Dead."

"I don't think they got here yet, man," Oswald remarked.

"They had to have been here." He sniffed the air. "I smell blood. The problem is that it's part human and part vampire." A look of revelation crossed his vampire features. "The prophecy is coming true."

"The Leader's gonna kill us," Oswald said, frightened.

"No, he won't."

"Why's that, Lewis?"

"Because he ain't gonna find out."

"All right, Lewis. I won't tell anyone."

"That's a good baby brother. Now get in the car. We gotta go."

Man! The vampires really did a number on this place. I wonder what happened to my counterpart in this reality. Patch's Pontiac turned into Sugarton, or what was left of it.

Most of the buildings that I knew were now piles of rubble; others were only partially standing. Mama's Corner Store was now a roofless group of walls. Patch drove toward Catston, a suburb of Sugarton. The village where his parents lived. The car stopped at the Sugarton Elementary School. I began my descent as they exited the vehicle. I landed about twenty feet away from them.

"So guys, why are we here at the school?" I asked. "Where's the camp?"

"It's in the school," Shauni replied as we headed to the gym doors. "The school was one of the last buildings left standing after the final battle. Remind me to tell you about it sometime."

"Come on, Shauni. It's getting late and the Hunters could be looking for us. You can talk to *him* inside," Tom said with a tinge of irritation in his voice.

"Yeah, Shauni," Patch replied, "we still have to show them where they're going to sleep."

"Whoa...ho...ho! 'Him!' 'They!' We do have names," Jason yelled, fed up. "It *would* be nice if you started to use them!"

"Trevor is the easy one," Patch said. "How are we going to distinguish between *us* in conversation. *Jason Pasner!*"

These two are like Jeckyll and Hyde. The problem is who's who.

"How about this, we'll call," I looked at the Jason that I arrived with, "you Jason, and we'll call you," I looked at the other Jason, "with no offense intended, Patch." I looked at the others in the group. "Is that good for everyone?"

"Kinda like Wolverine in Madripoor. It's cool with me," Patch said with a smile.

"Me too."

"Sure," Shauni said with a grin that was directed toward me.

"Yeah. Whatever," Tom remarked. "Let's go." He knocked on one of the double doors of the reconstructed school. A panel in the top of it opened. A familiar face appeared.

Dick! Good thing he's here. With the good guys.

"Who's there?" he asked.

"Boo," Tom answered as Patch looked around in anticipation.

"Boo who?" Dick asked. I noticed that both Jason and Shauni were getting nervous. I couldn't blame them.

"Stop crying, man. It's us."

"Okay." A few seconds later, the door opened.

"We gotta get a different password," Patch remarked to Dick as we entered.

We walked into the building. It was darkly lit and noisy. I was the last to go in.

What a mess, it reminds me of the bunkers in the future on Terminator. *I wonder where Arnold is.* As I walked with Patch and Shauni, I noticed that many of the people helping them were kids that I knew from school. Or, I should say, their counterparts. They all looked at Jason and I as we walked past them in the hallway.

"I'll show you where you're gonna sleep," Patch informed me and my partner.

"I guess I'll see you tomorrow," Shauni said as she stopped at an intersection in the hallway. "I have some things to do before I go to sleep. I have an early day tomorrow." She smiled at me. Jason just grinned.

"Good night, Trevor." She looked at my friend. "Good night, Jason." Shauni walked over to Patch. "Good night to you too, Jason." She kissed her cousin on the cheek and walked down an adjoining hall.

"Who are these guys?" Dick asked Tom as Patch and Shauni led us to our quarters.

"It's Trevor Wayne. Can you believe it?" Tom said excitedly. "Well, not ours. He has these powers. We might have a chance. I just wish I knew what happened to ours since the Leader arrived," he answered with a tinge of contempt. "The one with the hat is Jason."

"What do you mean 'our Trevor'? 'The one with the hat is Jason'? Where are they from?"

"Well, Dick, that's gonna be a little hard for me to explain." The two friends stopped in the middle of the hallway.

"Why? Are they like aliens or something?"

"You could say that. Try 'parallel universe.' I don't know the whole story, but from what Trevor said, he thinks something happened when the vampires first showed up. Something where he didn't defeat the Leader."

"It can't be that. I was there when he did it," Dick replied. "He came back and told us."

"Then maybe something happened after that?" Tom suggested.

"I don't know, Tom. We'll figure it out later." Dick looked at his watch. "Now if you'll excuse me. Since you're back, my shift's over, I'm going to check the perimeter." Dick turned and walked to the door.

"Watch yourself, man. There *are* still vampires around looking for us."

"I'll be careful. Trust me."

Jason led us into the basement of the old school house. "These are the only rooms we have left," he remarked. "They're not much. But we make do with what we have."

"That's okay, man. These are fine," I replied. I looked into one of the doorways. The classrooms were divided with plywood walls into small one-room apartments.

"It's getting late," Patch stated as he looked at his watch. "We have a big day ahead of us tomorrow. Shauni wants me to give you two a tour of the camp. She would do it, but she has to wash clothes."

"It sounds…" I tried to find the right word. "…educational."

"Yeah, a real class trip," Jason added with a fake smile.

"Good night, Patch. See you in the morning," I said to our host as I shut the door behind him. I looked at my friend. "What's up with you, Jason?" I walked over and sat on the cot across from my friend. "Ever since we got to this universe you've been on edge. What gives, man?"

"It's Patch. There's something about him." He put his arms up. "I don't know. Maybe it's his patch. But I just have this feeling that he's mad at me for something I did, or didn't do."

96

"Why don't you ask him about it tomorrow. See what's going on," I advised.

"Yeah. Couldn't hurt." He lay down on his mattress. "Shut the light off, will you?"

"Yeah. Sure." I got up and went to the lamp. As I flipped the switch I looked out the window. I saw Dick exiting the school.

Wonder what he's doing? Probably some kind of security thing.

I went back to my cot and lay down. I just stared at the ceiling, and reflected on everything that happened within the past twenty-four hours.

But, if it is a security sweep. Why is he alone? Less casualties if he gets caught I guess.

I closed my eyes. Every time I did, I could see Shauni, frightened. Being sucked into the rainbow colored portal to this world. And Samantha's calm look as the same thing happened to her. And her voice in my head saying that I'm the only one that can do what has to be done. I opened my eyes.

This sucks.

"Jason, I can't sleep." I got up and headed to the door. "I'm going for a little walk."

"Okay, man." He mumbled through his pillow.

I walked out into the hallway and headed for the cafeteria..

Hopefully, they keep food in the cafeteria. I'm hungry.

As I turned down the hallway, I heard someone coming. I floated up to a dark corner of the ceiling. The one who made the sound was Shauni.

She must be headed for some eats too. I floated down behind her.

"Shauni," I whispered.

"Aah!" she screamed. She turned around, breathing heavily with her hand to her chest. "Oh, Trevor? You scared me." Her breathing slowed to normal. She looked behind me. "What're you doing walking around the halls?"

"I couldn't sleep." As I looked at Shauni, I thought of my girlfriend that had her face. And how she must be scared out of her mind. The only difference between the two was that the Shauni from this universe had her hair cut short as opposed to "my" Shauni having hers past her shoulders. "I have a lot of things on my mind." I smiled. "Plus, I'm hungry."

"Yeah, me too. I was just about to go to the cafeteria for a midnight snack. I think I can rustle us up something."

"That'd be great." I followed her down the hall. We entered the dining hall and headed to the kitchen area. Shauni went into a stock room. She exited with a loaf of bread. She then got into one of the refrigerators and came out with a plate of meats and cheeses. "What do you'ns have to drink?"

"We have soda, milk and water," she answered.

"I'll take some water. Thanks."

Shauni got me a glass and put some ice cubes in it. She poured water from a pitcher that she got from one of the refrigerators. "Here you go," she said as she handed me the glass. As our hands touched, I could feel the attraction.

It's not your Shauni, I reminded myself. I quickly pulled my hand away.

"Thanks." I began to make a sandwich. "So. What do you guys do for fun around here?"

"We fight," Shauni answered solemnly as she retrieved two slices of bread from the bag. "I know this sounds morbid, but ever since the Leader arrived, we've been fighting the vampires and zombies."

"I just can't believe this happened. Surely I...my double would have found out and hauled ass back here. Didn't you'ns try to contact him?" I asked as I handed her the butter knife.

"Of course," she answered as she spread mayonnaise on a slice of bread. "I mean, he left us at the sand plant to go see Jace." This I knew. "After that, Jason said he went to California."

"I did," I remarked as I took a bite of my sandwich.

"I called his Aunt Martha the day after the vampires came back. She said he was dead and to quit prank calling," she continued. "The next night the war with the vampires started all over again. And since then, he, Trevor, hasn't been heard from. Jason and I think that he was taken before he left for California but after he left the hospital."

That can't be right. He would still have the powers of the DayWalker.

I flashed to "Jim Morrison" from the airport. And what he said in the Pizza Palace. *"Give up. I would in your position."*

I put down my sandwich. "No," I whispered, "it can' t be."

Oh, my God. No wonder my double isn't here fighting with the rebels. He's fighting against them, as a full-fledged vampire. "Jim Morrison" is this world's Trevor Wayne. No wonder he looked familiar.

It's seldom how often I look in the mirror at myself. I remembered the flash of light just as the Leader hit the "Holy Water" rain. *It was a portal.* I picked up my sandwich and took a bite. I took a drink of water and swallowed hard. "To get rid of his worst enemy as quickly as possible..."

"...he made him his right-hand-man as quickly as possible," Shauni finished for me.

Shauni and I talked for the next hour, while we finished our sandwiches. We would have awakened the "gang," but they needed their sleep for the upcoming battle. I was still a little freaked that my double was on the side of the Leader, and that I would have to take him out. Take them *both* out. The one thing that neither Shauni nor I could figure out was why the Leader decided to kidnap Samantha and my Shauni. After our conversation, I walked her back to her room.

"Maybe I'll see you tomorrow during the tour," I remarked.

"I'll be looking forward to it," Shauni said with a smile as she walked into her quarters.

Oh great.

I walked back to where Jason and I were to sleep.

Damn! I forgot to ask her why there would be animosity between Jason and Patch. Oh, well. We'll probably find out eventually.

I entered our "room" and lay down my cot. I was a lot calmer now than I was before I talked to Shauni. I guess seeing *her* safe somehow told me that my own Shauni was safe. I just wished that I could've been 100 percent sure. I stared up at the ceiling. Within ten minutes, I was asleep.

CHAPTER 4

I woke up the next morning, and succumbed to what I like to call the *"Quantum Leap* effect." All my surroundings were different than the ones I was accustomed to. I was used to waking up at my Aunt Martha's house or my bedroom in my parents' house. Hell, even waking up in Dick's sister's room while I stayed with him as Dylan MacLeod was easy to get used to. So when I woke up on a cot in the makeshift bedroom in an alternate reality, I was freaked. Especially when I realized that the events that happened the night before weren't from a dream that I had on the plane coming home. I sat up and looked over at Jason. He was still asleep. I looked at my watch. It showed me that it was twenty till ten.

"Hmmph!"

Sleeping the morning away. Some things never change, Jace.

I thought about waking my friend up, but decided against it. "He'll probably threaten to kick my ass if I do it. I'll just let him sleep."

I lay back down on my bed and thought of a plan to save Shauni. And exactly how to tell Jason that *my* twin was a full-fledged vampire. After about an hour, he woke up. Still half asleep, he looked around the room.

"Where are we, man?" he asked as he put on his glasses and flannel shirt. His eyes widened as he remembered the events of last night. "It wasn't a dream, was it?"

"Afraid not, man." I walked over to the window and pulled the curtains open. It was weird looking out the window to a place I was familiar with and knowing full well that it wasn't the same place. I turned back to my friend. "I finally figured out a way to save Shauni. I spent most of last night and part of this morning thinking about it. But getting back home…" I paused. I could hear Patch out in the hall. He was mumbling something about having to take us on this "freakin' tour."

"...that's gonna take some doing."

"Did you find out where your counterpart is in this reality?" Jason asked.

"Yeah. But he's not gonna be able to help much."

There was a knock at the door. "Come in, Patch," I said to the sound. The door opened and in walked he double of my best friend. "Morning."

"Morning," he grumbled. "How'd you know it was me?"

"I heard you coming down the hall." To answer the puzzled expression on his face, I pointed to my right ear.

"Oh yeah. I forgot." Patch straightened his sweatshirt and stood up straighter. "You guys ready for the tour?" Patch directed this question toward Jason with a look of contempt.

"Wouldn't miss it," Jason replied gruffly as he put on his baseball cap.

"Yeah, sure," I replied as I looked at Jason with a "Lighten up!" look on my face.

Patch led me and Jason into the hallway and toward the stairs that led to the ground floor. "There's not really much here." He absently pointed to the rooms around us. "There are the sleeping quarters. The dining hall." Patch walked to the door that we had entered last night. "During the day is when we get the most done. We have a truce with the Leader that the vampires can't harm us during the day." Our host opened the door and motioned for us to exit the building. "The legends say that's when they're weakest."

"Yeah," I stated. "Probably some kind of insurance policy."

"Whoa," Jason exclaimed when he stepped outside. "This looks like one of those Amish craft fairs. It's weird." I stepped outside with my friend and looked around the area surrounding the camp.

All I saw when I stepped outside was about thirty kids playing on the playground. There was a group of younger kids sitting down listening to Baby Jackson tell a story. I listened with my vampire hearing. The story was *The Little Engine That Could.* Behind the small group, in the grass, Dick and Tom were teaching some of the people closer to our age. It looked as though they were teaching hand-to-hand fighting techniques.

"What's going on, Patch?" I looked at Jason's double in disbelief. "Where are the grown-ups? There aren't any adults around here."

"The Leader had most of them killed. A lot of them he has as cattle in the old high school." Patch looked at Jason angrily. "My parents and Shauni's mother and sister were one of the first taken." He looked at me with sadness on his face. "Nobody knows if any of them are still alive."

"Hey, Jace!" Tom called from his class. "Bring those two over here so we can see if the stories are true," Tom said with contempt.

102

"No prob!" Patch said in a one hundred and eighty-degree mood change. He started walking to his fellow rebels. He waved for Jason and I to follow. "You didn't want this to be a 'regular class trip.' Now did you?"

Jason gave me a surprised look. "You asked for that one, dude," I said with a grin. "At least it won't be boring." We followed Patch to where Tom and Dick were teaching their class. Dick was showing the students how to turn the tables on an opponent when they have you in a headlock. One of the students, who I recognized as R.J. Rice, got up and put his arm around Dick's neck.

"Now what you want to do first is grab their arm," Dick explained as he took a hold of R.J.'s wrist. "And pivot around and bring their arm behind their back." Dick brought Rick's arm around and behind like he explained. Most of the class ooh'ed and aah'ed. Dick looked up and saw Jason and I.

"And if you want to get really fancy," he grinned, "you can trip them and push them off balance." He let go of Rick's arm and patted him on the back. "Now you try." Dick put his arm around Rick's neck. R. J. repeated the moves that Dick demonstrated. He released Dick from the hold. Dick looked up at our group.

"Here we are," he motioned at Jason and I, "Trevor Wayne, the one and only." *That's what you think.* "And his faithful sidekick." He stood up and walked over to some wooden swords that were lying on the ground. He grinned, picked one up and threw it to me.

"Care to take a 'stab' at it."

I caught the sword with one hand. "Sure." I began unbuttoning my flannel shirt.

"Are you sure about this?" Jason asked as he pulled me to the side. "I mean, you could beat him in about two seconds," he whispered.

"That's if I 'speed it up.' " I whispered back as I handed him my shirt. "Which I am *not* going to do." I stepped onto the mat on which Dick and R. J. were practicing. I got into my attack position. "Ready when you are."

Dick twirled his sword and swung it down at the top of the swing. I blocked it with my weapon and pushed him away with my free hand. Dick stumbled backward and regained his balance. "Nice shot."

"Thanks," I replied.

Dick aimed his sword for my chest. *Damn Dick!* He lunged toward me. When he was close enough, I deflected his sword and pivoted around to face my opponent.

"Whoa!" Dick sliced at my head. Only my vampire reflexes helped me block the attack.

"Damn!" I heard one of the Jasons say in disbelief. "This is getting intense."

Dick and I exchanged a few blows. Dick went to hit at my right leg. I blocked it easily. We exchanged five more blows. I thrust at his stomach and he deflected it. I thrust again but couldn't get past his defenses. We exchanged five more blows. Dick swiped at my legs. I easily jumped over his sword as he swiped. I brought down my weapon toward his head. He blocked my attack.

He seems more aggressive than the Dick from my reality.

He pushed me away in a similar fashion that I did to him.

"Turnabout is fair play," Dick said with a grin.

"Touché,." I replied as we once again began to exchange blows.

This is getting redundant. Time to end this.

Dick thrust at me. I brought my sword under his, lifting it up. I stopped then brought mine back over and pinned his to the ground. I pivoted around in a clockwise direction. As I suspected, Dick stood up to block my attack. I swung my sword and hit his hand.

"Ouch!" he screamed as his sword fell to the ground. While he was surprised, I crouched down and swept his legs out from under him. He fell to the ground.

"Oomph!"

I stood up and turned around. I walked over to Dick and put my sword to his neck. "Do you yield?" I asked with a grin. Dick had no other choice.

"Yeah. I yield." I threw my sword to the side. "Nice move. Where'd you learn it?" I put my hand out and helped him to his feet.

"T.V.," I answered. "*Highlander: The Series.* Season Two. Episode Three." Jason and Patch walked over to us.

"Nice move, Trevor," Patch remarked.

"Thanks, man." Jason handed me my shirt. "Thanks, Jace."

"No problem."

"Oh God! No!"

I didn't need super hearing to hear Shauni scream.

"Shauni!" Patch screamed.

Patch, Jason, Dick and Tommy ran to where Shauni was washing clothes. *Shauni!*

Her scream came from the other side of the playground. I immediately flew in the direction of the sound. As soon as I landed, I quickly scanned the area. It looked like a riot. A lot of people were running around like chickens with their heads cut off.

What I observed was something that I really didn't need to see. Patch's Sunbird, that he had since he was sixteen, was on fire. Flames licked out from under the slightly opened hood. Shauni and Nicole Watson were dragging the bathtub, which they used to rinse the clothes toward the car. I ran to the girls at super speed.

"Mind if I help?" I asked with a smile as I grabbed the tub.

"By all means," Shauni replied. Standing back to let me do my thing.

I picked up the tub with both hands and kicked open the hood. "Aargh!" I gasped as the flames spit out at me.

That was smart, you genius. I stumbled back and almost dropped the tub.

"Whoa." I regained my balance and dumped the water onto the fire. Steam rolled as it contacted with the hot engine. Everyone cheered.

"Nice save, Trevor," Patch said, wheezing. Winded from his run across the camp.

"Good job, man," Jason remarked as he patted my back. He leaned on me. Also winded.

"Yeah. Great jo…" Tommy was interrupted by Shauni screaming yet again.

I looked over to where Shauni was standing. Two guys that I recognized from my world, Chris Mazik and his cousin Leslie Suders, were holding her.

What now? These two are supposed to be with the good guys.

To answer my question, their bodies shimmered and they went from looking like healthy teenagers to thin, decaying zombies.

"Zombies! Everybody grab a weapon," Patch ordered.

"No!" Tommy yelled back. "If you do, they might hurt Shauni."

You took the words right out of my mouth.

Jason just stood there in awe. I couldn't blame him. I was a little caught off guard myself. Seeing Shauni being kidnaped again with nothing either of us could do. I had to do something.

"This is against the truce! You can't make an act of war during the day!" Patch declared.

"The rules have changed. And the Leader wants some more insurance for the battle that is to come," Chris slurred in an undead voice. He then looked at me. "You, Trevor, are to come with your 'gang' to the Dweller Valley High School tonight at sundown. If you want to see your girlfriend again." He smiled. He and Leslie, who was still holding onto Shauni, disappeared in a flash of rainbow colored light.

"Shauni!" Patch screamed as he ran to the location where she and the zombies disappeared. He turned and looked at me. He then ran at me with fire in his eyes.

"This is all your fault! If you would have made sure he was dead..." Tommy grabbed his friend before he reached me. "Let me go, Tom! Now!"

"Calm down, Jace," Tommy replied. "It's gonna be all right." He looked up a me. "Right?"

"I..." I wanted to say yes. But I couldn't give them false hope. My plan didn't exactly take this world's Shauni into consideration.

"We have to get a team together," Jason stated. He was scratching his goatee, the thing he did when he was trying to think through a situation.

"Patch, you and Dick get some guys and make as many stakes and crosses as you can. Tom, Jason and I are gonna rehash my plan to save the girls and anyone else that may be held at the school." Patch and Tom nodded in agreement.

"Dick, you ready?" My friend looked around the immediate area. "Where'd he go?"

Baby Johnson ran up to us. "He disappeared in a rainbow colored light the same time as the zombies left with Shauni," she informed us.

Oh no! Not again.

Jason's eyes met mine. We both knew what the other was thinking.

"Damn. They got him too," Patch said angrily.

I told Patch and Tom the truth. "They didn't get Dick. They've always had him."

"Come again," Tom replied.

"We better take this inside," Jason said as he headed for the doors to the elementary school. "We have a lot to tell you."

Patch and Tommy followed my friend. I was right behind them. Jason walked into one of the empty rooms and sat down on one of the desks.

"Dick is a werewolf," he said bluntly. "As I'm sure you're aware," he said to Patch, "when all this started last fall he was kidnaped by the Leader." Patch nodded an affirmative. "The Leader used his heritage to spy on Trevor." He looked at me and made a face as if to ask if he should continue. I nodded. "Trevor can't sense Dick like he can vampires, so we never knew he was working with the Leader until it was too late. Just like now."

"So what you're saying," Patch started, "is that we're going to be going up against two *very* powerful vampires, a werewolf and a couple dozen zombies and not-so-powerful vampires?"

"Yeah, pretty much," I replied.

"Good then let's get started. We have about five hours till the shit is gonna hit the fan," Tommy said.

"And we have a lot of work to do," Patch added.

That went well.

"What happens in five hours?" Jason asked as we walked to the armory.

"Sunset," Patch replied.

"Ask a stupid question…" Jason said under his breath, in spite of himself.

Shauni woke up in a cold sweat from the fourth nightmare she had since being captured. Getting kidnapped by vampires and being brought to another universe had taken a great toll on her. She leaned up on her elbows and looked over at Samantha who was sitting with her eyes closed and her arms on her crossed legs.

Holy moley! She looks like she's meditating. Trevor would get a kick out of that.

Shauni leaned her head back on her pillow and looked up at the ceiling. "Oh, Trevor, what happened?" She lay on her bed, waiting for Trevor and Jason to save her and Sam. After about two hours of counting the cracks in the ceiling, her attention was diverted by Samantha's voice.

"Damn! He's coming," she said as her eyes quickly opened.

"Who?" Shauni asked as she walked over to her cousin's girlfriend.

"That would be me." My double said as he opened the door to their "prison."

"What do you want now?" Shauni demanded as Sam stood beside her.

He looked from Shauni to Sam, then back at Shauni. He smiled revealing his fangs. "You just gotta love redheads. Such temper! Such fire!" He shook his head, as though he shivered. Then he took off his sunglasses and pulled his long hair into a ponytail. "Maybe this'll calm you down a bit." Shauni's mouth dropped open in awe. Samantha was unfazed by this new development.

"Trevor?" was all Shauni could say.

"Yes, I am. And as you know, I'm not *your* Trevor." His face took on the visage of a vampire.

Shauni gasped in fright. My double's face then turned back to the image of mine. He then went back to the door and tapped on it twice. "You can bring her in now," he called into the hall. He looked back at the girls. "Maybe you just need some more company." Chris and Leslie came into the old band room. The person that they were carrying was struggling with all of her strength. They turned her around so the other two girls could see her. Their new guest was the last person my girlfriend had expected to see.

Trevor looked at my girlfriend and her companion.

"Shauni Collins, I'd like you to meet a real good friend of mine..." He grinned again, "Shauni Collins."

"You're no friend of mine," the other Shauni said as she struggled free of the two zombies. She walked over to my girlfriend and looked at her in astonishment. "You're the *other* me." Was all she could say. My girlfriend was speechless.

"You won't get away with this, Trevor!" Samantha said as she stood up to my vampire twin. "The prophecy has foreseen this!"

Trevor pushed her away with a minimum of movement and effort. Samantha fell to the floor. "It *will* be changed, witch!" The forcefulness of his voice and the impact of Sam hitting the floor snapped the Shaunis from their amazement.

"Sam!" They said in unison as they ran to help her to her feet.

"I shall leave you three to get to know one another," the vampire said as he walked out the door. He shut and locked it after he exited.

The two Shauni's helped Samantha over to her bed. They laid her on the mattress.

"You're gonna be all right." My girlfriend assured. She looked at her double. "Could you get me a wet cloth please?" Her "twin" nodded and did as she asked. She came back and handed the cloth to Shauni. "Thanks." Shauni placed it on Sam's head. "You're gonna be all right, Sam." She then motioned for her "twin" to follow her. They walked over to Shauni's bed. "We need to talk," she whispered.

We arrived at the school with about ten minutes until the sun fully set. The sky in the west was slowly changing from a pinkish-yellow to a darker shade of red. Jason and I stood in front of a run-down copy of our high school with identical looks of awe. *This is really weird.* Patch and Tom checked out each other's weapons. I decided that Jason and I should do the same.

"Let me check your stuff," I informed him as he continued to stare at the building in front of us. "What's wrong, man?"

"Ah. It's nothing," he answered as he shook his head.

"Yeah right," I said as I checked the straps on the belt that held his stakes. "What's going on?"

"Do you have the sword?" he asked.

"Yeah, I got it." I looked at him quizzically. "Why?"

He turned to me with a grim look on his face. "I just have this feeling that we're definitely going to need it."

"Me too, man. Me too," I said as I patted the makeshift sheath that was strapped to my back. I checked the contents of his backpack. "I can't believe you actually picked that," I exclaimed as I noticed one of his weapons of choice.

"You never know when you might need one. Right?" he said with a grin.

I smiled back at my friend.

"You're crazy, man."

"I know." He looked over at our companions. "You two ready?"

"Yeah," Patch answered.

"Then we should get going," Tommy said as he led the way to the school. "But first we should split into teams."

Patch looked at Jason and me then back to Tommy. "What do you have in mind?"

"Yeah," Jason began as he looked at Patch. "What do you have in mind?" he repeated sarcastically.

"I'm just saying that it would be quicker if we split into two teams to find the girls and fight the Leader and Trevor's double."

"So who's on which team?" I asked.

As if I don't already know the answer. He must want the two Jason's to talk out their problems. Just like I do.

"You and me. And the two Jason's." My enhanced hearing picked up an "oh great" from Patch. "Is that okay with everyone?"

"Sure," I replied.

"Fine with me," Jason answered.

Patch was silent. "What about you, Jace?" Tom asked.

Patch gave Jason a cynical look. "Yeah, sure. No problem."

"Great. Let's get going." I motioned the two Jason's to a nearby corner. "You two go around back. Me and Tom'll give you three minutes to get to the back doors and then *we* go in." The "twins" nodded in agreement and went on to their part of the mission. Tom watched them with a look of apprehension.

I looked at my watch and started the timer. The next three minutes felt like they took forever. My watch "beeped," breaking the silence of the night. Tom looked at me.

"Well, let's get cracking," he stated as he reached into his backpack and pulled out a stake. "It's now or never."

I pulled out my sword and threw the sheath to the ground.

You can say that again. We walked up to the front doors. "After you," I said to my friend's double as I motioned toward the door. Tom's eyes showed surprise. "Just joking, man." I pulled my sword into a ready position.

"Whoa."

"Nice, isn't it?" I asked him.

I opened the door and stepped into the school. It was dark in the hallway. Only one of the overhead lights worked. *They probably think we're at a disadvantage.* But because of my vampire vision I could see everything very clearly.

"Watch your step, man." I scanned for a light switch. "I'll see if I can find a..." Suddenly, the hallway lit up. "...light." *That really annoys me when that happens.* I turned to Tom. "That helped."

"I'll say." Tom's facial expression said what the itching at my temples told me a half-second before.

"Look out!" With my vampire reflexes, I pushed Tom to the side and turned around. I sliced low, hoping to hit a vampire. The vampire that was closest to me jumped over my blade. What ended my slice wasn't the flesh his leg, but the broke down and busted trophy case to my right. "Shit." I stood up and dropped my sword to the floor. I reached to my belt and pulled out two stakes, ready to take on the next two vampires. One was a short chunky male whom I didn't recognize. The second was a female vampire that I had no choice but to know. "Kate?" I said in almost disbelief. I threw the stake at her chubby partner. It pierced his chest, and entered his heart.

"Trevor. What's up, lover?" she said, completely disregarding her fallen comrade. She stood like a statue, just staring at me. It was weird.

"Kate!" Tom yelled from behind me, where he was fighting the first vampire. His adversary punched at him. Tom ducked it and stabbed the vampire with one of his stakes. My friend stood up and walked over to me. His eyes were glassy and his body was completely relaxed.

Damn! I turned to Tom. "Tom! Snap out of it man." I waved my hand in front of his face. He dropped his second stake to the floor. All of a sudden, I was flying through the air. I smashed into the trophy case. It's metal stabbed through my flannel and into the flesh of my shoulder. "Ouch. That hurt," I managed to say as the hallway began to blur. I tried to sit up, to get the corner out of my shoulder. The pain only increased. *I...have to...get up.* I tried to sit up again.

"Kill him, my love," I heard Kate say.

110

"No problem, lover," Tom said in a magical stupor.

Tom walked over to me. *Oh man. This ain't good.* He picked me up by the collar. "Aargh!!" I screamed as the metal scraped against the wound as he lifted my body. I managed to grab my favorite basketball championship picture, the one I was in, as he lifted. I felt the wound start to close as he brought me to my feet. I swung the picture at Tom. He caught my hand before it connected with his face. *Damn! He's fast in this reality.* Tom punched me in the stomach. I executed a high kick for his head. He caught my leg and pushed me off balance. I landed on the floor, knocking the wind out of me.

"It's my turn now," Kate said as she walked over to her "puppet."

"Bring me across," Tom said. He looked at Kate and then at me. "Then you can have him."

In the blink of an eye, Kate ran over and stood between Tom and I. "If that's what you want." Her voice changed to the demonic one that I remembered from the night I got bit during halftime. "Who am I to argue?" She opened her mouth, revealing inch long fangs. Kate leaned her head back for her bite.

"Not tonight, Kate," I said as I stabbed her with my sword. I pulled the blade out of her back. She turned around and hissed at me with her fangs showing. "What the hell!"

"Gotcha," Tom said with a grin. I raised my sword and swung at her neck. The blade cut through the flesh and bone with little resistance. Kate's head rolled to the floor as her body fell, limp. The last expression frozen on her face was one of complete surprise. I looked over at Tom.

"This is my favorite shirt," I said as I lowered my sword.

Tom looked at me with an expression that was equal parts fear and surprise. "What took so long?"

"My shoulder didn't heal as fast as I though it would. Sorry." We walked to his backpack to retrieve the stakes. "I don't know. Something in this universe is just...*off.*"

"What do you mean?" Tom asked as we headed once again into the hallway.

"I'm not sure." We stopped beside the broken trophy case. I pointed down to Kate's corpse. "I just feel like my powers are fading the longer I'm in this reality. Or maybe I'm just getting tired."

"Maybe it's a cosmic fluke or something." He put his hand on my shoulder. "We'll worry about it later. Now we have to save the girls."

"You're probably right. I'll chalk it up to some kind of cosm..." As we walked past the auditorium, I sensed a very strong vampire presence. "He's here. In the auditorium."

"Who?" Tom asked as he reached into his backpack while looking for the enemy of which I spoke.

"The Leader," I answered as I opened the door to the auditorium.

CHAPTER 5

"Great. Let's get going." I motioned the two Jasons to a nearby corner. "You two go around back. Tom and I will give you three minutes to get to the back doors and then *we* go in." The "twins" nodded in agreement and went on to their part of the mission. Tom watched them with a look of apprehension.

Jason and Patch rounded the corner below the windows to the band room. They made good time to the back parking lot. As they went over the small fence separating the back quad from the back parking lot, Jason got a funny feeling.

"I have a weird feeling about this." As if on cue, a vampire and two zombies stepped out of the shadows.

"That was quick," Patch remarked.

"You're telling me," Jason said. They readied their weapons. Patch with his machete. Jason pulled out two stakes, looked at them thoughtfully and then threw them to the ground. "I guess this'll have to do," he said as he wrapped the end of a three-foot long, half-inch thick chain around his hand.

"Where'd you get that? It wasn't in the weapons' pile?"

"I'll tell you later," he said with a smile. The zombie, Leslie Suders, ran at him. Jason deflected the zombie's momentum toward Patch, who quickly stabbed the zombie in the chest.

"Ouch!" he growled as he slumped to the ground.

Chris grabbed Jason and threw him into Patch. The twins fell against the chain link fence.

"Why don't you two just give up," he said in his human voice. "It'll be a lot easier." His voice changed to his undead one. "For us."

Patch and Jason stood up, their backs to the fence. The vampire stepped more into the light. It was Doug Ewing. Jason's mouth dropped open. Patch just stared at the vampire with a look of complete anger and contempt on his face.

"You son of a…"

"Ah. Ah. Ah," Doug began as Chris stood beside him. "None of that, Jason." He looked at my friend. "And who is this? Your brother?"

"Something like that," Jason remarked. He never did like chitchat. "Did you come to fight, or talk?"

"Have it your way, Jason." He motioned to Chris. "Christopher."

Chris and Doug jumped at the "twins." Jason ducked the vampire and pushed Chris toward Patch. Patch did a roundhouse kick and knocked the zombie into the fence. He lifted up his machete and held it toward the vampire.

"Ewing!" Patch yelled. "Let's rock." He ran toward his enemy.

Jason stood up to catch his twin. "Pat…Jason! Don't do…" Chris suddenly Jason backward. "Oh boy."

Jason ducked the first punch. He then punched Chris in the stomach with all his strength. The zombie growled menacingly as he picked my friend up by the shoulders. Jason lifted his left arm, the one with the chain, and struck Chris on the side of the head.

"Oomph!" Chris moaned as he dropped my friend to the ground. Jason began to swing the chain in a circle above his head. He let go of it and thrust it at the zombie.

Chris grabbed the end of the chain. Jason quickly ran toward Chris, jumped up and wrapped it around the zombie's neck. When he landed behind Chris, he pulled the zombie to his knees. He then quickly wrapped the chain around Chris's neck one more time and pulled tightly. He then yanked Chris's neck quickly to the side. There was a loud pop as the neck broke.

"How'd it feel to kill, Jason," Doug asked. He picked him up by the neck. "Did it feel good?" The vampire grinned evilly. "Your *brother* is dead. And *I'm* hungry." Doug bent down to take a bite from my friend's neck.

"I don't think so," Jason said with a smile.

Doug arched his back and howled in pain as he reached around his back. His fingers lightly brushed the wooden stake sticking out of his right shoulder. He dropped Jason to the ground as his fingers tried to grasp the stake. Turning around, his face changed to the demonic one of the vampire as he laid eyes on the source of his pain.

"Hey, Doug. Miss me?" Patch said as he threw another stake at their vampire foe. Doug was too stunned to realize what was happening. His vampire reflexes did little to help him now. The wooden stake struck him right through the heart.

"Aargh!!" he screamed as he slumped to the ground. Patch walked over to Jason and extended his hand. Jason took it.

"Nice shot, man," he remarked as Patch helped him to his feet.

"I've been practicing," his double remarked with a grin as they headed to the back doors of the school.

"I know this is gonna sound stupid and isn't really the time, but," Jason began, "how'd you get the patch?"

Patch stopped in the middle of the parking lot. "If you *have to* know," he motioned toward Doug's completely lifeless body, "he happened. Back when the Leader first arrived, there were many small battles. In one of them, it was just Doug and me. One on one." Patch scratched beside his missing eye as he remembered.

He walked in the back doors of the school. Jason put the chain back in his pack and followed him inside. Listening intently.

"We fought for, I don't know, a good twenty minutes. He lost a lot of blood during the fight, I thought I had him weakened pretty good. We both did. I got cocky and decided to throw the stake like a knife." Patch sighed with a puff. "Doug caught the stake and threw it back at me." Patch shook the memories from his head.

"I've been blind in this eye ever since." He pointed to his left eye. The two teenagers walked the darkened hallway toward the gym doors. "Good thing is he was too weak to finish me off. He left." Patch snickered to himself as they rounded the corner.

The main doors to the junior high gym were closed. The Jasons reached for their weapons. Jason pulled out a Holy water squirt gun and a stake. Patch pulled out his machete and some stakes.

"You know, I just thought of something." Jason said.

"What?" Patch asked as he approached the doors. He pressed the latch. It was locked. "Damn!" They turned around and went back down the hall. "We can try one of the locker rooms."

Jason nodded in agreement. He went over and tried the girls' door. "Crap. Locked." He looked at Patch. "Any luck."

Patch attempted to turn the knob. He pushed on the door and it opened. "Yep." Jason hurried over to Patch. "Now what were you saying?"

"Oh yeah," Jason began. "Are you sure that," he pointed to Patch's machete, "*that* is gonna hurt Dick."

"It should. The blade is laced with pure silver." Patch opened the door fully and stepped in, his blade ready.

"After you," Jason said sarcastically, he held the squirt gun like a cop entering a building. Jason followed Patch into the locker room. It was dark, except for the few rays of moonlight that shone through some broken windows. The odor of mildew and stagnant toilet water permeated the room.

"There's a light switch in here somewhere," Patch said as he reached through the window of the gym teacher's office. He flipped the switch, the lights in the locker room came on.

"That helped," Jason remarked sarcastically. Only one of the four sets of overhead lights came on. He waved to his "twin." "Let's go." Jason walked to the back of the locker room. Patch followed with his machete at the ready.

"So far, so good," Patch remarked as Jason opened the door to the junior high gym room. It was good fifty feet by seventy-five feet and about fifty feet high. As the two guys walked through the door, they could hear an animal growling. "Look's like I spoke too soon." He pointed to the source of the animal like sounds. "Look!'

"Oh shit!" Jason said in disbelief as he watched the double of his friend Dick on the other side of the room. Dick was slowly transforming into a seven-foot-tall wolf.

"This *can't* get any worse." Suddenly the door slammed behind them. "I stand corrected."

The monster stopped howling in pain and stood up on its hind legs. Dick looked at the astonished "twins," then leapt toward them.

"Jason! Look out," Patch screamed as he pushed my best friend out of the way. They landed on the floor, underneath a nearby basketball hoop. Dick crashed through the door that they had come through. The two Jasons stood up, each readying their weapons as they made their way as far from the door as possible. Patch with his machete. Jason threw his gun to the floor and pulled out the chain. Patch looked at him questioningly.

"Whatever works, man," he said. Dick burst back through the doorway.

Jason once again wrapped the end of the chain around his hand, then began to swing it in a circular fashion as he ran full speed at the werewolf.

This guy is nuts, Patch thought as he watched his twin running toward the werewolf. He shrugged, raised his blade and charged his opponent. Dick swiped at Jason's head. A split second before the furry paw connected, Jason ducked and wrapped the chain around Dick's right leg. He went into a roll and knocked the werewolf off balance. Just as Patch swiped at the werewolf with his silver bladed machete.

"Damn!" Patch lost his balance and fell to the floor, right in front of Dick's snarling mouth. The machete fell a few feet in front of him, out of his reach. "Whoa!!"

Jason stood up, then fell down on top of Dick. Ramming a fistful of chain in the middle of his back.

"Jason! Roll now!"

Dick hit Jason to the floor as Patch rolled out of the way. The werewolf stood up and started toward my friend. "Rarghh!" he growled as he picked Jason up by the end of the chain.

"Oh crap!" Jason yelled as Dick lifted him with one arm so they were now face to face. Jason gagged as Dick breathed on him. "Man, your breath stinks."

Suddenly, Dick howled out in pain and dropped Jason to the floor. All Jason saw was a blur as Dick turned around and bit Patch in the arm. Patch dropped the machete as he screamed in pain.

"Patch! No!"

Patch kicked at the werewolf as he was raised into the air. Dick once again bit down on his arm then dropped him like a rag doll. Patch just lay on the floor, motionless. The last thing the werewolf saw as he turned around was the downward slice of the silver-laced blade of the machete in Jason's hands. The werewolf's head fell to the floor and rolled a few feet away from the body, which slowly followed.

There was a blinding flash of rainbow colored light and the scream of a name.

"Jason!" came Shauni's scream, in stereo. The two Shauni's, Samantha and Tom ran into the gym. My girlfriend's double ran up to Patch. "Oh God! Jason!" She picked up her cousin and rested him in her arms. "No," she cried.

Shauni ran over to Jason. "Jason, are you okay." Sam came over also and gave him a hug.

"Yeah. I'm okay. Hey, Sam."

Patch's body shuddered and his eyes opened.

"We have a slight problem." Jason took off his flannel shirt and put it on Patch's wound. He put his cousin's double's hand on the wound. "Keep pressure on that."

"Oooww!" Patch cried out. "Shauni?" He managed to say. "It hurts."

Tom watched the scene with skeptical eyes. "What kind of problem?" he asked. Jason looked at his double. Patch nodded in approval.

"Dick bit him."

"No!" Was all that world's Shauni said. Shauni and Samantha gasped. Tom just stood there and took it all in.

Jason looked at his cousin's double. "He did it to save me. To save us all." Patch nodded his acknowledgment of the truth and the fate that was now upon him: to live his life as a werewolf. Then Samantha broke in.

"I can use a spell to heal him somewhat." Jason looked at her in disbelief. "But I can't fully reverse the effects of the bite. Only change the rules pertaining to it."

"A spell?" Jason repeated.

"I'll explain later," Samantha answered as she knelt down beside Patch. She removed the blood-soaked shirt and placed her hands on top of the wound. Patch grimaced when she touched him. "Now just relax," she comforted.

She closed her eyes, bent back her head and began to chant in an unknown language. Jason was struck with awe. Then Sam's hands began to glow as small bolts of what looked like static electricity danced across the wound. Patch gritted his teeth in annoyance.

Jason's jaw dropped. Shauni held onto his arm in reassurance. A few seconds later Samantha stopped chanting and the "lightning" died down. Patch coughed and sat up slowly.

"Now *that* hurt," was all he said. He looked up at the woman who healed him. "Sam? You came back?" He managed a smile.

Jason stood back, watching everything with a wary eye. "What the hell is going on?" He was irritated, and rightfully so. "What just happened here?"

"I'll explain later, Jace." Shauni informed him. "We have to go help Trevor. Tom said he's fighting the Trevor from this world."

"I'm sure Trevor can handle...himself." He walked his cousin into a corner of the gym. "They have the same powers. More or less."

She put her arm on her cousin's shoulder and whispered. "No, Jason. Tom said that the Trevor from this world became a vampire and then killed the Leader from our world."

"But that would mean..." Jason face turned to one of great concern as the realization of Shauni's words dawned on him. "We have to go help Trevor."

He went into full "take-charge" mode. He put the machete that he was holding in his belt loop and made his way back to the group of our new friends. "Tom, you and Shauni take Patch outside." He pointed to Samantha. Even though he wasn't sure that he trusted her fully yet. "Sam, you're with us." Everybody nodded in agreement. Tom and the other Shauni helped Patch to his feet.

"I would put up a fight to go with..." Cough...cough...hack... "with you." He grinned meekly. "But as you can see. I guess I better go outside."

Shauni's "twin" took him by the arm.

"Let's get going." She looked at Jason, Samantha and my girlfriend. "Good luck." Tom just huffed to himself and helped with Patch. The trio walked to the exit in the back of the gym.

"We'll meet out front in about an hour. At the most," Jason told them as they stepped out the door. "Hopefully," he said under his breath.

"Let's get going," Samantha said to Jason. He gave her an icy stare. "We don't have much *time*," she said knowingly.

They exited through the doorway that the trio came through

"You're probably right. I'll chalk it up to some kind of cosm..." As we walked past the auditorium, I sensed a very strong vampire presence. "He's here. In the auditorium."

"Who?" Tom asked as he reached into his backpack while looking for the enemy of which I spoke.

"The Leader," I answered as I opened the door to the auditorium. I put my sword in front of me to guard against what ever tried to attack me. I walked into the darkened room with Tom right behind me. We started toward the stage.

The auditorium was just as it was on my world. Except that there were no seats and it was decorated like a medieval throne room. Drapes hung down from the high ceiling.

"This is unbelievable," Tom said in disbelief.

"Thank you, Thomas," My voice boomed sarcastically.

"Oh..." Tom said.

"My," I added.

"God? I don't think so," My double concluded as a single large throne-like chair in the middle of the stage rotated to reveal his smiling vampire face. "Come here. Sit down." He motioned to a couch to his right.

Tom, with a blank look on his face began to walk forward. I put my arm in front of him to stop his advancement. "Tom! Snap out of it!" I looked up at my double. "Stop it! Now!"

"So touchy." He stood up and walked to the edge of the stage. "You'd figure, Well I figured, that you'd have a better sense of humor about the whole situation." He floated down to the floor and advanced toward Tom, who was still oblivious to his surroundings. "I do."

I maneuvered Tom behind me. "Leave Tom out of this."

I stood inches from my double's face, unflinching. *I hope this is a good idea.*

"Your fight is with me," I remarked, frightened of what my "mirror duplicate" was capable of.

"You don't know how right you are, Trevor." He waved his hand in front of Tom's face. Tom shook his head as if he had just been punched in the face unexpectedly. Trevor looked me in the eye. "You are right. *Our* fight *is* with you, Trevor."

He flew back to his throne in the blink of an eye. Suddenly sitting down with his hands in a steeple like posture.

"And to show you how nice I am." He spread his hands apart as if to offer me anything I wanted. "I'll tell you where the Shaunis and the witch are before I kill you. You can even let Tommy here save them."

Witch? What the hell is he talking about? Don't matter. As long as I can save Shauni, both of them…I'll deal with the witch later.

I looked at my double. Then I looked at my friend and back to the vampire. "Okay, you have my attention. Where are they?"

"Trevor, what are you doing?" Tom grabbed my arm and pulled me to the side.

Like he's not going to be able to hear us anyway, Tom.

"How do you know that Jason and Patch didn't already save them?"

"How do you know they *did*?" I replied as I looked to the throne. "I don't know, but I just don't want to take that kind of a risk with their lives. And besides I have a feeling that there's more to him," I tilted my head to the stage, "than meets the eye."

"How right you are, Trevor." Tom and I both looked at my double at the same time. "I was just waiting for the right moment to tell you."

"Tell us what?" Tom blurted out.

Oh no! "Our fight…" and the Leader hasn't shown up yet. This is not good. I hope he doesn't say what I think he's going to.

"I killed the Leader from your world when he first arrived here and brought me across." Tom and I looked at him in surprise. *Oh man. Here it comes.* "And to get all his power…"

"…you drank his blood," I finished for him.

"See now, Trevor, buddy, you're not as dumb as…well you know the rest."

"*You* were the powerful vampire I sensed when were came in." I looked at him in disbelief, even though I knew this new development was true. "You're the new Leader."

120

"Yep. I have all his memories too." The Leader smiled. "And boy is he pissed at you."

"Oh shit," was all Tom could manage.

You got that right.

I had to get rid of Tom. I couldn't trust Trevor/Leader with his life if he was in the same room. I put up a brave front. "Well, are you gonna tell us where the girls are? Or are we gonna have to do some damage?"

"Fine. Fine." He stood up and then instantly appeared at the front of the stage with a fang-revealing smile. "If it'll make you happy to get Thomas to safety. The girls are now being held in the band room." He absently waved to his right. Then pointed toward Tom. "He can save them if he wants to."

I nodded to Tom. "Go on. I'll catch up." He looked at me with a skeptical expression as I handed him my backpack. "Here. You'll need them more than I will."

Yeah, right. Keep telling yourself that.

My friend looked at me. "Ill be back as soon as I can." He shook my hand. "Good luck," he remarked as he looked back to my double.

"Thanks. I'll need it." Tom turned around and ran out the doors that we came in just minutes before. Leaving me and my "evil twin" together for a final confrontation.

"Come on up, Trevor." He motioned to me with his hand. "I won't bite you." He grinned evilly.

This guy is sick.

I patted the folds of my coat that covered my sword then floated up to the stage. The Leader/Trevor smiled in approval. I stood in front of my adversary. I evaluated him. He had my dimensions and build.

I can take him. Yeah right. I made my way to his face and our eyes locked. Suddenly, the familiar "red haze" began to cloud my vision. *Damn!* I shook off the familiar sensation.

"I know that trick, Trevor." I started to circle around him. "Or did you forget."

"I didn't forget. I just figured I'd give it a shot." He began to circle around with me and grinned evilly. His fangs grew longer than they were a moment before. "You know. It's like Jekyll and Hyde," he said in his demon voice. His eyes glowed red as they widened with excitement. "Or God and the Devil."

I was getting fed up with the way my double was acting. It downright scared me, and I wanted to get the show finished as fast as possible.

"Or Clark Kent and Superman in the third movie." I readied my sword. Hiding my fright behind my blade. "What's your point."

"Still in the *Highlander* phase?" At super-vampire speed, The Leader ran behind his throne, then was right in front of me. He was holding a cavalry saber that I recognized. "I can deal with that." He pointed the saber to the ground. He also noticed the look of surprise on my face. "I figured you'd know this blade."

"It's Jason's," I answered.

I wonder why he has it now.

"You're probably wondering why I have this now." He raised the sword to his face.

"The thought *had* crossed my mind." My double did a few experimental swings. I instinctively went to block an attack.

"Whoa! Sorry." His face went back to his human one. "Not quite yet. I still have to tell the story."

I humored him. "Yeah. What is it?"

"I took it from our cycloptic little friend." His face turned back into his vampire visage and his voice became demonic. "Right after I beat him to a pulp." He gave a wide, fang-showing smile.

"You son of a bitch!" I swung my sword for his neck at super speed. My double instantly blocked it.

"Tsk tsk." He grinned in his evil way. "What a temper *we* have." He then swung at me.

I just barely blocked it. *Damn! That was close.* I stepped back a few feet at super speed to catch my breath.

"What's the matter, Trevor? Don't you think you can take me?" My double swung at me and I ducked, falling backwards as the sword whizzed over my head. I stood up in the blink of a *normal* eye.

Damn! That was a close one.

I ran at The Leader, swinging my blade at his right shoulder. My opponent blocked the attack. I then sliced at his left, then his right. I then swung the blade down to his left leg. He blocked all of my attacks. The Leader sliced at my left shoulder. I raised my blade and barely blocked the attack.

He then swiped toward my leg on the same side. I brought my sword down to block, then I thrust toward his chest. My double instantly parried the blade.

"Touché, Trevor," he said mockingly. My double attacked my upper body. He sliced at my left shoulder and I blocked it. He then thrust quickly to my stomach and then quickly sliced at my head. I blocked both attacks easily. I sidestepped and sliced him on the right arm.

"You're going down, Leader." I attacked his shoulder again. My opponent blocked the attack. I once again sliced at his left, then his right. He continued to block my attacks. I repeated my attacks and again he protected himself. I then swung the blade down to his left leg. I never connected.

"I don't think so." He sliced at my left side. I stepped back and brought my blade down on his.

"I do," I said mockingly. *This should do it. There can be only one.* I pivoted on my left foot in a clockwise direction. I brought my sword up to connect with his neck. My cockiness had overridden my quick reflexes. Before I knew it my evil twin ducked and slammed the point of his blade into my chest.

"No!" I heard Shauni scream as I fell to my knees.

I could see Jason, Samantha and Shauni through my pain-clouded eyes. My vampire hearing picked up Sam's voice.

"Jason. Throw as many stakes as you can into the air." Samantha nodded to my girlfriend. "Shauni, you do the same."

Jason and Shauni each grabbed a handful of stakes, ten total, and tossed them into the air. The wooden weapons froze in mid air, caught in a rainbow-colored bubble.

"What the..." I exclaimed through teary eyes. Not believing what I was seeing.

The Leader looked in the direction of my friends. He looked back to me with a look that was equal parts of anger and fear.

"This is where it ends, Trevor," he said as he pulled the saber from my chest. He grinned evilly. "There can be only one." He swung down at me. Before the blade reached my neck, The Leader was thrown to the side and to the floor.

Five of the ten stakes were sticking out of his back. There was one in his right shoulder and another in his leg.

He's not getting back up. But I am.

I used my sword as a crutch and staggered to my feet. I waved to the group of friends that miraculously saved my life. Shauni was running to the stage with tears of happiness in her eyes. Without warning, her eyes changed from tear-soaked happiness to complete horror.

In the time it takes a normal person to blink, a dozen thoughts went through my head. *Damn!* Everything slowed down to a snail's pace. In slow motion, Jason and Samantha began to run toward the stage. Both of their mouths were open in the beginning of a warning.

With my vampire reflexes working overtime, I pulled up my sword, pivoted and sliced behind me. I felt very little resistance as the blade sliced through the skin of The Leader's neck. It exited and continued through his raised arm. There was a loud crack as my sword hit bone and sliced through it as well. My pivot stopped and I was faced with a headless corpse standing in front of me. The head was only at the middle of his back. I stood there staring at The Leader's body, catching my breath. As I calmed down everything returned to its normal pace.

"Trevor!" Jason and Samantha screamed in unison. "Look out!"

The Leader's body slumped to its knees and the body fell forward. The head hit the floor with a thud and rolled to the side. It was stopped by the throne on which my evil double had sat. The fangs were still extended. The eyes, which had lost their evil-red glow when the head was severed, stared back at me. I was transfixed on them and it scared me to the bone. I shivered. *It's far from over, Trevor.* My voice echoed in my head. Whether it was my voice or a psychic imprint from my other self...I'll never know.

The next thing I remember was a hand on my shoulder.

"Come on, honey," Shauni's voice said sympathetically. "It's over."

I hope so, Shauni. I hope so.

I attempted to walk, leaning on Shauni for support. I could feel the wound in my chest knitting itself back together. Jason jumped up onto the stage and came over to me.

"Come on, Trev. Let's get you out of here," my best friend remarked as he put my left arm around his shoulder.

"Careful, man." I forced a grin. "Whatcha doing? Trying to bruise me?"

"Very funny," he replied.

We walked down the small set of stairs to the floor of the auditorium. Sam walked over to us as we descended.

"The prophecy is fulfilled," she stated. "It's time for you to return to your own dimension." She looked at us and smiled. For some reason, I knew she could feel our sadness. "But I'll let you say good-bye to the others."

We walked to the main doors of the auditorium. The wound in my chest stopped bleeding a long time ago and the pain was subsiding. "It's all right, guys," I said to my supporters, "I can go it on my own." Jason and Shauni stopped helping me stand. I put my hand in Shauni's.

We walked outside, past Kate's body and that of the other vampires. The corpses were now dried up, almost mummified. Shauni looked at them in a mixture of disgust and fright.

"Oh my...," she gasped.

Jason wove around the dead bodies. When he got to the front doors he opened one and held it open for us. Samantha walked though the doors. Next was Shauni, I lifted her hand to let her go through the door ahead of me. After everything that happened in the past few days, there was no way I was letting go. I was amazed at how much pain I *didn't* feel as I raised my arm. My wound was almost gone. *Damn cosmic flukes.* Tom, Patch and the other Shauni ran toward our group. Samantha stepped to the side and leaned up against the side of the school. "I take it the good guys won," Patch said as they neared us.

"Yeah, we won," Jason replied as he sat down on the railing for the wheel chair ramp. Patch joined him. The two young men, who were so much alike and yet so different, began to talk as if they were lifelong friends. Both groups convened on that spot.

"Don't you mean Trevor won it for us?" Tom asked.

"No, Tom," Shauni retorted. "We won. It was a team effort." Shauni closed in on him with fire in her eyes.

Oh man, Tom. Don't get her pissed.

I flew down between the both of them.

"Shauni?" I said in a mocking sternness with my arms across my chest. I looked my girlfriend in the eyes and smiled. She smiled and gave up.

I'm getting good at that.

"Tom," my girlfriend's double said as she pulled him to the side, "behave yourself." She began to talk to him. *I wonder what she's saying.*

"Trevor, don't even try it."

I looked at my girlfriend. "What?"

"You have that 'I'm getting ready to use my *super-hearing*' look on your face." She smiled. "So ignore *them* and kiss *me*." I took my girlfriend's head in my hands and kissed her on the lips. Something I had wanted to do for a the past two days. Our lips parted.

"I love you, Trevor."

"I love you too, Shauni." Somehow I heard not only my voice say it, but also Tom's. I smiled when I realized what was happening. "What did you do?" I grinned.

"I just helped her realize that there was a chance for her to find love." She stroked my hair. "Without Trevor Wayne, and the way she talked about Tom's protectiveness, I *knew* there was a chance that they'd be perfect together."

"You never cease to amaze me. You know that?"

"I know," she said with a smile.

Tom and Shauni walked over to us. *That looks so weird. No wonder he always had something smart to say about me.* The two Jasons jumped from the railing. We all walked back to Samantha, who had been watching the last few minutes unfold.

"The prophecy is fulfilled," Samantha announced. Her voice turned somber as she looked at our new friends. "They have to go back."

I looked at Samantha, then at Shauni and then back to Samantha. *This is nuts.*

"I guess I really was your best bet for this situation?"

"That you were, Trevor," Samantha answered.

"So you've known pretty much what was gonna happen this whole time," Jason began. "Why didn't you just come out and help us? It would have saved us a lot of trouble, Sam."

"I would have only gotten Trevor into *this*," Samantha's voice answered. But her lips did not move. The six of us stood and watched in awe as the girl from the airport, minus her glasses and the hair bun, walked out from the shadows. "But you were actually punctual for once, Jace."

"Oh my...," the two Shaunis said in disbelief.

Jason and Patch looked on in awe. The young woman walked up and stood beside her blond twin. I began to process everything that happened within the last few days and came to only one conclusion. *This is nuts.*

"So you *are* a witch," I explained to Samantha. "Like on *Bewitched.*"

"Not exactly." She grinned. "I don't wiggle my nose."

"I'm happy that you guys are just *now* getting to find out who's who. So tell me, oh fearless Leader." Tom pointed to the newcomer. He directed this to me. "Who the hell is that?"

"I'm Phoebe. That's all you need to know for now, Tom."

"We really should be sending them on their way, Pheebs," Samantha informed her sister.

"Yeah. Yeah, I know."

"Are you ready to go?" Samantha asked my group.

I nodded. Shauni smiled. "Yep," she answered.

Jason looked at his ex-date. "Yeah sure. No prob, Sam," he replied with some irritation.

"Jason," she said with hidden sadness, "I'm sorry. When you get back to your own world you'll forget all about me." She walked over to him and looked into his eyes. "Trust me."

Jason shrugged her hand away. "Lets get this over with." He walked over and stood beside Shauni and me. Shauni interlocked her arm in her cousin's.

Sam turned to our right and started to speak in a mixture of what sounded like Latin and Spanish. As she spoke a small point of rainbow-colored light emerged. The longer she spoke, the bigger the light became. The wind began to blow harder and harder as it grew. In less than a minute the colored circle was more than eight feet in diameter. We walked over to our new friends. Shauni and Jason went to their counterparts. I walked over to Tom.

I shook his hand. "It's been real." I glanced over at the other Shauni who was hugging my girlfriend. "You'd better take care of her, Tom. You got a good girl."

"You too, Trevor." He grinned. "I'll see you around."

"Good-bye, Shauni," my girlfriend said to her "twin." "I enjoyed our talk." She kissed her on the cheek. "I'll see you in the mirror."

"Same here, Shauni," she replied with a grin.

I looked over to Jason and Patch. They looked like they were having trouble getting out their feelings. I decided to listen.

"…your life and all that. You're welcome." Jason grinned. "I knew you'd have done the same thing."

"Maybe." Patch smiled then patted my friend on the back. "Just joking. I just hope I can get used to this whole werewolf thing."

"You will, trust me."

Time to go.

It was as though I had a sixth sense about the situation, because Samantha spoke up.

"You better go now," she called over the roaring wind. "Trevor, I think you should hold onto them when you go through. That way you'ns won't get separated."

That's a comforting thought. I nodded to Sam. Jason, Shauni and I walked over to the portal. *I just hope I don't pass out this time.* I put my arms around each of their waists.

"You ready?" I asked them.

"Yes." Shauni kissed me on the cheek.

"Let's blow this Popsicle stand," Jason joked. I felt his head turn as he looked behind us. He turned back to the portal.

"Let's go." I held my friend and his cousin tighter. I floated into the air and flew into the portal.

The rainbow lights swirled around in all directions at once. The power of the vortex carried us like going down a water slide at the Wavetown Water Park. Within the space of a minute, there was a large circle of white light that we seemed to be heading toward.

Oh man, I think I'm gonna be sick.

Suddenly the white light engulfed us and then everything went dark.

"Jason, he's awake," I heard Shauni say. As my eyes began to focus in the darkness, which I saw as early morning, I saw Shauni lean down. She kissed me on the mouth. "Welcome back, sleepy head."

"Thanks for the landing ,Trev," Jason said as he held a slightly bloodied cloth on his head.

"Sorry about that, Jace. How long was I out?" I looked around. We were in the front quad of the high school. "We did make it back, didn't we?"

"Yeah. We made it."

"You've been out for about five minutes," Shauni answered as I sat up. My girlfriend helped me to my feet.

"Well, since we're back," I grinned at my friends, "and the car is at the Pizza Palace."

"Oh man, you know I don't like heights."

That's right. He was unconscious the last time.

"Jason, it'll be fun." I smiled at my friend. "Trust me. I won't drop you," I remarked with a smile as I indicated his forehead.

"I'm looking forward to it," Shauni said with a smile.

"You would," Jason remarked to his cousin. He sighed in defeat. "Let's get this over with." He walked over to Shauni and me.

"I knew you'd see it my way," Shauni said. She put her arms around my neck. I put my arm around her waist. Jason did the same as his cousin. I held onto him also.

"Well, let's get going."

"Up, up and away!" I joked as I lifted into the air and headed toward the Pizza Palace.

After about a minute of flying I looked over at Jason. His eyes were closed.

Vampires he can handle. Flying... I laughed to myself. I looked over to Shauni. She was looking around the city.

"Penny for your thoughts."

"I was just wondering what you got me for my birthday. That's all."

"I'll give it to you when after we drop Jason off at the car." I thought of the small velvet box in my backpack at Jason's house.

"Huh? What?" Jason asked through eyes that were closed tightly.

"Nothing, man. I'll tell you later," I said as I flew my friend to his car. And I flew, once again, to my uncertain future.

BOOK III

THE PACK

CHAPTER 1

It was pretty difficult trying to get back into school under my real name. But after a three-day explanation to the school board, and six weeks of seeing a shrink after school, I was allowed to resume the life of a normal teenager. Well, a normal teenager with the powers of a vampire.

Without warning, someone hit my shoulder, snapping me from my reverie.

"Trevor, wake up. The speech isn't *that* boring," Jason joked.

"Shut up, man," I replied. "I was just thinking about this last year. All the stuff that happened with the Leader and then our doubles in the other universe."

"Hey, I used to think about that all the time. When it was going on." He smiled then looked at Shauni and Baby. "But then I realized that there was no use in dwelling on all that stuff."

Wow! I thought. *Jason has changed a lot since this crap with the vampires started.* "Wow, man. You've really grown up a lot in the past year."

"Grow up nothin'!" He smiled. "I had to buckle down and make sure I'd graduate with you'ns."

"You're messed up. You know that?"

"Yep," he said as he looked around in the direction of the bleachers across from us. "We're still jumping off the Bridge tonight? Right?"

"Yeah. Whatev—" I was cut off.

"Uh oh. Shauni's giving us 'the look.' "

I looked down to my girlfriend. She was turned around looking at Jason and me.

"What?" I mouthed as I made a "what'd I do?" gesture.

Baby pulled at her to turn around. It was now their row's turn to get their diplomas.

"Don't give me that, Trevor," Shauni whispered. My vampire-enhanced hearing picked it up clearly. "I know you and Jace are plotting something."

"What'd you say?" Baby asked her as they began to march to the end of the bleachers.

"Nothing." Serves you right, dear. I smiled.

"Do you know Shauni thinks we're plotting something."

"Oh, she always thinks we're plotting something," Jason replied.

"Because we usually are." I watched Baby get her diploma. Shauni took a step forward. "She's next, man."

"Shauni Renee Collins," said the Principal.

Shauni was handed her diploma in her left hand as she shook the principal's hand with her right. She then went down the line of officials, the vice-principal and then the school superintendent. I smiled with pride as she stepped off the platform to head back to her seat on the bleachers. The ceremony continued through the rest of Shauni's row and the one in front of mine.

Well, let's get this over with.

"Well, let's get this over with," Jason repeated aloud. We stood up. I just smiled to myself.

Jason and I began to walk toward the end of the bleachers. We were the last two to be called. Lucky us. Me being the final one. *Figures.* We slowly moved closer to our diplomas. Dick's name was called off. Then Tommy Bayer's.

Five more till they call us.

The next few minutes crawled by slowly. Making me more nervous by the second. Then it happened.

"Jason Scott Pasner." My friend stepped up to the three school officials. I moved up to the steps. Jason repeated the actions of the almost one hundred classmates before him. He stepped off the platform.

My turn.

"Trevor Jonathan Wayne." I stepped up and took my diploma. "Congratulations, Trevor."

"Thank you, sir," I replied as I shook his hand. I stepped to the vice-principal.

"Congratulations."

Oh no. This isn't redundant, I thought sarcastically.

"Thank you."

I moved to the superintendent. A friend of my mom's.

"Good job," he said with a smile.

"Thanks." I shook his hand and walked to the edge of the platform.

What the hell.

I quickly turned around and did a backward somersault onto the grass. I landed perfectly, thanks to my supernatural abilities. There was a collective intake of breath from the audience. All the students including my fellow classmates, cheered, clapped and yelled encouragingly.

I bowed to the audience then walked the path back to my seat. As I walked by the fence, I saw R. J. standing with a camera.

"Hey, Trevor. Smile!!" he yelled. "Nice flip," he whispered. I grinned. R. J. was one of the few select people that knew how I pulled off the somersault. I walked farther along the fence.

"And there's Trevor, my baby," Mom said into the camcorder.

Another video for Dad. Figures.

I turned toward her when I got close enough and made a slight wave to her.

I walked back to my seat. Everyone else was now standing. Zachary Walter, the class president, went to the podium to give the final speech.

"Nice little stunt, Trevor," I heard Shauni say.

Oh great. I chuckled.

"What?" Jason asked in a whisper. Trying to keep still.

"Shauni's yelling at me for my flip," I whispered.

"She doesn't waste any time. Does she?"

"Nope. Never."

"…just saying that if you keep doing stuff like that in public, people are gonna start wondering."

"Shauni, ssh. It's almost time."

I looked over at the podium. Zach was just finishing his speech.

"…I now give you the Dweller Valley High School class of 1999."

He reached his right hand to his tassel. Every one of us in the bleachers did the same. He then pulled the tassel to the right side of his cap. My fellow classmates and I once again mimicked him.

The audience of our family and friends cheered and clapped. Louder than when I did my flip.

Go figure.

After the ceremony, everyone gathered to get pictures taken. For the usual post graduation-get the picture taken with the family-picture. Before the parents got to us, Rick Rice, R. J. to the Gang, came up to Shauni, Jason and me.

"Hey, guys. Smile for the camera," he said cheerfully as we looked in his direction. I had my arm around Shauni. Jason just gave one of his "cool" smiles.

"Well. I know which picture is going in the supplement for the yearbook. If I have anything to say about it." He walked over and shook my hand. "Congratulations, Trevor."

"Thanks, dude," I said. He extended his hand to Jason. "Good job, Jace. Didn't think you were gonna make it there for a sec," he joked.

"Thanks for the vote of confidence," my friend said with a smile. We all laughed at the exchange. Rick turned to my girlfriend.

"Sweetheart." He leaned into her with open arms. "Congrats," he said smoothly as he kissed her on the cheek.

"Thanks, R. J," she said as she hugged him.

"Hey," I said jokingly, "you better watch it, man." I stood up straighter, my arms across my chest. "That's my girl you're messing with," I said in a deep voice. Trying to sound menacing. I cracked a smile. "Damn. I just can't act mean with a straight face."

Shauni put her arm around my waist. She looked into my eyes.

"But you get an *A* for effort." She kissed me full on the lips. With no care as to who saw us.

The clearing of a throat snapped us back to reality. It was my Uncle Bob and Aunt Pam, Doug's parents. Shauni and I pulled out of our liplock and smiled meekly at my relatives. Jason was a few feet away talking to Rick about something.

"Congratulations, you two," my uncle said.

"Thanks, Bob," I replied.

"Thanks, Mr. Ewing," Shauni said.

"Now, Shauni, call me Uncle Bob. You're almost one of the fam…"

"Let's get a picture of you two before I forget," Pam fussed, saving my girlfriend and me from being embarrassed any further by my uncle.

Thanks, Pam. I owe you.

Shauni and I stood and posed for my aunt. I stood behind my girlfriend and put my arms around her waist.

"Smile," Pam ordered. She then pressed the button and the flashbulb went off. She put her camera back in her purse. "Have you two seen Doug anywhere?" she asked.

"I think he was talking to Bill." Bill's his cousin on his dad's side. His mom and my mom are sisters. "Over by the flagpole." I pointed in the general direction.

"Where's Mom?" I asked before they headed off.

"She's coming," Pam answered. "I think she's putting another tape in the camcorder."

"Oh. Okay," I acknowledged as they walked to where I pointed. I glanced at Shauni who made a small sigh of relief.

"I'm glad that's over with," she said as we walked back over to Jason.

"Are they gone?" he asked with a smile.

"Shut up, man," I said with some irritation. I looked around the crowd, in the direction that my aunt and uncle took. In a nicer voice I said, "Yeah, they're gone."

Jason, R. J. and I laughed at the joke. Shauni hit me on the arm. "Trevor!"

After a few minutes of planning out the rest of the night, my enhanced hearing picked up my mom and Maggie talking. They were talking about the prospect of Shauni, Baby Jackson, Jason and I living in my uncle Tom's townhouse on the Keystone State Campus.

Uh oh.

"Our female parental units are on their way," I said to Shauni.

"How do you know?" Rick asked me. I just tapped my right ear. "Oh yeah."

"Well I'm getting outta here while I…"

"Not so fast, J. P." Maggie said. "I want to get a picture of you and Shauni together," ahe ordered. "And one of all three of you."

"Yes, ma'am," he replied in submission.

Mom, like Rick and I, just stood back and watched the exchange. *I love it when Maggie orders him around like that.* I laughed to myself. Maggie escorted the cousins to the fence that surrounded the football field.

"I'm gonna head, man," Rick informed me. "I have a few more pictures to shoot. I'll see you tonight at the Bridge."

"Okay. See ya." My friend started to walk into the crowd, camera at the ready.

Mom just looked at me with a loving smile.

"What?"

"Nothing. It seems like just yesterday I was sending you off to kindergarten, and here I am at your high school graduation."

"Well, we knew it had to end sometime." I smiled at her and gave her a hug.

"Yeah, I know. I just wish your dad could be here to see it," she said over my shoulder.

"Me too. Me too." I kissed her on the forehead. "I love you, Mom."

"I love you too, sweetheart. Now let's get some pictures taken for my albums."

I spent about fifteen minutes getting different pictures taken with Mom and a few with Shauni and Jason. Mom even got a picture of me and Shauni together. Pam and Bob finally hunted me down and got the picture with Doug that they wanted. After she was done doing her photographer thing, Mom left with Uncle Bob and Aunt Pam. I hung out at the school getting more pictures taken. Shauni exchanged phone numbers with Nichole Watson and some other girls from the band. Tom Bayer gave Jason and me his address at the Fichenton College. He said that we could visit any time we wanted. Shauni swiped Maggie's camera and got a picture of Jason and me. She said it was a "must have."

The horde of graduates died down at about eight-thirty. The different groups of friends went to their separate parties. The Gang, as I had come to call them, went to Uncle Tom's campsite. We built a fire in the fireplace and sat around drinking and talking. Thanks to my vampire-like metabolism, alcohol didn't stay in my system for very long. So I had the ability to sober up faster than everyone else did. Especially my best friend.

"Come on, Jace. Why is it that the only time you wanna jump off the Bridge is when you're drunk?" I asked my friend.

"I'm fine, man. Seriously," he said with a smile. "Besides," he took another swig, "back when I cut you with the sword, you promised me that if we made it through the whole thing without getting into trouble, you'd jump off the Iron Bridge before we graduated." I looked at my girlfriend for help. She just nodded in agreement.

Great. They're ganging up on me.

"And by my watch," he looked at his watch, "you have twenty minutes till midnight. And the end of graduation day." He smiled.

He gets so logical when he's drunk.

"Fine. I'll do it."

I really hate it when he gets like this. Sometimes the only way to put him in his place is to do it.

I got up from the picnic table, ran up to the cabin and locked the door.

"Well? Are we going or not?" I asked my friend as I returned to the picnic table.

"As much as I'd love to go, man. I have to get up early for work tomorrow," R. J. explained.

136

"I'll take you home," Dick suggested. "I have some stuff to do early tomorrow too." He looked at Shauni, Baby, Jason and me. "And I think five is a crowd anyway."

"Okay, man. Whatever floats your boat," Jason said. Dismissing Dick's apparent discomfort. "See you later." Shauni and Baby both gave him a mean look. I walked Dick and R. J. to Dick's Camaro.

"You sure you're alright to drive?" I asked. Concerned for my friends. "I can take R. J. home." I made a flying motion with my hand. "Stay here. Have fun."

"No really, I'm okay." He opened his car door. "Werewolf metabolism. Remember."

He got in and sat down. Rick did the same on the passenger's side. I smiled to myself.

Dick just beat me at my own game.

I, more than anybody else in our small group of friends, understood what he meant. Along with Dick's werewolf heritage came the immunity to most sicknesses and an increased healing factor. Not as fast as my own though.

"Okay, I understand," I said as I shut the car door. "Drive safe."

"Yes, sir," he answered with a mock salute as he started the car. Dick put the car in reverse and backed onto the road. He started driving toward the main road and into town. I waved to my friend as his taillights faded in the distance. When he was out of sight, I went down to my other friends. I looked at Jason and the girls.

"All right. Let's go." *I can't believe I'm gonna do this.*

I didn't really want to, but I made a promise a few years before, and I try not to go back on my word.

Good thing I can't get hurt.

I looked at Jason, who was quickly climbing to the top of the bridge. I turned to Shauni. She smiled at me and motioned toward her cousin.

"Well, get going, mister."

"I'm going. I'm going." Shauni and Baby stood by the railing as I followed Jason the ten feet to the top of the bridge.

Jason was standing on top of the metal structure. He was leaning over the edge, looking at the flowing river below.

"You better watch it, Jace," I warned. My friend jumped back. I had surprised him. "Whoa."

I made a move toward Jason to catch him, but he righted himself. My vampire hearing picked up both girls gasping in surprise and fright.

"I'm okay." He waved his hands in the air to back me away. "I'm okay." I glanced over the edge of the bridge to the water below.

Oh man. How far's this? Fifty feet into twenty feet of water?

"Maybe we should reconsider," I said as I looked at Jason. *Guess not.* He was already sitting down taking off his shoes. He then removed his T-shirt and stood up in his oversized swimming trunks.

"No way, man." He grinned. "You're next."

"Come on, honey," Shauni called up to me. "You're not *scared. Are you?*" She smiled. In part of because our past with the Leader and my evil twin from the alternate reality and because she liked to pick on me now and then.

"No," I said with a returned smile.

"Yeah right," Jason replied. He looked down at the girls. "Trevor's scared. Ha ha. Neener, neener, neener," he teased musically. Jason began to dance on the twelve-inch wide metal railing.

"Come on, Jace. Stop it," I warned. "Be caref…"

"What's the matter, Trevor? *Scared?*" He said as he began to get bolder in his performance. He began to dance wildly now. I took off my T-shirt.

"Okay. Let's go." Jason stepped toward me.

I remember this next part so well because, to me, most of it happened in slow motion.

"Now you're talkin'." Jason laughed. "Let's get go…" Jason's right foot hit a puddle of water and he fell backwards. "Ah! Shit!" He yelled as he fell over the side, toward the river.

"Damn!"

"Jason!" Baby screamed.

"Ja…" Shauni began as everything slowed.

The last part of his name was stretched out. It seemed to go on for a full second. I looked down at the girls. Expressions of fear were frozen on both their faces. I quickly looked back at my best friend. In what seemed to me about five seconds, Jason had only fallen about three feet. I then looked back at the girls.

With Baby here or not, I have to save him.

I jumped off the bridge and flew down toward the river and under Jason's falling body. Jason landed in my arms. The force of catching him knocked me three feet downward. Just enough to get my sneakers wet.

Great, it's gonna take forever to dry these suckers.

As I realized this, time returned to normal.

"Going my way?" I asked with a grin as we made our way up to the road.

"Very funny smart-ass," Jason replied after his breathing slowed to normal.

"Oh my God!" I heard Baby yell.

"Baby." He looked at me. "Did she…?"

"Uh huh," I answered as I flew to the bridge.

"Oh boy," My friend remarked as I flew him through the support pillars and the railing on which our clothes laid. I sat him down in the middle of the road. Shauni and Baby ran to him. Baby kept her eyes on me. They were wide with amazement and wonder.

I looked at my girlfriend. Our eyes met. She was thinking the same thing that I was.

This is gonna be interesting.

"Ann." Her eyes went from Jason, who was still lying on the road, to me. I had to tell her the story of last summer and this spring. Vampires, zombies and the alternate realities included. "You're not going to believe this…"

"Okay, Trevor. If you get this one, you win the game." Jason looked at Baby, who pulled out one of the TriBond cards and handed it to Jason. "Thanks. Okay man, what category do you want?"

I looked at Shauni, then back at Jason. "Riddles and wordplay," I said with a smile.

"You always pick that," he said with mock disgust.

"Go with what you know, man." I took a drink of my Pepsi.

Jason looked at the card. He grinned, put his hand to his head and showed the card to his game partner. Baby just grinned.

"Come on, Jace. Read the card," Shauni ordered politely. She reached across me to my right side and took a drink of my soda.

"Okay. But just let me say that I don't think it's fair."

"So what are the clues?" I asked impatiently.

"Okay. Riddles and wordplay," he started. "Sunlight. A wooden stake." I smiled. Shauni did the same. "And Holy water." He finished with at tone of mock irritation.

"Heh. Heh." I laughed. *Oh I wonder what it could be,* I thought sarcastically.

"Hmm. Let me think," I said jokingly. "Things that can hurt vampires?"

Jason threw the card onto the board.

"Very funny, smart ass," he retorted. He grabbed his can of Dr. Pepper and took a big swig.

"Oh, Jason. Don't be such a sore loser," Baby said as she gave him a kiss on the cheek.

Whoa. Go for it, Jason.

I smiled and looked at Shauni. She gave me a sly look that spoke volumes. She quickly looked away and started to gather up the game pieces and put them in the box.

Shauni, what are you up to?

Baby handed her the cards. She put them in the box and put the board in also. Then she put the lid in place. I took the box, and stood up. At super speed, I put the game on my uncle's desk on the other side of the living room and returned to Shauni's side. Baby gasped when I sat back down.

"Sorry about that," I told her. "Force of habit."

She smiled. "That's all right. I mean," Baby sat up straighter, "I *did* notice that you and Dylan looked *somewhat* alike in the face. But the hair and glasses threw me off," she explained.

"You're not the only one," Jason said under his breath. My vampire hearing picked it up clearly. I laughed out loud.

Yeah, you, Shauni and Lois Lane.

"What's so funny, Trevor?" Shauni asked.

"Huh? What?" I gave Jason a knowing glance and then smiled at my girlfriend.

"Oh nothing. I just remembered an old joke."

"Why don't I believe you?" she said.

I leaned closed to my girlfriend and quickly kissed her on the mouth. "Because you love me so much," I answered.

"Yeah. You're probably right," she replied with another kiss. This one was longer and was more passionate than the previous one. Until she remembered that we were not alone. Out lips parted and we looked sheepishly at our friends. Shauni faked a yawn. "Whew, I'm bushed. I think I'm gonna go to bed." She stood up and extended her hand to me. "You coming, honey?" she asked with mischievous grin.

I took Shauni's hand and stood up.

"Yeah." I looked at Jason and Baby. "The extra blankets and pillows are in the closet in the other room." I grinned at Jason. "Unless you two are sleeping in the same bed."

Fortunately, I knew more about Jason liking Baby than she did. So hopefully, she would take me as just joking. Baby blushed and Jason bit his bottom lip to keep from smiling too wide.

Shauni slapped me in the stomach. "Trevor?"

"Oomph! Sorry." I smiled. "I just meant that…"

"You better quit before you dig yourself a hole that even *you* can't fly out of, Trevor." Shauni grabbed me by my T-shirt. "Now off to bed you go."

Why do I have a strange feeling about this?

"See you in the morning." I followed my girlfriend into the bedroom.

"Good night, you two," Baby said with a smile.

"Good night, guys," Jason said.

I walked into the bedroom. Shauni smiled back at them and shut the door behind me.

I can't sleep.

I gently placed Shauni's arm across her stomach and slowly untangled myself from the sheets. Careful not to wake up my girlfriend, I floated into the air and landed on the floor. I picked up my T-shirt from the doorway and my jeans from beside the bed. I put both articles of clothing on at vampire speed. Shauni's body stirred. I froze in place.

Damn!

Shauni just rolled over and kept sleeping soundly.

Whew. Now where did I put my sneakers?

I scanned the darkness of the bedroom. To me it wasn't a problem.

Oh crap! That's right. They're by the fireplace. I hope they're dry by now.

I quietly opened the door and scanned the living room. Everything was in the same place as when I went to sleep. Except that Jason was sleeping on the couch. I held in a laugh.

Oh, Jason. You're such the gentleman. I grinned.

I floated over to the fireplace so I wouldn't make any noise on the old wooden floor. Sure enough, my shoes were where I left them. I sat on the hearth and grabbed my shoes. They were now only partially dry.

At least they're not soaked.

I slipped them on and tied them. I stood up and floated to the door. I opened it and flew outside and to the one place where I could sort things out, the Iron Bridge. I had been at the bridge for about fifteen minutes, using my flight powers to walk on the side of the railing. I heard someone approaching and quickly flew to the farthest edge to hide from whoever it was.

"Trevor? Are you here?" Jason called out in a loud whisper.

"Yeah, I'm here," I answered as I stood on the top of the bridge. I looked down at my friend. He was looking up at me. "Come on up."

Jason began to climb up the middle of the bridge to the top. After about a minute, he finally made it. I walked over to him and sat to his right. He moved to a sitting position beside me. My best friend reached into the pocket of his hooded sweatshirt and produced two cigars. He offered me one. I looked at him skeptically.

"Come on, Trev." He grinned, "They're Swishers."

"Then how can I refuse," I joked. "You got a lighter?" I asked as I unwrapped my stogie.

"Hold on a sec, will ya," he said as he undid the plastic on his cigar. He put it in his mouth and reached into his right pants pocket. He pulled out a small black cigarette lighter. He positioned it in front of my cigar tip and went to light it. Jason used too much force and the lighter flew from his hand. In the blink of an eye I caught it. "Thanks."

"No problem," I replied as I lit his cigar and then my own. I handed him back the lighter.

"Then why'd you come out here?" he asked bluntly as he puffed on his cigar.

"What's that supposed to mean?" I took a small puff.

"You know that the only reason you come out here to sit is when something's troubling you. You've been doing it since we were kids." Jason flicked his ashes over the side. "Is it Shauni?" he asked in a concerned voice.

"Yes," I said, as I looked him in the eyes. A look of knowing concern flickered across his face. "And no. I don't know." Surrendering, I put my hands in the air. I decided to change the subject. "By the way, what are *you* doing here?"

"I was lying on the couch half asleep. And *No!* Baby and I aren't sleeping together."

"Yet," I said slyly.

Jason gave me the middle finger.

"Anyway. Then the door shut and I sat up. I thought someone broke in." he explained. He then took another drag and breathed it out. "I noticed that your shoes weren't in front of the fireplace, so I got dressed, took a guess on where you'd go and then I walked out here." He flicked his ashes again. And looked at me. "So what are *you* doing out here? You and Shauni didn't have a fight, did you?"

I smiled to myself as I remembered what happened after me and Shauni went into the bedroom after the game of TriBond.

"Far from it." I took a pull from my stogie, let it out and flicked my ashes.

"No, man. Nothing like that. It's just that…" I sighed "I don't know what to do about us." He looked at me strangely. "Me and *Shauni,* retard."

"I know, man," he said with a smile. "Don't have a coronary."

"I mean, I love Shauni with all my heart. It's just that I've been thinking about my powers lately. The Leader is finally dead. There's been no vampire activity around here for the past three months. And *I'm* still the same."

In a fit of anger I punched the iron plating on which I sat. I put a small but visible dent in the half- inch thick metal. "I don't even feel pain. What if I don't age, man? What if I never grow old?" I could feel a lump beginning in my throat.

I reached under the place on which we sat and pulled out a small velvet box from my secret hiding place.

"I couldn't even give her this for her birthday."

"Is this what I think it is?" Jason asked as I handed him the box. He opened it to reveal a one-half-carat diamond engagement ring.

"Yep."

CHAPTER 2

For me, the summer went by way too quickly. Before I knew it, the day we were to move into my uncle's town house off campus, two days before classes started, had arrived. He was letting us use it for our time in college. As long as we cleaned up, and didn't destroy anything, we could stay in it as long as we liked.

After loading my last box of stuff into our Ford Bronco, I shut the tailgate. I preferred to do it alone. Mom offered to help, but with her in the house and me in the garage loading stuff I didn't have to act like the boxes were heavy. I was finished in about fifteen minutes. I walked into the kitchen through the door in the garage. Mom was in there making tomato sandwiches.

"You're done already?" she asked.

"Yep. All done. The boxes weren't as heavy as I thought." I smiled as I took a bottle of water out of the fridge.

"Oh, Trevor," she said sweetly as she handed me a sandwich, "you've matured so much in this past year."

You have no idea.

I took a bite of my sandwich.

"What do you mean?"

"Loading all your boxes yourself. Last year at this time, I could even get you to clean your room. Your time at your Aunt Martha and Uncle Tom's really helped you get your act together. And Shauni seems to have had a positive effect on you also." She sat down at the table and took a bite from her sandwich. I smiled at her comment.

"Yeah, you could say that." I smiled. "I've learned a lot of things this last year of high school too." *More than I can tell you now.* I remembered last year at this time and what happened that made me leave the house. I looked at Mom. "I'm sorry about leaving last year. I didn't mean to scare you and Dad like that. I should've left a note. I guess I just wasn't thinking clearly."

Not really but I have to tell her something.

"That's okay, honey. I'm just glad that you're okay now." The phone rang. I got up to answer it. "Sit down and finish your lunch." I took another bite and washed it down with some water. She went over to the phone and picked up the receiver.

"Hello." I used my hearing to listen to the other person.

"Is Trevor there?" Shauni asked. I smiled knowingly and Mom saw it.

"Yeah. He's here." She smiled. "Hold on a sec." Mom brought the cordless phone over to me. "It's Sha…"

"Hi, honey," I said, cutting her off. She looked at me in amazement then walked over to the sink and started to do the dishes.

"Are you ready to go?" my girlfriend asked.

"Yeah. I'm just having lunch. I'll be ready in a little bit." I took a drink of water.

"Would you make it quick please. Mom and Candy went to the store to get lunch and I'd like to be gone by the time they get back." She sighed. "Trevor, I can't take another minute in this place," she said with irritation.

"Candy back to her old self? Huh?" I said with a smile. Mom grinned.

"Her and everybody else."

"I'll be over as soon as I'm done. Okay, sweetie? Give me a half hour."

"Okay. Thirty minutes. No more."

"All right. Thirty minutes. And, Shauni?"

"Yes."

"I love you." I know I was getting mushy in front of Mom. But I'm funny that way.

"I love you too," she replied. I could picture her smiling in my mind. "Buh-bye."

"Bye," I said as I pressed the button to end the conversation. I laid the phone on the table.

Mom looked at me. "How'd you know it was Shauni?"

I decided to play with her. "Shauni and I have a psychic connection." I took a bite and grinned. "Plus I told her to call."

Mom threw a T-towel at me. "Very funny, Trevor."

I finished my sandwich and the last of my water. I stood up and walked to my mother and handed her the plate and towel.

"I know." I kissed her on the cheek. "That's why I said it." I walked back to the table and picked up the keys to the Bronco. "Hey, Mom, do you have the keys to Uncle Tom's house?"

"Yeah, honey." She looked up from the sink. "They're in my purse."

"Where's your purse?"

"It's in the living room, on the coffee table."

I walked into the living room and around the couch to the coffee table. Sure enough, Mom's purse was there. I went over and unzipped the main compartment. I searched through the clutter.

Man she's got a lot of junk in here. At least I know why I'm such a packrat. I finally found the keys.

"Bingo." I grasped the keys in my hand and walked back to the kitchen. Mom was finished with the dishes and was drying her hands when I walked in.

"All set?" she asked with a slight smile as she put the T-towel on the counter.

"All set," I replied as I held up the keys. I looked at my watch. "I guess I better get going." I grinned. "Don't wanna keep Shauni at home any longer than I have to."

"I'll walk you out." Mom walked over to me and we walked out to the garage.

"You know your dad wanted to be here when you left," she began, "But you know, 'duty calls.' "

Heard that before.

"Heh heh. Yeah I know." I opened the driver's door of the Bronco and then turned to my mother. "I guess I better get going." I leaned over and gave her a hug.

"Bye, honey." She squeezed me. I faked being squeezed too hard. "Call when you get there."

"I will, Mom." I stepped into the truck, shut the door and started the engine. I rolled down the window. "Bye. Love ya." I waved at her as I put the truck in reverse and backed out.

"I love you too. Be careful," she warned.

"I always am," I replied as I cleared the garage doors.

I pulled the Bronco into Shauni's driveway ten minutes later. I stepped out of the truck and walked up the stone walkway to the porch. Shauni was at the door to greet me when I was about to knock.

"Hey, sweetie," she greeted with a kiss and hug. "You're early," she added as we stepped inside.

I acted like I was stepping back outside. "I can drive around the block for another ten minutes if you want." I grinned.

"I don't think so." She pulled me back inside and to her room. "If we hurry, we can get everything in the truck and leave before Mom and Candy come back from Sheetz."

"Don't you want to say good-bye to them before you go?" I asked as I picked up her two suitcases and a basket of clothes.

"Mom, yeah. Candy, no." She grabbed another basket of clothes and put her clock radio on top. "Candy started a big stink about us all living in the same house. Then Mom sort of started to side with her," she continued as we walked out the door. She held the door for me as I maneuvered my way outside with my load. "It's just been a rough morning. Then *she* started in on me. That's why I called. I just have to get out of here."

I walked to the back of the truck and set the suitcases and the basket on the ground. I reached in my pocket and produced the keys. I rolled down the back window and opened the tailgate. Shauni handed me her basket.

"Shauni, don't you think that the reason that they're acting like this is that they're just sad to see you go." I put the basket in the back with my stuff. I bent down to get the other one. "You're the first of you two girls to go to college." I smiled at my girlfriend. "Candy's just jealous."

"Yeah right, Trevor." She picked one of the suitcases with both hands and balanced it on her leg as she tried to flip it into the back of the truck. I reached over and took it from her with one hand and placed it in the back. I got the other one and did the same. We walked back into the trailer to get her other stuff.

We walked into her room. Shauni unplugged her 25-inch color television and unhooked her VCR. She picked up the VCR and I grabbed the TV. Balancing the television with one hand, I opened the door for her. My hearing picked up a car moving on the cobblestones of the driveway. I snickered.

"What's so funny?" she asked. I switched the television to both hands. "And why are you holding that with both hands?"

"Your mom and Candy are back," I answered. As if on cue, the two older Collins women walked in the trailer.

"Hello, ladies," I greeted with a smile. Shauni looked at me knowingly.

"Trevor, so good to see you again," Maggie said as she shut the door behind her.

"Hi, Trev," Candy said with a smile as she moved past me and Shauni into the kitchen.

I balanced the TV against the wall to make it look like I was getting tired. "Hey, Candy."

"You getting packed so soon?" Maggie asked.

"Yeah, Mom. I am," Shauni replied tersely. "We have to do everything quicker than we planned," she lied. "Jason's ready to go and we have to pick up his stuff before we go."

I made an audible sigh. "Oh Trevor, I'm sorry," Maggie said as she walked back and opened the door.

"That's okay," I said as I maneuvered the television through the narrow doorway, using my vampire strength to keep from dropping it. I walked down to the truck and used my super-hearing to listen to Shauni talking with her mother. *"...is picking up Baby and all their stuff won't fit in the back of the Daytona."*

I put the TV in the back of the truck and shut the tailgate. As I walked back to the trailer, Shauni continued her defense for leaving early.

"And we want to get most of our things unpacked and set up as soon as we can."

Pretty flimsy, Shauni, I thought as I stepped onto the porch.

I opened the door and walked in. The voices coming from my girlfriend's bedroom said that's where she and Maggie were. I didn't want to be an actual participant in the conversation so I made my way down the hall to the kitchen. Candy was taking groceries out of the bags and putting them in their rightful places.

"Want some help?" I asked.

"No, that's all right," Candy replied as she opened the refrigerator. She placed two jugs of milk inside. "So, Trevor, you ready for school?" she asked, as the rumblings from Shauni's room became loud murmurs.

"Yeah, I guess so." I grinned. "As ready as I'll ever be. And all that stuff." I leaned against the counter by the sink.

"You four are lucky," she started as she placed a large jug of Sunny Delight in the fridge. "To get that house all to yourself. And for free too."

"My uncle said it's my high school graduation present." I moved to the side so Candy could put two boxes of cereal in the cupboard above me. "I lose it when I graduate." We laughed at the truth, which in itself was funny.

"So, you're plotting against me too, babe," Shauni said as she entered the kitchen.

I put my arm around my girlfriend and kissed her on the forehead in front of her sister.

"Trevor!" Shauni joking slapped me in the stomach.

Candy smiled at our playful exchange. Maggie entered the kitchen from the bathroom. Shauni, Candy and I turned to their mother.

"You all set?" she asked.

"Yep. Pretty much," Shauni replied as she got a can of Pepsi from the fridge.

"We just have to put my stereo in the truck." She opened her soda and took a drink.

"Can you get it for me, honey?" she asked sweetly.

"Yes, dear," I said with a joking smile. I walked back to Shauni's bedroom and unhooked the stereo from the speakers. I then wrapped the cords and wires with rubber bands and placed all of it in a cardboard box. While I was doing this, Shauni, Maggie and Candy went outside. I picked up the box and head out to join them.

"Well, that's the last of it," I said, shutting the tailgate for the last time during my visit to Shauni's. I turned to the trio of Collins women as they said goodbye to each other. After hugging her daughter, Maggie walked over to me with her arms extended.

"And you," I stood up straighter. "Take care of my baby."

"Yes, ma'am," I replied with a mock salute. I hugged Maggie. "You know I will." I kissed her on the cheek.

Shauni walked over to me after saying goodbye to Candy.

"Ready?" she directed to me. I nodded. Shauni walked over to her mom and gave her a hug. "Bye, Mom. Love you."

"Love you too." Maggie kissed her daughter. "Be careful."

"We always are," Shauni replied as she opened the passenger's side door and hopped in. I opened the driver's side door and stood on the step on the side of the truck.

"Bye, Maggie. See ya, Candy." I got in as they waved goodbye.

Maggie made a motion for Shauni to roll down her window. I turned on the engine and rolled it down.

"Just remember..." Maggie began.

"I know, 'Call when you get there.' " They said the order at the same time.

"I will, Mom." She waved again as she rolled up the window.

I put the truck in reverse and backed out of the driveway. I honked the horn as we headed off to Jason's house.

"What's going on, guys?" Jason asked as Shauni and I got out of the Bronco.

I walked over to my friend. We did our usual handshake.

"You ready to go, man?"

"Yeah. Baby's in the house." Shauni walked past her cousin and to the house. "She should be almost done."

"Hey, Jace," Shauni greeted her cousin with a hug. She opened the door and walked in the house.

"So. Where's your stuff?" I asked as I stood with my hands in my pockets as I leaned against the truck.

"Oh, it's in the garage." He motioned for me to follow. "C'mon." I followed him through the side door of the garage. "Dad made me put all the boxes and stuff in here. He said they were junking up the living room." I bent down and picked up one of his big boxes of clothes. I laughed at my friend's statement.

"How long did you have them in there?"

He opened the main garage door. "Just this last weekend," he answered.

I balanced the large television box full of clothes in my left hand as I fished in my pocket with the other. I threw the keys to my friend. He caught them with one hand.

"Roll down the back window and open the tailgate." Jason nodded. He bent down and picked up his two suitcases and walked outside.

After opening the tailgate and putting his stuff in the back. We headed back inside. As I picked up the last two boxes of stuff and Jason picked up his gym bag and his backpack. He said he wondered what the girls were doing.

"Don't know, man," I replied as we walked to the truck. I stopped and cocked my head to listen for the girls. *That's nuts. I can't hear them.* All I could hear was scratching and giggling. "Something weird is going on. All I can hear is scratching and giggling. They're plotting something," I said with a grin.

I put Jason's box of knick-knacks in the back of the truck. Jason put his gym bag and his backpack in the back of the Daytona. He then shut the garage door and we headed into the house.

"I *guarantee* they're plotting something," Jason said as we walked inside. "Baby told me earlier that she and Shauni were gonna come up with a way to talk to each other without you hearing them. Especially when we're gonna be living in the same house." He smiled as we walked into the kitchen.

Our girlfriends suddenly stopped what they were doing. Shauni quickly hid a note pad under her arm.

"Hi, honey," Shauni said innocently with a smile.

"We all set?" Baby asked. Jason went to his girlfriend and gave her a kiss on the cheek. He nodded.

We left for the townhouse. Shauni and I were the first to arrive. I pulled the truck into the garage and started unloading our boxes. Shauni went into the house to call her mom to tell her that we made it. Ten minutes later I had Jason and Baby's stuff and ours in the living room. Shauni walked in when I was in the middle of sitting on the floor unpacking our third box. I had everything laid out in the middle of the floor in organized groups.

"You know something," she said as she walked over to me, "I'll never get used to how fast you do everything."

I stood up and smiled at her. "Hey, I resent that." I moved over to her at vampire speed. I put my arms around her. "There are *some* things I like to do slowly." I pulled my girlfriend to me and gave her a passionate kiss. After about a minute we came up for air.

"Okay, I take it back," she said with a grin. She looked at the clock on the wall.

"We still have about fifteen minutes until Jason and Baby get here. We could..." She winked at me.

I picked her up in my arms and walked her to the couch. I laid her down and began to kiss her on the neck. She reached down and started to pull my shirt out of my pants. I stopped kissing her long enough to pull it over my head. I pulled her shirt bottom up a little and began to kiss her exposed stomach. I lifted it higher. As I leaned down again to kiss her, my enhanced hearing picked up the sound of a car. I could also hear the theme song to *RedHaze: Blood Reign* playing on the radio. I got Jason the CD for his birthday.

"Ah shit," I remarked, lifting my mouth from Shauni's body.

"What is it?" she asked in an irritated voice.

"Jason's early for once," I said with the same irritation. I stood up and put my shirt back on.

"Oh," Shauni replied as she rose to her feet.

There was a quick knock on the front door and then Jason and Baby walked in.

"Honey, I'm h..." Shauni and I gave our friends identical looks of anger mixed ever so slightly with humor.

Baby had a smile on her face. "We catch you two at a bad time?"

She's been around Jace way too long.

"Something like that," I answered.

"No. Not at all," My girlfriend said at the same time.

We spent the rest of the afternoon unpacking and putting away the rest of our stuff. At about six-thirty we finished. Afterwards, we decided to relax at The Eight Ball, a campus pool hall.

Too bad I can't use my powers to help me out.

We were playing doubles pool. It was Shauni and I against Jason and Baby. I aimed my cue with the ball, lining up the ball and the pocket for my shot. I moved my stick to judge how much power I was putting into it.

"Eight ball corner pocket," I announced. I executed my final thrust.

"Hi, guys," Dick called over the sounds of the pool hall. I hit the cue ball with too much force on hits lower side. It flew off of the table with great force. I looked up to see which of the other people in the pool hall it was about to hit.

Damn. It looks like Dick is in a gang.

There were four guys with him. They all wore what looked like the same type of brown leather jacket. The guy standing closest to Dick was holding the cue ball in his right hand.

"Lose something?" he said with a smile.

"Yeah, thanks," I said as he handed me the ball. I put the ball back down on the table.

"Who's this, Dick?" Jason asked. Shauni and Baby each gave him a mean look.

"Sorry. I mean…Dick, who's that with you?"

"Oh. Guys," Dick walked to the side of the table that we were on, "this is Dave, Frankie, Marty and Joe. They're my brothers." We all gave Dick a look of astonishment. "No, my fraternity brothers. And the weird part is, is that Frank use to date Jeanie."

"Oh," we all sighed in unison.

"That's weird," Jason said matter-of- factly. Dick looked at his "brothers."

"Guys, this is Trevor, Shauni, Baby and Jason. The Dweller Valley Gang I told you'ns about."

We all acknowledged Dick's new friends. "What's up?" Jason and I shook each of their hands. The girls just waved "hello."

We hung out with Dick and his friends for a few hours. They seemed pretty easy to get along with. Frank and Dave were seniors in college. Marty was a sophomore and Joe was a freshman who just so happened to have the same chemistry class with Baby. At ten o'clock Frank's watch started beeping.

"Well, time to go," he said to the others after looking at his watch. They stood up. Dick stood up also. "No, Dick, you can stay here. Catch up on things with your friends. It's cool."

"Okay. See you later," Dick replied.

"See ya." Frank turned to the rest of us. "It was nice meeting y'all."

"Nice meeting you too," Shauni replied.

"Likewise," Jason said as he shook each of their hands a second time. I shook with them also.

"Nice meeting you," Baby said as she gave a wave.

I stood up and shook Frank's hand. "Later then," was all I said. I waved to the others. "Bye guys."

Our new friends left. The rest of us continued to hang out. We played a few more games of pool, catching up on the how our summers went.

Dick headed to Keystone State early to get some of his general study courses out of the way. Two weeks into his stint he met Joey in his Calculus class. Joey then introduced him to Frank, whom Dick recognized from Jeanie's pictures. In part because he was Jeanie's brother and Frank was still an acquaintance of hers, Dick had no problem getting into the frat.

He also told us, after revealing his nature to Baby, that he rented a storage shed for his "time of the month." After catching up and telling asking Dick to come over for breakfast before going to our racquetball class with Jason and I, we all headed to our respective houses.

CHAPTER 3

Finally it was the first day of our college classes. Dick came over at six-thirty to eat breakfast with Jason and me before our first class. Shauni and Ann were sleeping in because their first class, English, didn't start until ten.

"Morning, Jace," Dick said as he walked in the kitchen door. He was holding our newspaper. "Morning, Trevor." I picked up my glass of orange juice and took a sip.

I indicated the newspaper as I sat at the table. "Can I have the paper. Or are you gonna hold it till the news is in the history books?"

Dick threw the rolled up paper to me. I caught it with not so much as an upward glance.

"Whoa!" Dick looked at me in surprise. "Are your reflexes getting faster or something?" he asked as he leaned into the refrigerator.

"Something like that," I said as I opened the paper. Jason sat down beside me with a bowl of Fruity Pebbles. *I can't believe he still eats those.* I pulled out the comics' section and handed it to my friend. "Here you go."

"Thanks," he said after taking a big spoonful of his cereal.

I started to leaf through the newspaper. I always started with the obituaries. It's a little weird. After that, I'd read anything that would catch my interest. As I read the paper, a section in the Police and Fire Log caught my eye.

"CAMPUS MANGLER STRIKES AGAIN." What the...

It was the first time that I heard of a mangler on campus. I took another look at the article and read it to myself.

"...was found dead in an alley behind The Eight Ball, a local college hangout."

"Hey, guys, look at this," I said as I pointed to the paper. My friends leaned in to get a closer look at the article. I read it to them as they looked at it. *"K.*

S. U. freshman, Joe Rivers was found dead behind The Eight Ball, a local college hangout, last night at around twelve-thirty a.m. His hear..."

Oh man this is sick. I stopped reading.

"What is it, Trevor?" Dick asked.

"Why'd you stop?" Jason asked.

I continued reading. *"His heart was removed from his chest. A spokesman for the police would not make any statements at the time. A private source for the paper did say that the murder is almost identical to the ones committed last year."*

"Sounds like something out of the *X-Files* if you ask me," Dick remarked.

"I know. The full moon always brings out the crazies." Dick and I looked at our friend. "What? What'd I say?" Then Jason realized what he said. "Oh sorry, Dick."

The alarm on my watch started to go off. I set it ten minutes ahead so I'd always be early. Jason looked at the clock on the microwave when he heard the sound.

"Oh, man, we better get to class. Don't wanna be late on the first day."

"You got that right." I took another look at the headline and threw the paper on the table. "I think I'm gonna start patrolling campus just to keep an eye on things." I grabbed a notepad and a pen and I wrote Shauni a quick note to tell her I'd meet her after her Art Class. Then I left for racquetball.

"Excuse me," a female voice that I didn't recognize said from behind me as I sat on the bench waiting for Shauni. "Do you believe in love at first sight?"

I turned my head. What I saw was a young woman about my age with short blond hair with highlights. She was wearing blue jeans and a black *RedHaze: Blood Reign* T-shirt.

"I do, actually," I began. "That's why I'm waiting for my girlfriend." I smiled.

"Good answer, Trevor," Shauni said as she walked out from behind a tree. The blond girl turned to my girlfriend. "Nice job, Sue." Shauni gave me a kiss on the cheek and put her left arm around my waist. "Afternoon, dear." I was confused.

"You know her?" I asked, indicating Sue.

"Yeah. Trevor Wayne, this is Susie Devlin." She turned to her friend. "Sue, this is my boyfriend Trevor."

"It's nice to meet you, Trevor." She extended her hand. I shook it. "Shauni's told me a lot about you."

"She has, has she?" I gave my girlfriend a "How Much?" look.

"Not everything. You know better than that." She gave me a playful smack on the back. Sue must've thought we were talking about intimate stuff. I personally was talking about my powers. "Sue and I have Art together. She's a really good artist."

"Come on, Shauni, it was only the first day," Sue remarked bashfully. "I just let the paint reveal what's already there."

"That's a philosophical way to put it," I remarked.

"Wiccan's prerogative," Sue answered back. *Great. Another witch,* I thought to myself. "And before you say it, I'm not that kind of witch. We're not magical. That's a fictional stereotype."

"Oh," I said dumbfounded. *That's what you know.*

"I invited Sue to the house tonight for dinner," Shauni informed me.

"That's cool. No biggie. Well, let's get going then. I'm hungry." I started to playfully drag Shauni in the direction of the car. Sue followed us with a smile on her lips.

On the way to the car we continued more small talk. As we were driving to the townhouse I found out that Sue, as she likes to be called, was at K.S.U. working on her Associates Degree. She was a child genius who graduated high school at the age of thirteen. She decided to take the freshman art class because she likes to paint. She also told us that she practices Wicca mostly for the meditative aspect.

After eating our dinner of spaghetti, salad and garlic bread, we went into the living room to play some board games.

"Let's play Tri-Bond," I suggested with a smile as we walked into the living room.

"How 'bout we don't," Jason shot back.

"Come on, Jace," Shauni said to her cousin. "That was three months ago."

"Okay. Okay. Fine," I defended. "What do you suppose we do?"

"I don't know," Jason said. "Just not Tri-Bond."

"I could read your palm," Sue suggested.

"Nah, that's okay Sue," he said. "I...I have to go do the dishes." He winked at his girlfriend. "You coming, Baby."

She nodded and followed Jason into the kitchen and closed the door behind her.

Man. They're worse than me and Shauni. Sue looked at Dick.

"No thanks. I think I'll keep my life private thanks." Dick shook his head.

"I'll do it." Shauni looked at me and smiled. "It'd be nice to know what the future has in store for me."

"All righty then," Sue said. She scooted in beside Shauni on the couch, pushing me against the edge. She then turned and faced my girlfriend. I got up and stood by Dick. "Hold out your right hand, palm up," Sue told her. Shauni did as she said. Sue waved her hand in a circle above it. And closed her eyes. She opened them again and looked at Shauni's palm. She ran her finger along the lines in Shauni's hand. Shauni looked around with a smile. "Oh this is nice." She looked at me. "You're gonna have two kids." I could feel my ears getting warm, something that always happened when I got embarrassed.

"Go, Trev," Dick called out with a laugh.

"Ha ha. Laugh it up fuzz ball," I retorted with a slap to his chest. Dick got a jokingly frightened look on his face. Shauni smiled at the half-Star Wars/half-werewolf joke.

"Shh," Sue ordered. She went back to examining Shauni's palm. "You're also going to go through a period of despair to get to unending happiness. You will be the glue that holds your family together."

What the hell is that supposed to mean?

"Okay. That's enough of that," Shauni said shakily as she took back her hand. Sue noticed Shauni's reaction.

"I'm sorry. I said something to trouble you."

No shit? I thought.

Sue's heartbeat began to beat faster. I used my enhanced vision to check her palms, which were starting to sweat. "I was just playing. It's only a game." Shauni smiled at her friend.

She's hiding something.

"How about I do Trevor's?" My girlfriend perked up at this. I didn't think it was a good idea until I knew more about Sue's abilities.

"No, that's okay," I said turning to go toward the kitchen.

"Come on, honey. It's only a game," Shauni repeated with a wink.

Why do I have the feeling I'm gonna regret this.

I walked over to the couch and sat between the two young women. I looked at my girlfriend pleadingly. Sue wiped her hands on her pants and took my right hand. She looked at it and ran her finger along the lines in my hand like she did with Shauni.

"Holy shit!" she gasped.

"What!?" Shauni, Dick and I said in unison.

"You've got the longest lifeline I've ever seen," she explained.

"Is that good?" I asked, curious.

"Yeah, if you plan to live forever," Sue joked. We all smiled. Those of us who knew my secret knew that it was always a possibility. Sue went back to reading my palm. "This is interesting too." I looked at her questioningly. "You come from a long line of great warriors. And you yourself are one."

"Cool," was all I said. Sue's watch alarm started to go off. She looked at it and pressed the button to stop it.

"Oh. It's eight already? I have to get going. I have a study session at the REC building." She gave me back my hand and stood up.

"I better get going too." Dick looked at Sue. "Do you mind if I give you a ride home?"

"Sure," she replied. I looked at my girlfriend as she put her arms around me from behind. She was smiling like she did when Jason and Ann started dating.

Perfect. Just perfect.

We got up off the couch and said our good-byes to our friends.

"And don't forget, ou four are gonna help the Pack with its monthly blood drive this month. Right?"

I started to say something against it, but Shauni cut me off before I could speak.

"Of course we will," Shauni answered. I looked at her. "Except for Trevor. Being diabetic and all." We both hoped that Dick got the hint.

He winked at her. "Oh yeah. Sorry. I forgot. Don't forget to tell Jason and Baby."

"Will do," I replied.

Dick looked at Sue, getting out of the hole that he had dug for himself. "You ready to go?"

"Yep," she answered. She came over and hugged Shauni. "I'll see you tomorrow in class."

"Buh bye," Shauni said. Dick opened the door and motioned for Sue to go out.

"Later, guys," Dick said as he walked out the door after her.

Being the nosy people that we are we watched them walk to Dick's Camaro and leave. Shauni once again warned me about using my enhanced hearing to listen to what they were talking about. Sometimes it makes me mad when she does that. Except when she distracts me with a really good kiss. Like she did this time.

Jason and I were put in charge of handing out snacks to the people that were giving blood. He was in charge of the drinks and I was in charge of

159

making the sandwiches. I couldn't donate because of the vampire nature of my blood. I told the officials that I had a rare blood disorder that prevents me from donating. Not exactly lying. Jason told them that he wasn't feeling good and that he'd help me distribute the food. Shauni, Baby and Sue were going to help when they were finished giving blood.

"How did we get stuck with this?" Jason asked as he poured the Tropical Punch Cool-Aid powder into the five-gallon jug, preparing another batch.

Why the Pack, as Dick's fraternity was known, picked that particular flavor for this blood drive, I'll never know.

"Because I have partial vampire blood and you're afraid of needles," I answered.

"Very funny, smart ass," Jason said as he filled the jug with cold water. "Now where did I put the wooden spoon?" he asked me as he looked around the counter top.

"Don't know." *We have to stir it somehow.* I smiled. "Jace, put the ice in and put the lid on, I have an idea." Jason did as I asked. I looked around the area to make sure no one was looking and grabbed the five gallons of unmixed Cool-Aid. Holding the lid tightly, I began to shake the jug. After I was sure the drink was mixed enough, I stopped.

"Boo!" a female yelled from behind me.

"Whoa! Oh my God, Ann," I said, surprised as I almost dropped the container of Cool-Aid. Jason was beside me with his hand on his heart.

"Give a guy a heart attack, why don't you," I said as I sat the Cool-Aid on the serving counter.

"Sorry, Trevor." She kissed her boyfriend on the cheek. "Sorry, sweetie." She looked back at me. "Good thing it was me that caught you doing your little stunt. You know Shauni'd throw a hissy fit if she was the one to catch you."

"Catch him doing what?" My girlfriend added as she walked into the pantry where we were.

"Floating up to the top shelf to get more sugar," Jason told her.

Thanks, Jace. I owe you one.

"Uh huh," she replied, not believing one word. I grabbed two sandwich wedges and moved closer to her at faster than normal speed.

"Sandwich wedge?" I offered. Holding one of them in front of her face. "You need to keep your energy up." I grinned changing the subject.

"Oh really?" she said with a smile.

"Yes, really." I leaned into her and gave her a peck on the mouth. "Now scoot on out there and take a seat." I made brushing motions toward her as I said this. I turned back to Jason and Baby, who were in a very passionate lip lock. I coughed out loud to get their attention. "That means you too, Baby."

They disengaged from their kiss and sighed. She walked over to my girlfriend and they both left to sit on the outside of the serving counter. There was a guy standing at the counter deciding on which sandwich to take.

"I'm partial to ham salad myself," I commented. "But we have egg salad and chicken salad too."

"I'll take chicken salad," he said. I handed him two wedges of chicken salad and a paper cup of Cool-Aid. "Thanks." He walked over to the table where the girls were sitting.

I tuned in my vampire hearing to listen. He seemed like a nice guy, but I still wanted to make sure he didn't try to hit on the girls.

"...and this is Ann Jackson. Our boyfriends are the ones handing out the sandwiches and juice," Shauni said, then took a bite of her sandwich.

I love it when she establishes that at the beginning of a conversation.

They continued to talk for a few more minutes. During which Sue came back and their new friend got up and left. The girls came back into the pantry to tell us that they were ready to leave. "Baby and I are gonna take Sue to her dorm and then we're gonna get dinner. Pizza okay?" she asked me. "By the way," She gave me a secret smile, "I have something to tell you when you get home."

Oh crap. Naahh.

"Hey, Jace. Pizza okay for tonight?" Shauni yelled back to her cousin.

"Yeah," came his reply.

"We'll be home as soon as we're through here." I kissed my girlfriend good-bye. "We should be done around seven."

"See you then. You ready, girls?"

Sue and Baby followed Shauni to the main doors. I turned back to my best friend who was carrying the other jug to be filled with Cool-Aid. Jason unfastened the lid on the jug and smiled at me.

"Guess what I found?" he asked. Almost laughing as he reached in. He pulled out the wooden spoon that he couldn't find a few moments before.

The next two weeks went by relatively peacefully. Not much in the way of crime fighting happen. I only patrolled every other day. Sue had integrated herself into the Gang fairly quickly and was hanging out with us all the time.

After the blood drive, Shauni told me that she found out that she has a rare blood type. "One in a million" she told me. And that the guy that she was talking to, Jake Daniels, had the same type also.

And that's *really* rare. All I could tell her was that I found it fascinating. Good thing she couldn't tell that I was being sarcastic.

The last Thursday of the month we all decided to go to The Eight Ball for dinner. This included not only the Gang, but also The Pack. We figured we could make this an ongoing thing that each month, we would all go to a different restaurant. To kick back and have a good time. Sue said that she'd be about an hour or so late and that she'd try to make it in time for dinner.

When we were finished bowling, Dave, Marty and Joe left. They said that they weren't staying for the food because they had to get back to the house and study for an early morning test for R.O.T.C. Jason told me when we were in the restroom washing up before our food came, "For a first monthly meeting for our groups they weren't being very friendly."

"At least they got to bowl with us," I commented to my friend as I pulled some paper towels from the dispenser. "From what Dick told me this morning, R.O.T.C. takes up a lot of their time."

Jason opened the door to go back the table. "Oh. Then I guess that's okay. But you know I still think there's something weird about these guys."

"Come on, Jace." I smiled at my friend as we arrived back at the table. "That's the Army for you." We sat down at the table. Shauni was on my left. Then Baby, Jason, Dick and Frank. There was an empty seat between Dick and Jason, for Sue. She and Dick were becoming quite the couple, despite the age difference.

We continued to talk with Dick and Frankie as we waited for our food. Shauni was doing her usual "pumping for information" bit. We found out that Frank and Jeanie use to date during their whole freshman year. Then for some reason she broke up with him and quit school. There wasn't any bad blood between them. From what Frank said, the relationship was slightly "rocky" when she left anyway.

Then by some strange set of circumstances, we got on the subject of *Highlander* and when Jason and me used to sword fight. Shauni told Frankie about the time that Jason accidentally cut me with his sword. She did her best to keep from embarrassing us too much.

"Come on, Shauni. Why do you always have to tell people this?" Jason asked. Almost whining.

"Because it's funny," she remarked. "Now hush." I smiled to myself.

162

"Yeah, Jace," Baby said as she kissed him on the cheek. "Be quiet and let Shauni tell the story."

She looked back to her eager listener.

"So I get this call and it's Jason. 'Shauni, it's Jace. I need you to pick me up at The Circle. Trevor and I were sword fighting, and he got cut.' " She started to giggle as she continued, "'I need you to take us to the hospital.'"

"So what did you do?" Frankie asked.

"I took Trevor to the hospital." She smiled at me. "I had to. I owed him for hitting him with a snowball with a rock in it two winters before."

I smiled back at her, remembering that that was one of the first things she did to show that she like me. I took a drink of my root beer. As I was putting the glass back on the table my enhanced hearing picked up sounds of an argument.

"How about you just give us your money and we'll call it even?" a male voice suggested. I heard a metallic click of what I guessed was a switchblade knife. "Or we can take it by force," another gruff sounding voice commented.

Well, that's not fair. I gotta help this guy out.

"Oh man." I started to get up from the table, then I remembered our new friend. "I...uh, just remembered that I have to...uh, pick up my insulin prescription before the drug store closes." I know it was a weak excuse. "I'll be back in a minute." I scooted out from the table as Frankie looked at me in wonder. Everyone else at the table knew that I heard trouble and that I was going to see if I could lend a hand.

Our food finally arrived.

"Thanks," Shauni said to the waitress.

Damn. And I was hungry too.

Shauni looked at our new friend, averting his attention away from me. "So, Frank what are you gonna major in?"

"I don't know really," he answered. "I may go to medical school or get a degree in Biochemistry or Journalism."

"That's interesting," I heard her say as I stepped out into the street. I turned left and headed for the nearest alley. When I was sure that I wasn't being watched I pulled a ski mask out of my pocket, Shauni's idea of a secret identity, and put it on. I then lifted into the air.

I concentrated my hearing for the sounds that I heard while in The Eight Ball. Then I saw it, a half a block away, there was a young man being picked on by three men in long black trench coats. They each wore ski masks to cover their faces.

What is it with girlfriends nowadays? I remarked as I started my descent to break up the scuffle.

Two of the guys were holding the man while the other was about to stab him with the switchblade. I landed behind him as he was in his back swing.

"Didn't your mother ever tell you not to play around with sharp objects?" I said with a grin.

The bully turned around to face me. His buddies threw their proposed victim to the ground and jumped toward me, pulling baseball bats from underneath their coats.

Great.

Their prey ran away hysterically. I tripped the knife wielder and grabbed the bat of the attacker that was closest to me. I pushed it hard back into his face.

"Son of a bitch! You broke my nose," he said as his mask began to glisten with his blood. Suddenly, there was a sharp pain in my right side. His buddy had hit me with his bat.

Damn! He's fast.

I recovered from the blow and did a backward flip, landing ten feet away from them. The batboys came at me at the same time. I used my enhanced speed to catch the one's bat, using it to block his partner's. I then kicked him in the stomach. The force of the blow caused him to lose his grip on his weapon.

Out of the corner of my eye, I spied the knife wielder. In one fluid motion, I pivoted around and hit his partner in the kneecap. He fell to the ground in pain. As I twisted one more time, I blocked the knife that was coming for me at an incredible speed.

The force of the combined speed caused the blade to go deep into the wooden bat. We both looked at it in surprise.

Wow.

I looked back to my opponent, using my super-human reflexes to slow time.

This may be my only chance, with these guys being as fast as they are. I grabbed his free arm and brought his elbow down onto my knee. My vampire hearing made the popping sound almost deafening. He howled out in pain. The sound reminded me of when I staked Dick in his wolf form the year before. *Naaahhh.*

Somehow he still had the strength to hit me with the bat. "Ouch," I said as I fell to my knees.

"We have to abort. The mission's been compromised," the second batboy said. "Let's go." As I was about to get back up, I was hit again. "Stay down." As I watched through tearful eyes, the trio ran into the night despite their injuries. My healing kicked in and I stood up.

I better get back before I'm missed. I flew back to The Eight Ball and my friends.

I walked into the restaurant/arcade, stuffing the stocking cap in my pocket I made my way back to my friends at our table. I slid beside Shauni. She gave me a peck on the cheek as I sat down.

"Everything okay?" she asked.

"Yeah. I got there just in time." Shauni, Jason, Ann, and Dick all gave me identical looks showing that they knew what I was talking about. I took a bite of my meatloaf platter. I swallowed it with a smile, even though it was now only slightly warm.

We continued to eat and talk about stuff for the next few minutes. Then I heard a beeping sound.

"Oh, that's me," Frank said as he pulled out a cellular phone. I chose not to listen to his conversation. Frank's personal life wasn't one that I was all too set on invading. Plus Shauni would have known if I tried.

I took another bite of my rapidly cooling food and a drink of soda. Frank shut his phone and put it back in his pocket. Only I noticed that his expression changed to a mix of anger and concern.

"You'll have to excuse me, I have to get going." Then he saw the faces that were waiting for a reason. "Uh. That was Dave back at the house. There was a leak in the bathroom. And me being the one in charge, I have to be there when the plumber shows up."

Everyone seemed to acknowledge that as a good enough reason. For some reason, I noticed that Jason looked a little skeptical. Dick rose to go with his friend.

"I'll go with you," he said to Frank.

"No, Dick, that's all right." He motioned for Dick to sit. "Stay here and catch up with your friends. I can take care of this." Dick nodded in agreement. "See you later."

"See ya," I said.

"Later," Jason remarked.

"Buh bye," Shauni said with a wave.

Ann just waved, being unusually shy. Frank headed to the door and the rest of us sat down to talk with Dick. Taking Frank's advice to catch up on stuff.

CHAPTER 4

After eating our spaghetti dinner with salad and garlic bread, we went into the living room to play some board games.

"Let's play Tri-Bond," Trevor suggested jokingly as we walked into the living room.

"How 'bout we don't," Jason replied quickly. I think he was still a little sore from Trevor beating him with a vampire association clue.

"Come on, Jace," Shauni told her cousin. "That was three months ago."

"Okay. Okay. Fine," Trevor said in his defense. "What do you suppose we do?"

"I don't know," Jason said. "Just not Tri-Bond."

"I could read your palm," Sue suggested.

"Nah. That's okay, Sue," he said. "I...I have to go do the dishes." He winked at his girlfriend. "You coming, Baby?"

She nodded and got up and followed Jason. I watched the two lovebirds from behind the couch where I was standing. Jason smiled at me as Ann shut the door. Sue looked at me with the same question on her face.

"No thanks. I think I'll keep my life private. Thanks," I said, shaking my head.

"I'll do it." Shauni looked at her boyfriend and smiled. "It'd be nice to know what the future has in store for me."

"All righty then," Sue said.

I got up from my seat and walked behind the couch. Sue scooted in beside the redhead, pushing Trevor against the couch's other arm. She then turned and faced Shauni. Trevor slid off of the couch and stood beside me.

"Hold out your left hand, palm up," Sue told her. Shauni did as she said. Sue waved her hand in a circle above it, and closed her eyes. She opened them again and looked at Shauni's palm. She ran her finger along the lines in Shauni's hand. Shauni looked around with a smile. "Oh this is nice." She looked at me. "You're gonna have two kids."

I looked at Trevor, his ears were getting red. It always happened when he got embarrassed.

"Go, Trev," I said with a laugh.

"Ha ha. Laugh it up, fuzz ball," he shot back as he slapped me on the chest.

Oh, bring up the werewolf thing. I acted like I was scared. Shauni smiled.

"Shh," Sue ordered. She went back to examining Shauni's palm. "You're also going to have to go through a period of despair to get to unending happiness. You will be the glue that holds your family together."

I wonder what she means by that?

"Okay. That's enough of that," Shauni said shakily as she took back her hand. Sue noticed Shauni's reaction.

"I'm sorry. I said something to trouble you."

With my werewolf-enhanced sense of smell, I could tell that Sue was getting nervous and uneasy. "I was just playing. It's only a game." Shauni smiled at her friend.

"How about I do Trevor's?" Shauni's "time to get back at you" expression crossed her face.

Poor Trevor.

"No, that's okay," he answered as he headed toward the kitchen.

"Come on, honey. It's only a game," Shauni repeated with a wink.

Trevor walked over to the couch and sat between the two girls. He looked at Shauni pleadingly. Sue wiped her hands on her pants and took his hand. She looked at it and ran her finger along the lines in his hand like she did with Shauni.

"Holy shit!" she gasped.

"What!?" the three of us said in unison.

"You've got the longest lifeline I've ever seen," she explained.

"Is that good?" Trevor asked.

"Yeah. If you plan to live forever," Sue joked. We all smiled. We always knew that because of the part of Trevor's DNA that was now vampire that it was always a possibility. Sue went back to her palm reading. "This is interesting too." I crossed my arms as I watched intently. "You come from a long line of great warriors. And you yourself are one."

"Cool."

Sue's watch alarm started to go off. She looked at it and pressed the button to stop it.

"Oh. It's eight already? I have to get going. I have a study session at the REC building." She gave Trevor back his hand and stood up.

"I better get going too," I informed them. I looked at Sue. "Do you mind if I give you a ride home?"

"Sure," she replied. Out of the corner of my eye, I saw Trevor look at Shauni. She put her arms around him from behind. She also had a big grin on her face.

Oh. That's so sweet, I thought sarcastically. The two of them got off the couch to see us out.

"And don't forget. You four are gonna help the Pack with its monthly blood drive this month. Right?" I reminded them.

Trevor opened his mouth to say something but Shauni cut him off before he could say anything.

"Of course we will," she answered.

Trevor looked at her in surprise. *How's she gonna get around his blood problem.*

"Except for Trevor. Being diabetic and all."

I winked at her.

"Oh yeah. Sorry. I forgot. Don't forget to tell Jason and Baby."

"Will do," my friend replied.

I looked at Sue. "You ready to go?"

"Yep," she answered. She came over and hugged Shauni. "I'll see you tomorrow in class."

"Buh bye," Shauni said.

I opened the door, and being the gentleman I am, motioned for Sue to go out.

"Later, guys," I said as I walked out the door.

"She sent me an e-mail the next day saying why she left." Sue looked out the window. "As soon as I read it, I ran to her dorm. When I got there she was already gone. Our neighbor from three doors down, Briana, said that she tried to find out why Jeanie was in such a hurry. But she couldn't get anything out of her. Bri said I was only ten minutes late." She looked back at me. "Ten minutes too late to give her the gift that I'd made for her."

"A gift?" I repeated. "What kind of gift?" Sue kept quiet. I nudged her shoulder. "Come on, Sue. You can tell me. After all, she is my sister."

She looked at me with a mixture of sympathy and reluctance.

"It was a necklace," *That's not that bad.* "More importantly, a medallion, a talisman. To repress her lycanthropic transformation during the full moon."

I swerved into the left lane as what Sue said sunk in. "Oh shit!" I turned the car back onto the right side of the road. "How...whuh...she *told* you?"

"Not exactly." We pulled into the parking lot of Jordan Hall, Sue's dorm. "We were walking back here for study group the night before she left." I pulled into an empty parking space as she continued her story. "The sun had set about ten minutes before and the full moon was just beginning to rise. We walked inside and Jeanie...she doubled over." Sue got a look of fear and sadness in her eyes as she remembered. "I bent down to help her. Part of me, at the time, was sorry I did."

"She was 'wolfing out,'" I said, as if that was the only explanation. Which it was. Sue nodded and continued her story.

"When she looked up at me I jumped back. Her eyes were all black. No color at all."

The description of what happens during the first stages of the change made a chill run down my spine.

"She looked at me pleadingly. I think she had too much on her mind and lost track of the days. Considering her relationship with Frank was on the rocks." She ran her fingers through her hair. "She told me one thing before she changed completely. 'Run!' she growled. Then Jeanie turned and ran through the main door. Her clothes shredded off her body as she grew and completed the change."

I looked from Susie to the street in front of us. I rubbed my face with my hands to clear my mind. What she just told me was like a blow to the head. It was also a little bit of a relief to know that someone outside the original "Dweller Valley Gang" knew my secret. I looked back at Sue.

"The next day I got the e-mail from Jeanie saying that she was leaving school to find out what happened to her."

This was an unexpected turn of events. I had finally found a way to stop the transformations. Something that I had hoped, prayed and all to often wished, would happen. Sitting there, I came to the conclusion that there was only one plausible reason for me to have met Susie Devlin.

"Can you make one for me?" I asked her, looking into her eyes.

"I've already started," she answered bluntly. "When I found out that you were Jeanie's brother, I knew it was only a matter of time." She gathered her books. "All I need is three strands of hair to weave into the string of the necklace."

I felt a little weird for going along with it, but after going through all the stuff I had in the past year, I decided that if feeling weird once was enough to get rid of this curse, then I was all for it. I grabbed a few pieces of hair and gave a quick tug.

"Ouch." Sue smiled as I handed her the hairs. "Here you go."

She put them in an envelope that she got out of one of her textbooks.

"How long will this take?" I asked anxiously.

"It should take a week or two." She put the envelope back in her book. "It takes forever to weave in the hairs."

"Oh," I said.

"I'm kidding," she said with a grin. "It'll take me two days. I'll give it to you at the Eight Ball on Thursday. Just before the Full Moon on Friday."

"Okay then." I looked at my watch. "Well. I best be going. I'll see you later."

"Bye, Dick," she said as she kissed my cheek. "See you Thursday." She opened the car door and stepped out. She shut it and walked into the dorm.

This is gonna be interesting, I thought as I drove back to the fraternity house.

We all sat in profound silence as Dick finished his account of when Sue told him that she knew he was a werewolf. And that she had a way to stop his monthly transformations.

"...And then I drove back to the frat house to get some sleep."

Shauni was the first of us to say something. "That's really great, Dick. I'm happy for you."

"Thanks, Shauni," he replied.

"Yeah, man, congratulations," Jason said with a smile. They did a little handshake thing.

I didn't know if what I felt for Dick was jealousy for getting rid of the burden of his curse or the resentment I felt for not having a cure for my own. I took a long drink of my soda.

"Congratulations, Dick. I'm happy for you." Shauni interlocked her hand in mine and squeezed it reassuringly.

"So when's Sue gonna show up?" Baby asked.

Dick looked at his watch. "She should be here anytime now."

As if on cue, my enhanced hearing picked up Sue's voice.

"...looking for...forget it. I found them."

"She's here now. She just walked in," I remarked. Ten seconds later Sue walked up to the table.

"Evening everyone," she said as she took the seat next to Dick.

Jason, Baby, Shauni, Dick and I watched Sue intently as she picked up her menu. Everyone was silent as she chose what she wanted to drink. Sue decided on what she wanted, put the menu on the table, called over the waitress and told her what she wanted. When she was finished, she looked up to see five pairs of eyes staring at her.

"What?!" she said loudly. Then the realization hit her. She looked at Dick. "They know?"

"Of course they do. They were all there when it first started." Dick smiled and gave Sue a quick account of what happened the year before, with the Leader.

"So, can we see it?" Jason asked excitedly.

Sue nodded as she got into her pocketbook. She pulled out a small wooden box with different symbols on it. I recognized some of them as runes, others as signs of the zodiac. She slid the box to Dick.

"Consider it an early Christmas present."

Dick smiled. We all looked at the box in anticipation. We knew what it was, or more importantly, what it was supposed to be. Dick opened the box. In it was a necklace with a metal circle attached to it. On the circle were more of the same designs that were on the box.

"Put it on, Dick," Jason encouraged.

"Yeah, Dick," Baby said. "Put it on."

Dick took the necklace from the box. He slipped it over his head. He then lifted the medallion in his hand. "It's beautiful, Sue. Thanks."

"You're welcome, Dick," Sue said then kissed him on the cheek.

I looked at Shauni and the other two during the exchange. She and Baby were just smiling, like their greatest plan was coming together. Jason had the same mixed look of dread and knowing on his face that I did.

These two just don't stop, I thought, remarking about our girlfriends.

"All I'm saying," I began to explain to Dick as I chose an apple for my fruit, "is that you shouldn't really put faith in this, if you're not really sure that it's going to work."

"Well, I'm not saying that," Dick said as he filled up his soda cup, "I'm gonna lock myself in the basement on the next full moon." We walked over to the cashier. Dick handed her his college I.D. and meal ticket. "If it works, it works. If it doesn't, it doesn't. No skin off my back."

"Don't you mean hair," I replied as I paid for my lunch.

"Very funny, Trev." We made our way to a table. "I mean, I trust Sue. It's just that I really don't trust this whole *magic* thing." I tried to say something. Dick looked at me. "*Even* after everything we've seen."

Dick and I continued to eat as we waited for Jason. His Algebra class ended ten minutes after Dick and my American History class. When Jason got there, we talked about the upcoming Full Moon party that the Pack was having. It was partially for Halloween, partially for the full moon that was that night and more importantly, just to have one.

We all decided that since we had significant others that we would dress up in costumes of famous pairs. And since Jason and I were comic book fans and we outvoted Dick, it had to be some kind of fictional character or superhero.

It was finally time to get ready for the Pack's Full Moon Party and to see if Dick's medallion was going to work. We had about an hour to get ready for the party. The girls were in me and Shauni's room getting dressed. Jason and I were downstairs in the living room. I was waiting for the Aerosmith version of "I Don't Want to Miss a Thing" to download onto my computer.

"So do you think this medallion is going to work out for Dick?" I asked Jason as he got a can of soda from the fridge.

"I don't know. I've seen a lot of things in the past year to tell me it should." He threw me a can of Pepsi. "When Samantha healed Patch in the other Dweller Valley, I was freaked. I didn't think something like that could happen." We sat down and waited for the song to finish downloading. "But Phoebe showed me something before we left that convinced me that the whole magic thing is real and everything happens for reason."

"What'd she show you?" I asked as I took a drink of my soda.

"She showed me my future."

"Whoa." Was all I could manage to say.

"She showed me my life after college and who I would marry."

"Baby," I finished.

"Yep," he replied with a grin. "So if Sue's magic is even ten percent of what Sam and Phoebe's is. I think Dick has a good chance of not seeing the Wolf anymore."

"I hope so." I checked the computer. My song was finished. Jason and I headed upstairs to get ready for the party.

"What if it's some kind of trick to make Dick evil?"

"That's not funny, Jace." We walked into Jason's bedroom. Then the realization hit me. "If it happens, which I'm sure it won't, I'll just have to take him down." I grabbed my suit and the rest of my costume. "Susie is Shauni's friend. I like the girl. I'm pretty sure she won't try anything like that."

"I hope you're right," Jason said as I handed him his costume.

"Me too," I said as I started for the bathroom. Jason looked at me with a "what the hell you doing" look. "I'll be out in a few minutes." I walked in the bathroom. I took my shower and got dressed. I was back out in the hallway before Jason was finished getting his stuff ready for his shower.

"You know, I just thought of something during your three minutes in the bathroom," Jason said as he got a pair of underwear from his drawer.

"What?"

"When do you plan on asking Shauni to marry you?"

"Keep it down, man," I said as I concentrated my enhanced hearing to listen to the girls. They were writing on the notepad again. *Oh great, the notepad treatment.* "I want it to be a surprise." Jason gave me a disbelieving look. "I'm going to. I just have to wait for the right moment."

"Uh huh," he said shaking his head. "You're scared. Big bad, Day Walker, with the powers of a vampire, Trevor Wayne is afraid to ask his girlfriend to marry him."

"So' Mr. I already know I'm gonna marry my girlfriend because a witch showed me my future,' when are you gonna ask Ann?" Jason stuck up his middle finger in response. "Good. Now go get ready." Jason walked out of the room and into the bathroom. I headed down to the living room to watch some television. After watching a few videos on VH1, Shauni came down the steps.

"Hey, sweetie," I said as I stood up. "You look *wonde*rful."

"Thanks," she said as she kissed me. "You look *super* too."

"I don't feel to super. This Superman suit feels like long underwear."

"How do you think *I* feel." Shauni indicated her costume for the party. "I'm wearing a bathing suit as a costume. And this wig itches a little," she finished, scratching her head.

"I'm not the one that suggested that you go as Wonder Woman." I smiled because I knew that Shauni was starting to get a little defensive. "I said go as Lois Lane. And you said, 'That's not much of a costume.'" Shauni stuck her tongue out as I continued. "And I said you can put the Ultra Woman costume under it.' And you said, 'Ultra…' " Shauni pushed me onto the couch and shut me up with a kiss.

"The one good thing about being Wonder Woman," she said as we exchanged kisses, "is that I have this." She held up a lasso made of gold spray-painted clothesline. "For later."

"For later?" I said with a smile as I kissed her again. Then I realized what she meant. Just then, the doorbell rang.

"I'll get it," Shauni said as she jumped up and headed for the door.

"Not wearing that you won't." I floated up from the couch and headed to the door at super speed. I stopped and turned to my girlfriend.

"No fair. That's cheating," she said, then stuck out her tongue.

I looked through the peephole. "It's Dick and Sue," I said as I undid the lock and opened the door. In walked my friend and his new girlfriend. They were dressed as Frankenstein's Monster and the Bride of Frankenstein.

"Whoa, Dick. What'd you do? Get a facelift? You look good."

"Trevor!" Shauni scolded.

"And hello to you too, man," he said with a smile as he shook my hand. "Hey, Shauni."

"Hi, Dick. Hi, Sue."

Sue waved at my girlfriend. "Hello. Evening, Trevor." Then she looked at Shauni again, as with a double take. "Shauni, are you sure you're going to wear that to the party tonight. It's a little chilly out."

"See, Shauni, I told you. But you never listen," I said with a smile.

"Do you have any clean white sheets?"

"Yeah," Shauni answered, ignoring my comment.

"We'll make a toga to go with it. And you can stop at the drugstore and get some skin-colored panty hose to keep warmer. Unless you already have a pair." Shauni shook her head. "Then I guess you should stop and get some before you'ns get to the party."

"That could work," Shauni agreed. "Let's get to work on the toga aspect. Trevor and I can get the panty hose when we leave." Shauni always knew how to volunteer me for a job without really asking.

The two girls headed upstairs, leaving Dick and I alone to talk. We headed to the couch to watch some TV. Dick was the first to speak. "Did you notice what time it is?"

"Don't worry, man," I used my enhanced hearing to listen in on Jason and Baby. What I heard made me wish I didn't. I made a face that Dick read pretty well. "We'll all be ready in time."

"Jason and Baby are at it again, aren't they."

"Yep."

"But seriously, look outside," Dick told me. I went over to the window and pulled back the curtain. The sun was just setting and the moon would be up in about half an hour. *Oh great.* "Are you sure you wanna go through with this?" I asked my friend as he went to sit down on the couch.

"I guess I'm as ready as I'll ever be," Dick replied. "But I need you to do me one favor." He looked at me pleadingly.

"Anything." I had a good feeling of what he was going to ask.

"I trust Susie and everything," he said as I sat down on the chair in front of him. "But if this...if this shouldn't work." Dick continued as he pulled the medallion out of his collar. "I need you to keep me..."

"In check," I finished for him.

"Yeah."

"Understood."

"Thanks, man," Dick replied.

"Anytime," I said as I shook his hand. Jason and Baby chose this time to finally come downstairs. Jason had on a Batman costume. Baby was dressed as Catwoman. "Evening, Bruce," I said.

"Hey, Clark. Where's the glasses?"

"Damn," I said. "I left them upstairs. Be back in a sec." I flew upstairs to my bedroom. I knocked on the door. "Hey, Shauni. You decent?"

"Yes, Trevor. Come in."

I opened the door and walked in. Shauni was standing in front of the mirror. Sue was putting the last touches on her toga.

"Wow, babe. You look good." I looked at our friend. "Good job, Sue."

"Thanks," she said as she fastened the last safety pin. "There. All done." She handed Shauni the tiara and the black wig. "Here you go."

"Thanks." Shauni put on the wig and fastened it with the tiara and bobby pins.

"Jason and Baby are finally finished getting ready." I smiled as I went over to the nightstand. "If that's what you want to call it."

"Trevor."

I opened the drawer and pulled out the last piece of my costume, the glasses that I wore as Dylan MacLeod. Clark Kent just wasn't "Clark Kent" without them. I put them on and turned to the girls.

"What do you think?"

"They look good," Sue said.

"Perfect," Shauni said as she gave me a quick kiss.

"Thats what I was going for," I replied. "Now for the cool part." I started to unbutton the shirt of my tuxedo. I opened it to reveal the S shield of the "Man of Steel."

"Now it's prefect," Sue said with a smile.

"Okay. Let's get going," Shauni said as she headed for the door. Sue and I followed her downstairs to our friends and to the party that awaited us.

CHAPTER 5

"Thank you. Come again," the cashier said as she handed Shauni the bag containing her panty hose.

"Thanks," she replied. I just waved to the girl as I walked toward the door. Smiling, I opened the door and held it for my girlfriend. "Don't even say it, Trevor."

"I didn't say a word," I replied, half-laughing. Shauni gave me a half-angry look. We walked down the street on our way to the party. "Come on, sweetheart, I'm not thinking anything out of the ordinary."

"I heard that one before," she said as she put her hand in mine. "So where am I supposed to change?"

"We can go into McDonald's and use the bathroom," I suggested.

We turned down an alley and headed to the fast food restaurant. When we were halfway down the alley I heard footsteps behind us. I turned around to see a man in a ski mask and a brown leather jacket.

Not him again.

"Oh shit," I exclaimed.

Shauni squeezed my hand harder. "What?

"Nice night for an evening. Don't you think?" I said to the masked stranger.

"Nice enough to kill you and take your girl," he replied.

"Shauni, stand back while I take care of this yahoo." I pushed my girlfriend behind me and looked back at the thug. "Lets go," I said as I stepped toward him.

He pulled a baseball bat from his coat. And pointed toward me. "Just bring it," he said as he motioned me to advance.

I ran toward him. He swung the bat and I ducked his attack. Shauni stood beside a nearby dumpster. I punched the attacker in the stomach twice and then gave him an uppercut. He flew off his feet and fell to the ground. I turned to walk back to my girlfriend. Standing about ten feet behind her were the other two masked men who tried to kill Jake Daniels two weeks before.

Great!

"Shauni! Duck!" I ordered. She did as I said. I flew at the two new guys, grabbing the smaller one by the shirt as I clothes lined the other. I then landed on my feet and held him in the air. He struggled to get out of my grasp, kicking me in the stomach and clawing at my hands.

"Trevor, in here," Shauni said as she held the door to the dumpster open.

I carried my foe toward the opening. Before I got there, the first attacker tackled me. *Damn it.* I dropped the other one as we fell to the ground. We rolled around punching each other with little jabs. I finally made my way on top. As I held him down I reached up and pulled off his mask. I was caught by surprise when I realized who it was, Joey King, one of Dick's friends from the Pack.

Shit. That would mean...

"Hey, Trevor. What's up?" I looked up just in time to see the short one, who I realized was Dave Samuels, swinging down toward me with Joey's baseball bat. I caught it before it connected with my head. I swung it down and smashed him in the knee. "Mother fu...Shit!" he screamed as he fell to the ground.

While my head was turned Joey punched me in the stomach. I fell back. Joey and I then stood up at the same time.

I looked over toward the dumpster. To my dismay, the tallest of the three was holding a stylized knife to Shauni's neck. *This must be Marty.* Joey walked over to them and faced me.

"Good show, Trevor," Marty said as he took off his ski mask. "But that still isn't enough to save little Shauni here." He tightened his hold on my girlfriend with one arm as he moved the knife a little closer to her throat with the other.

"What do you want, you son of a bitch?" I tried to buy some time to figure out a way to attack them without getting Shauni hurt.

"Just her. For now," Joey replied. "As for you. You're expendable." As he said this, I suddenly felt a sharp pain in the middle of my back. I turned to see Dave leaning on his good leg with a bloody switchblade knife in his left hand.

"Trevor!" Shauni screamed as I slumped to the ground.

Joey walked up to me with his bat. Ready to strike. "And this is for my arm." He swung down and hit me across the side of the head. It dazed me but didn't knock me out. "Damn he's resistant."

180

"This'll definitely stop him," Marty said as he took the blade from Shauni's throat. "I won't need this anymore after tonight."

He threw the knife at me. It connected with the middle of my chest. The last thing I remember seeing before I blacked out was Marty carrying Shauni away and Joey helping Dave to the end of the alley.

"They're fifteen minutes late," I told Dick as I looked at the clock on the wall. "This isn't good."

"Would you relax, Jason, we're at a party," he reassured me. "It's a full moon. And best of all, I'm not a wolf."

"I'm real happy for you, Dick. But that's not the point," I replied. "Trevor said he'd be here at eight-thirty. It's ten-till-nine now."

"Don't worry, Trevor can take care of himself." My friend smiled. "He and Shauni probably stopped back at the house for some fun. If you know what I mean."

"Yeah, maybe you're right." I began to look for my girlfriend and wife to be. "You see the girls anywhere?"

"They're over there talking to a girl from Sue's dorm. I think her name is Briana," Dick said as he pointed toward the refreshment table. Ann and Sue were talking to a girl dressed up like Elvira. What I could tell from her outfit, her boobs were real. We walked over to them and heard the tail end of their conversation.

"...they were both named Seth. One was really good and the other could have learned something from him," Briana said as we walked up to them. "The bad thing is, I can't remember which was which."

"Always two Seths there are. A master and an apprentice," I remarked in a Yoda-like voice as I put my arms around my girlfriend. Her skintight Catwoman suit turned me on.

"But which was destroyed? The master or the apprentice?" Dick remarked as he did the same to Sue.

"Would you two quit it," Ann said in response to our *Star Wars* joke.

"Sorry, sweetheart."

"Bri," Sue nodded toward the werewolf, "this is Dick." She pointed to me. "And this jokester is Jason."

I waved to the girl, trying my best to take my eyes off her chest. "Sorry about the joke," I apologized as I shook her hand. *Man, her skin's cold.*

"That's okay," she said with a smile. "I've heard worse."

"Good one, Bri," Baby said as she gave her a high five. "Shauni and Trevor get here yet?" she asked me.

"No. Haven't seen them," I answered. "I was just about ready to call the house to see if they were there." I told her. "Care to join me?"

"Sure," Baby said as I took her hand. She then looked at Briana and shook her hands. "It was nice meeting you, Bri."

"My pleasure." She looked at me. "Jason." I shook her hand. Then Baby and I walked to the living room.

"This party's not exciting enough for me," Baby said as we exited the recreation room.

"Be careful what you ask for, sweetie," I told her as I kissed her cheek. "You just might get it."

"I hope there's no one in there," she replied with a wink.

"You're a bad girl. You know that?" She nodded as we walked onto the porch for better reception. I opened my cell phone and dialed Trevor's. His voicemail picked up so I ended the call. "This is not good. I got the voicemail."

Baby put her arms around my neck and kissed me on the lips. "Well, maybe he don't have it with him. We *could* go back to the house and have our own party," she said with a mischievous grin.

"As much as I'd love to," I began as I took her hands and put them to her side, "I think something is wrong. It's not like Trevor, or Shauni for that matter, to be this late."

"Well let's head back to the party and see if they're here yet," my girlfriend suggested. We walked out of the living room and back to the recreation area. I immediately found Dick and Sue. "Did they show up yet?" I asked them as I approached. Dick shook his head.

"Damn it."

"Relax, Jace. Everything'll be fine," he said reassuringly as he scanned the room. "Hey, there's Marty. Maybe he's seen them." Dick waved to his frat brother. "Marty," he called out, "can you come here for a sec?"

"Yeah sure," he said as he came over.

Something about the way he was dressed made me uneasy. He was wearing pretty much all black. He had on a black T-shirt and a pair of black jeans. His face was made up to look a lot like Jack Nicholson's did in that movie *Wolf.*

"What is it, Dick?" he asked calmly. A little too calmly for my taste.

"Have you seen Trevor or Shauni tonight?" I asked for Dick, who was frozen in place like he could quite understand the way Marty looked.

182

"No, why?" he said as he looked around the room, avoiding eye contact with me as he spoke. "Aren't they here yet?"

"No," Baby answered. "If you see them can you tell them we'll be right over here."

"Sure," he answered.

"Marty! It's time," Frankie's voice yelled from somewhere inside the room.

"Well, it's time for me to go. The 'master' beckons," he said with a wink.

"See ya," I said. I looked at my friend, who had the thousand-yard stare going for him.

"Dick, what's wrong?"

"We got trouble," he answered as he rubbed at his chest where the medallion was.

"What's the matter, Dick?" Sue asked. "What going on?"

"His face *looked* like a *really* good make-up job," he started.

"It looked pretty damn good to me," I commented. Dick looked at me with a 'get real' expression.

"That's just it. I couldn't smell any glue to hold on the hair or ears. And he *smelled*," Dick got a weird expression on his face, as he found the right words, "like *me*."

"Oh shit," Sue said as she looked up onto the stage beside the DJ booth.

We all looked in that direction as Marty, Dave and Joey pulled out a hospital cart that was covered in a sheet. Frankie was dressed in a robe like something a monk would wear. He walked up to the podium as the other three members of the Pack stood by the hospital cart. Frank walked up to the podium and took the microphone.

"My friends," he said with a evil looking smile, "I have come before you not as an equal, but as…the man in charge. Of the party that is." Everybody else in the room laughed as if it was the funniest thing they had ever heard. They were all drinking the same thing, some kind of liquid that was bluish in color. My three companions and myself just stood there and watched.

"I have brought you all here tonight to witness the greatest accomplishment of my life," Frankie continued. "Tonight is the night that I will once again be like each and everyone of you."

"Fully human," I heard Dick whisper.

Holy Shit.

Suddenly, it all made sense. The murderers that took the hearts of their victims. Hell, I watched *An American Werewolf in Paris*. The members of the pack all wearing the same type of costume that looked amazingly like wolf-men, with no scent of spirit gum or any other adhesive for their "masks." Frank picking the night of the full moon to again be "one of us."

"They're all werewolves too," I said out loud.

"Jason, don't be ridiculous," Baby said.

"He's right, Ann," Dick relied. "Remember, I'm an authority on these things."

"How can you be so sure, Dick?" Sue asked him.

"The nose knows."

"So what do we do?" I asked. And it seemed that Frank answered that for me.

"To do what you have to do. You have to make a few sacrifices," Frankie said, and pulled back the sheet to reveal my cousin.

"Shauni! Oh my God!" Baby screamed. I looked in the direction of the stage.

"Jason, it's Shauni," she said as she pointed to my cousin.

"Son of a bitch," I said.

"Well, at least we know what to do," Dick said.

"Yeah," I replied, "we fight." I looked at my girlfriend. "Baby. You and Sue get everybody out of here. However you can."

I reached behind my back and pulled out the batarang that I made for my costume. I used the blade from the machete that I got off of my double when Trevor and me went to save the girls in an alternate Dweller Valley. *Good thing it's laced with silver.* I ran toward the stage. Dick was right behind me. The girls began to usher everybody else outside.

"Get them!" Frankie ordered, pointing the knife that he was going to use to cut my cousin at Dick and me. Marty, Joey and Dave jumped down and headed for us. I ran for Joey. He growled at me to show me his fangs.

Damn!

He went to punch at me. I ducked his attack and punched him in the leg. The only place I could reach. A lot of good that did me.

It took me a good twenty minutes to get to the Pack's frat house. The wound in my back had completely healed. The bruises from the bat were good as new. And best of all, the stab wound to the chest had just closed as I made my way up the cobble stone walkway. I could hear the sounds of the party even without my enhanced hearing.

Time to crash the party.

As I went to open the door, it flew open. I moved out of the way at super speed. A whole horde of people ran out screaming and yelling. *What the hell!* I stopped one of the guys from the college football team, he was dressed as the Crow.

"What's going on, man?" I asked as I grabbed his shoulders.

"They're…they're…cra…crazy," was all he managed to get out. He ran with the other scared people.

I looked up at the full moon. *Not crazy, Danny—werewolves.* I looked down toward the door.

I guess it's time to play superhero.

Just then, as the last wave of people came out of the house, I sensed a vampire. *Oh shit.* The feeling was strongest when a female dressed as Elvira walked past me. I grabbed her by the arm.

"What the hell is going on in there?" I demanded as I held up the knife that I pulled from my chest earlier. "Or I kill you now."

"You don't have time for that now, Trevor," she said. This amazed me. Because I was sure that I had never seen this girl before. "Jason and the others need your help." She pulled a metal pin from her hair. She then extended it to me. "It's silver. You're gonna need it." Just then I heard Shauni scream. I looked back to the door. Then back at "Elvira." She was gone.

"Don't say I never gave you anything," her voice said in my mind.

I shook the voice from my head and walked into the house, in the direction of the noise. As I passed a mirror I got a good look at my outfit. The pants were dirty and soaked with water from the alley. The jacket was ripped and bloody.

"There goes my deposit." I heard a large crash coming from the party area. I smiled at my reflection. "This looks like a job for Superman." I took off the glasses and spun around at superspeed. I took off my tuxedo and stopped spinning.

I stood in front of the mirror. I was no longer dressed as a mild-mannered reporter. I was now dressed as the Man of Steel.

I flew through the doors to the party room. What I saw didn't help my attitude much. Many of the tables and chairs were turned over. Jason was fighting Dave with what looked like a bat shaped knife. *He goes all out for Halloween, doesn't he.*

Dick, who was still in his human form, was fighting Joey. This was a plus. Marty stood with Frankie up on the stage. All six people saw me when I entered. I looked to my friends who were battling members of the Pack.

Jason sliced Dave's throat with his "batarang." Dave then slumped to the floor. Dick was trading blows with Joey. They were pretty evenly matched as fighters, but Joey fought dirtier.

He kicked Dick in his right knee, as my friend was about to punch him.

"Jason, go check on the others!" I called out to my friend as he wiped the bloody batarang on a nearby tablecloth. He looked to me and nodded. He then headed out of the room.

"Marty," was all Frank said as he pointed to me, "I thought you killed him."

"I will this time," Marty said as he jumped to the floor.

We ran toward each other. We stopped right in front of each other. We then began to throw punches. A series of rights and lefts to the chest area. All were blocked. We then aimed for the stomach. All of these were blocked also. I decided to pivot around and hit him with my right fist. Marty anticipated it and blocked with his forearms. He hit away my hands. And punched me in the stomach. *Ah shit.* I thought as the pain registered. I looked up behind Marty, to the stage. Frankie had the knife poised above Shauni's chest.

Damn! I have to get to her.

"Frankie!!" Dick yelled from the other side of the room. He was standing over Joey's body. His hand reached for the medallion around his neck.

"Dick! Do..." I was cut off by Marty punching me in the face.

"It ends now!" Dick finished as he ripped the medallion from his neck. My friend doubled over in pain as the change began. Even as I fought with Marty, I managed to see Dick running toward the stage. As he neared it, he grew larger and his hair lengthened as he changed into the Wolf.

Frankie took the blade away from Shauni's chest and reached inside his robe. He then pulled out what my enhanced vision recognized as a medallion identical to Dick's. He yanked at it and threw it to the floor. Just as the last of the change completed, Dick jumped the last ten feet to his adversary.

Son of a bitch.

Damn it! I thought after getting punched in the head by Marty. *Focus, Trevor.* I jabbed him in the ribs a few times then used as much of my strength as I could to punch him in the jaw. His head snapped back with a crack. A half second later he slumped to the floor.

I ran up to the stage and began untying my girlfriend. I ripped the ropes from her hands and then her ankles. I helped her to her feet. The makeshift toga that was part of her costume fell to the floor. Suddenly, the darker of the two werewolves flew backwards up against a nearby wall. Shauni screamed in my ear. He then looked up at her and growled.

"Let's get you out of here." I picked my girlfriend up in my arms and quickly flew her outside with everyone else. Jason, Baby and Sue were standing out on the front porch.

"Jason, take the girls home. I'll be back with Dick as soon as I can." He nodded. I looked at Shauni. "I *have* to go back in."

"Be careful, man," Jason replied.

"I always am." I looked at my girlfriend's waist. *I gotta have that.* I reached for it. "I'm gonna need this," I said as I took the spray-painted clothesline. Shauni looked at me.

"Trevor," she said, almost pleading, "be careful."

"I will. Trust me," I replied with a smile. I flew back inside.

"Frankie!!" I yelled from the other side of the room as I reached for the medallion around my neck. *God, I hope I'm doing the right thing.* "It ends now!" I warned as I pulled on the medallion.

The leather strap snapped and I felt the change begin. I doubled over in pain, dropping the medallion to the floor.

For Jeanie.

I ran toward the altar. Feeling my blood grow hotter as my lycanthropic heritage manifested itself in the form of the Wolf. I could feel the muscles of my body stretch and grow as the fur began to cover my body.

I looked up through the eyes of the Wolf to see Frankie take the blade from above Shauni's chest and reach inside his robe. He pulled out a medallion just like mine.

Son of a bitch. I have to kill him, I thought with extreme pleasure. *Suits me just fine.*

Frankie yanked at the necklace and threw it to the floor. As I felt the last of the change finish, I jumped the last ten feet toward Frankie.

"You're a dead man," I growled as I tackled him to the floor that was five feet below the top of the stage.

"You first," Frankie replied, halfway through his change. I rolled on top of him and began to claw at his chest. He cried out in pain, but I didn't stop. When the Wolf takes over, Dick Harshburger no longer exists. Frankie was nearly through the change as he grabbed my paws. He smiled at me, showing his fangs in an evil grin.

"My turn," he growled as his change completed. He bent his legs up under me and kicked out. I flew into a nearby wall at the back of the altar. I heard a scream. It was Shauni. I looked at her. "Get out of here! Please!" I growled.

"Let's get you out of here," Trevor said as he picked Shauni up in his arms and quickly flew her outside with everyone else.

"Good boy," I said with a smile. Just then Frank jumped up onto the stage with me. I rose to my feet quickly, ready to continue the fight. We began to circle each other. "Why'd you do it, Frank? Why kill all those people?"

"You should know, Dick," Frank growled as he swiped a paw at me. "Your sister did this to me."

"What?!" I yelled as I kicked at him. Frank caught my leg and threw me backwards.

"Two years ago," he started as he ran toward me. Before I could dodge his fist, it connected with the side of my head.

"The day after Jeanie broke up with me because she didn't believe me when I told her about your family 'problem' I was sitting in my room trying to call her to tell her to lock herself up for that night's full moon."

He went to punch at me again as he continued his explanation, "After my fourth attempt in an hour I walked over to my window, wondering if she had enough sense to go somewhere safe."

I caught his fist and kicked him in the knee.

"Son of a bitch," he said as he fell to the floor.

I jumped on top of him and began to claw at his chest again. He was pissing me off trying to make it like he was the good guy and he was only looking out for Jeanie's safety. I just wanted to tear him apart.

"Now I wish I wasn't so concerned about your sister." Frank rolled us over and began to beat and claw my chest.

"She jumped through the window from the ground that was twelve feet below. I never had a chance."

Frank then bit down on my shoulder, digging his sharp teeth into my fur-covered flesh.

"Aargh!!" I howled in pain. "She gave you this gift. And this is how you repay her!" I yelled as I kicked him off of me. "By killing innocent people. By almost killing Shauni. She considered you a friend."

"I wasn't so lucky, *Dick*." He began to circle me again. "Jeanie almost killed me, since I wasn't born this way, but acquired it through a bite." He picked up one of the speakers from the DJ's booth and threw it toward me. I batted it out of the way. "I have to have the heart of normal human with AB-negative blood because a certain protein in it keeps my own protein levels normal." I charged him. "Well, normal for a werewolf."

"You're sick," I said as I pushed him against the DJ's booth.

When I flew back into the recreation room, the two werewolves, Dick and Frank, were still fighting.

That's a plus. Sorta. Now all I have to do is figure out which one is Dick.

They began to circle each other. The one with the lighter-colored fur growled, then picked up one of the speakers from the DJ's booth and threw it at the other one. The darker one batted it away like it was nothing. I ran over at super speed and caught it before it hit the nearby wall. *Those things gotta be expensive.* I set it gently on the floor. As luck would have it, I put it down right beside Dick's medallion.

Someone's looking out for me, I thought as I put it down the front of my suit.

The lighter of the two werewolves growled then charged at the darker one. He growled again. The darker one charged at him, lifted him off the floor and pushed him against the DJ's booth.

"I gotta stop this." I jumped up behind the werewolves.

How am I gonna figure this out. I tried the direct approach.

"Hey Dick," I called out. The darker one turned to me and growled. This gave the light one a chance to catch his enemy off guard. He punched "dark fur" in the side of the head. "Dark Fur" stumbled and fell to the floor. "Lightie" went to jump on him.

"Whoa!" I said, putting a hand to his chest. I didn't judge my strength well enough. What was going to be a simple gesture to hold him back, turned into a super strong push.

Where the hell did that come from? I bent down and pulled the silver hairpin from my sleeve. *God! Please don't let this be Dick.*

I raised my hand to deliver the final blow. "Darkie's" eyes opened wide as he growled. My enhanced vision helped me see the reflection in his eyes. I used my speed and reflexes to turn around and throw the silver pin into the chest of the light haired werewolf.

In slow motion, he let go of the speaker he was going to use as a weapon and reached for the pin that was now embedded in his chest. I flew into the air and grabbed the speaker. I gently let it to the floor as "Lightie" slumped beside it.

When my reflexes allowed for time to flow normally, "Dark Hair" was on his feet and heading for the body of his fallen enemy. "Lightie's" fur was receding into his body as he grew smaller. In seconds I recognized him as Frankie. I turned back to the werewolf that I now knew was my friend.

"Dick?" I said. He just continued to walk toward Frankie's body. "Dick!"

He turned toward me and jumped. Using my enhanced speed, I dodged him, grabbed the rope from around my waist and tied his hands together. I pulled hard while Dick was in the air. He flipped backward and landed to the floor. I dropped down and put my arms around his neck, cutting off his air supply just long enough for him to pass out, which for a werewolf is about five minutes. I picked up my friend and flew back to the townhouse.

I hope no one is watching, was my last thought as I lifted into the air.

"Morning, sleepy head." Were the first words I heard upon waking up the next morning. Shauni was sitting beside me on the couch in the basement. She handed me one of the two cups of coffee that she was holding.

"Morning to you too," I said, kissing her on the cheek as I took my coffee. I looked over at the makeshift cage where I had laid an unconscious Dick the night before.

I concentrated my hearing to listen for a heartbeat. Luckily, it was there. *Whew! I thought I broke his neck.*

"What's for breakfast?" I asked as I took a sip of coffee.

"Thats what I'd like to know," Dick said as he lifted his head off the mattress.

"And can I get some clothes please?" he asked as he wrapped the sheet around his waist and stood up.

"I'll get you some of Trevor's," Shauni said as she started upstairs.

As Shauni opened the door at the top of the stair, I took the key to the cage out of my pocket. I unlocked the gate and opened it. "Thanks, Trevor," Dick said sincerely as he walked out. I gave him a weird look.

"Not just for the door. Also for keeping me in…"

"Check," I said with a smile. We sat down on the couch and waited for Shauni to come back with his change of clothes.

"I do have one question though?"

"What's that?"

"How did you know which of us to stab with that big needle?"

"I saw it in your eyes." Dick gave me a weird look. "Not that way. When you growled when I was about to stab you, I saw the reflection in your eyes. I saw Frankie getting ready to crush us both with the speaker."

"Kill two birds with one stone," Dick said.

"Exactly." I took a sip of coffee. "With both of us out of the way he could continue his killing spree. Without resistance."

"I guess somehow you knew I was trying to warn you." I shrugged my shoulders. Dick shivered and looked up to the top of the steps. "Man. Where's Shauni with those clothes?"

Just then, the door opened and my girlfriend walked down. She was holding the morning newspaper, a pair of sweatpants and the burgundy "Sunnydale High School" T-shirt that I got when I was in California. She handed the clothes to Dick.

"Thanks," he said. He then walked into the small bathroom to our left and shut the door. Shauni sat down beside me on the couch. She unfolded the paper. And showed me the front page. "Guess who's little escapade made the paper?"

Oh great, I thought as I looked at the front page.

The headline read "WILD DOGS CRASH FRAT PARTY. FOUR DEAD." I quickly read the article.

"Good."

"What?" Shauni asked as she took a sip of her coffee.

"No mention of Superman saving the day." I folded the paper and put it on the floor. "That's real good." I grabbed Shauni's coffee cup and placed it on the floor beside mine. I then kissed my girlfriend on the mouth. Just as we were about to get a little more hot and heavy, we heard a cough. I raised my head to see Dick standing beside the couch.

"Did Sue come back with you'ns last night?" he asked.

Shauni bent her head up to look at him. "Yeah. She's up on the couch."

"Guess I should go wake her up," he said with a grin. He then headed for the stairs.

I reached into the pocket of my jeans and threw Dick's medallion to him. "I think you might need this." Dick caught it without looking.

"Thanks." He tied it to his neck and headed upstairs.

I turned back to my girlfriend. "Now. Where were we?" Shauni lay back down onto the couch as I kissed her on the mouth and made my way to her neck.

"Right about here," she replied with a smile.

It had been a little over three weeks since the events of the full moon party. It was my birthday and decided I'd pick that day to do the one thing that I had been planning for almost a year. I flew Shauni into Dweller Valley and landed on top of the roof of the First United Methodist Church. I figured it'd be the perfect place to ask her to marry me.

After we got a spot settled on the edge of the roof Shauni handed me a small package.

"Happy Birthday, Trevor."

I ripped off the wrapping paper. It revealed a small white box. I then opened the box. Inside was a small silver cross on a chain.

"Oh, sweetheart. It's beautiful. Just like you." I kissed my girlfriend on the mouth. "Ill wear it all the time."

"You're welcome, Trevor." She hugged me and kissed me on the cheek. She smiled. "And you better keep it on all the time. It's pure silver."

"Yes, ma'am." *I guess it's a good a time as any.* I pulled from Shauni's embrace. I looked into her eyes. "There is one more thing I'd like for my birthday."

"And just what would that be, Mr. Wayne?" she said with a mischievous grin.

I stood up and pulled her to the edge of the roof. I then took a step off the edge of the roof. I was floating in the air, I reached behind my back and pulled out the small velvet box that I'd had since my trip to Los Angeles. My girlfriend's eyes got bigger as she realized what it was. I moved into a kneeling position and opened the box.

"Shauni, will you marry me?"

Tears welled up in both our eyes. "Oh yes, Trevor. Yes," she answered through sniffles and tear-soaked eyes.

I took the ring out and placed it on her left hand. She stood up on the roof and I stepped back onto it. "I love you, Shauni."

"I love you too, Trevor."

I put my arms around my fiancée. I kissed her on the mouth, lifted her into my arms and I floated into the air. We had class the next day, so we flew back to the townhouse and my now, crystal clear future.

Printed in the United States
23593LVS00007B/344

9 781413 760941